DOCTORS, BODIES AND SNATCHERS

HECTOR BRYSON

Doctors, Bodies and Snatchers

CANONGATE

First published in 1978
by Canongate Publishing Ltd.,
17 Jeffrey Street, Edinburgh

ISBN 0 903937 49 2

Typesetting by G. Sanderson, (Phototypesetting)
44 Constitution Street, Edinburgh

Printed and bound in Great Britain by
Morrison and Gibb Ltd, London and Edinburgh

1

My medical studies began when Father came home from Waterloo with three legs. He brought back the standard complement of everything else, but the spare leg clearly had a special place in his heart even if there was no room for it on his person.

"I got it from the Earl of Uxbridge," he explained as I helped him one evening to wire the extra bones together and it was, I recall thinking, a curious thing to give your surgeon, no matter what he has done for you, or indeed, if he has done for you.

Actually, the facts were not quite like that, for you see Father had been masquerading as a corpse behind a dead horse, at one time on the fodder roll of the Scots Greys before they had charged themselves into oblivion. He was suddenly brought back to life by a cluster of gorgeous uniforms cantering out of the cannon smoke. Wellington's nose of course gave him away at once but the gallant beside him turned out later to be Lord Uxbridge. At that exact moment however he was turning sideways out of his saddle shouting,

"Bigod, I've lost my leg."

"Have you bigod?" barked the Duke who had no high regard for people who lost anything.

Then followed one of those stiff lipped charades that blossom in the wake of British disasters. There was Wellington desperate to settle the French hash, but hoping not to appear so, and Uxbridge trying to pretend that he was in the habit of being blown to bits every afternoon and just about this time too. They carried him away, his stump spouting like a fountain while the Iron Duke rode off to see what the Imperial Guard was up to.

Fine details of the tale at this point fade away into a haze of old Madeira, emerging irregularly to lend colour to whatever military reminiscence took Father's fancy. It would seem though that he had stuffed the leg into a large sack made up of stretcher blankets, resumed his ghastly disguise and avoided enough flying metal to pose as a martial hero for the rest of his life. He returned home shortly afterwards on half pay, with a mysterious leg-shaped package, a thrilling after dinner repertoire and a resolve never again to wear uniform and he put this desire for an unwarlike existence to the test as surgeon apothecacy in Dalkeith, a small town lying some eight miles from Edinburgh. The work was ceaseless and remuneration rather less so until the timely demise of a rich aunt made him think more kindly of her than he had during her lifetime. Thus with his family no longer dependent on his competence he attended his patients in their front rooms when they were not too ill, in their bedrooms when they were not too well, and in the graveyard when his remedies had finally proved useless.

When he was not pestling in his mortar or settling accounts with importunate tradesmen or curing himself with whisky after a night out in the rain, he would bring the leg from its oaken cask to amuse me with anatomical instruction. In no time at all I could talk freely about sciatic nerves, hamstrings, femurs, housemaid's knee and coachboy's aneurysms, long before Beattie, the village dominie had even broached the subject of frogs and rabbits and their families. For doctors' children have as much chance of escaping a career in medicine as they have of escaping chicken-pox. By the time I realised that my sister was different from me, I had already begun to model myself not on a man but on a country doctor. I would accompany Father on his rounds which he conducted in a sort of gig. He was a changed person at the ribbons, exploding into a froth because the roads were choked with madmen who always passed on the wrong side. He felt these rages might convince our wilful mare that he was in charge, but she for her part ambled if whipped, trotted if cold and stopped when it suited her. While Father was barely controlling himself on the driving seat, I used to amuse myself guddling round his bag of instruments. One day I pulled out a coiled tube shaped like a hard worm.

"What is this, Father?" I demanded pushing it beneath his nose.

"Ah", said he, tilting back his head to bring the tube into line with his aging focus, "that is a catheter. It is for thrusting into the bladders of old men who cannot pass water." I examined it closely. Its construction was wondrously simple and if, as seemed likely, it had only one mode of entry it struck me as being a rather cruel weapon and I said so.

"Well, maybe you're right," said Father, "but it's not so cruel as the pain it relieves. Man, you've never seen a bladder that won't empty, or heard it; they lie there after a good Saturday night at the beer, just praying to burst."

There was another tube in his bag made of silver that formed a close fitting open ended scabbard for a mobile plunger pointed in the style favoured by the Borgia family for their more intimate supper parties. I had not the chance to ask him its purpose because I saw him use it before I had discovered it on my travels through his bag. I must have been about thirteen at the time, perhaps more. It was the year Walter Scott was made a Baronet I remember, for our minister, a good Calvinist, had sent him a grovelling letter of congratulations. I can still see the scene in an outlying farmhouse that overlooked the Jedburgh road. Father had been summoned by a breathless messenger to attend a wee lad with the fever and a sore throat, which his parents had at first believed simply to be the croup. We descended into a farmyard quagmire of squawking hens, dropsical pigs and inquisitive children. This was all quite normal, but inside the kitchen there was nothing at all normal about the atmosphere of jagged desperation. The mother had collapsed across the bed in terror, the father was bravely hiding his own terror behind a masculine facade, whilst the little waif was tearing at the sheets in weakening efforts to drag air past the putrid membrane in his windpipe. I had forgotten Father could move so fast. No-one could protest before he had plunged his Renaissance dagger into the boy's throat. Nor could one protest afterwards for as he withdrew the plunger the sheath hissed now with a regular breathing that was already turning the livid cheeks and lips from blue to pink,

"Now, mother," said my father, diverting her emotion into memorising his instructions, "that tube will need to stay in place until Willie's throat clears again. Cool him if he gets hot, with cold compresses, and you can wash his mouth out with this mixture of squill and opium," and more besides—his deliberately lengthy recommendations soothing Willie's mother even more than following them would soothe Willie. She was near to smiling by the time we left, and her husband's code of honour allowed him a tear or two now that they were tears of relief and not of despair. The Borgia family could never have caused so much simple joy with all their stabbing as did Father with just that one.

In time I learned the contents of the bag by heart. There was the catheter for letting fluid out and a clyster tube for letting fluid in. There was laudanum, a blend of opium and cinnamon, as an anodyne to make your pain a dream and as a soporific to make you dream in the first place. And, wonder of wonders, there was a mixture of ginger, magnesia and rhubarb devised by the celebrated Professor Gregory of Edinburgh University. Father said that it had just been included in the new Edinburgh text of recommended draughts and mixtures. "Though," he added, "this is not to be wondered at, Gregory edited the book after all. Aye, and a wild lad he was too," he added, snuffling in amused recollection.

I resisted my father's coachmanship though not his persuasion, but when he saw how much fruit his teachings had borne he took fright at the windfall. One bleak February morning he yanked in the mare from the path of some buffoon at the gallop, gave me a droll look and shook his head through a sigh,

"You know this is not for you," he said, "you don't want to spend your life fighting for survival on the turnpikes." He meant, of course, that he did not want me to be an apothecary which entitled him to enter the larger houses by the back door. Rather he wanted me to go to Edinburgh to become a real physician, with an M.D. from a University, permitting me to condescend to the likes of himself or to confer with my distinguished colleagues in Latin before deciding that a case was hopeless after all.

Whatever Father's inner misgivings might have been, our family with its extended circle of expert acquaintances fell to discussing my future with overpowering relish. The spiritual aspects were dealt with by the Reverend Gideon MacWrath, our parish minister, a gaunt and wild fanatic straight from *Deuteronomy* or *Old Mortality*. The Scots, for ever at the throats of their kinsmen over the choice of available roads to Hell, had great need of such men to show them the best way and he was prepared to do this for them by example in return for a good meal. He was always appearing at the house around supper-time to give us unsolicited advice on my career, savouring the duty of unpalatable counsels with a commendable indifference to his host's profession.

"Aye," he would say benignly to my mother, patting his belly the while. "Aye, spiritual balance can only be reached when the vulgar needs of the stomach have been satisfied. But I fear for your son's welfare if he follows a profession that concerns itself with our fleshly turpitude. He should follow Christian interests; he should not inflame the baser passions which it is his bounden duty to suppress." He continued to fear for my welfare all evening, or at least until the decanters were empty. His concern was irrelevant, except to his appetite, for my slide into medicine had become inevitable from the day Father had shown me the structure of his titled leg.

There was another slide in my life, downward this time, and one that caused me rather less pleasure, for the Reverend Gideon had a daughter, a pumpkin in dun ringlets, whom he had seen fit to christen Grizel, and it was generally understood that at some hallowed time in the future we would be man and wife. What was not generally understood was why.

The "why" happened one day not long after the disclosures of Sandy Leer, of whom more later, and the scene was on the banks of the Esk, which around Dalkeith tends to meander through dense birch woods that afford thick cover from prying eyes; they also afford thick springy turf under foot. Grizel and I used to scamper through these woods as children, and one summer afternoon, when I assumed I was still a child, I discovered that Grizel was not. I have now no doubt that she had known this for a long while already and I still blush at the memory.

In short, we found a sylvan glade where the fair Grizel invited me to help her suffer a fate worse than death. There may well have been an element of coercion, for Grizel was a big girl. Now Sandy Leer's accounts, despite his wealth of descriptive detail, left me in some doubt exactly what to do. Grizel, however, with no doubts at all managed to fill in any necessary gaps left in Sandy's instructions. I can recall thinking that the nettles must have caused her grievous injury from the vast area of flesh in contact, but I am not inclined to think that it was just the nettles that caused her to cry out.

Then we rambled along the riverside, hand in hand, love's little angels blowing dandelion fluff, sniffing the wild mignonette and searching for another rustic bower, free of nettles this time. The air was drowsy with the hum of fat bees and the undergrowth alive with rabbits and squirrels and stoats who quite unmoved by our activities, were scuttling about in a ceaseless quest for something to eat. It was idyllic, almost.

The shock came as we were wandering home. Grizel wanted me to kiss her again, and thrust me against the trunk of a convenient tree. She then put a quietening finger to my lips and murmured sweet nothings, among which were scattered bitter somethings. I caught the words "marriage", "taken against her will", "famous in Edinburgh", "wife of a famous man", and herself smiling sweetly the while as if to emphasise her helpless fragility.

I was caught. To impugn her honour was unthinkable; to impugn my own by suggesting that she had overpowered me, which was not far from the truth, was equally unthinkable. Home we came, and Grizel skipped skittishly past the fir trees to the whitewashed manse, bursting through the front door.

"Father, Father," she shouted, like a farmer issuing his final warning to a feckless bull. "Father, I have been sought in marriage. What do you say to that?" What he said to that came down as a bellow from on high.

"I have been sought in marriage, Father," she bawled again, "and with your approval I would like to accept. And my love is to go on to Edinburgh to become a professor." She squeezed my ear playfully, leaving a red weal across my cheek and rhapsodised a bit in this vein while her father struggled down the stairs, snorting and gasping and putting on a great show of paternal sternness. I can now realise that he could only have been relieved and delighted that he would not have to go on feeding his hefty daughter. As one not familiar with grocers' bills I was not to know that then. He put a fatherly hand on my shoulder and led us into his study.

"This calls for a wee thochtie celebration," said he, untopping an empty decanter of whisky. "Och no," he went on, retopping the container, "we had best go and celebrate the good news with your father and mother instead."

Father's decanters were full of whisky, and his and my mother's eyes

5

were full of questions. He graciously toasted the happy couple we would make, "when my studies were completely finished."

Here we were talking of marriage when my studies, far from being completely finished or even started, had not even been decided or arranged. Mr MacWrath continued to air his doubts before, between and after meals for he was now running short of excuses to ruin our family evenings which in summer we tended to spend in the upper reception room.

There were countless such gatherings, but a particular one remains with me because the setting contrasted so grotesquely with these forebodings of domesticity. From the bow window I could feel mysterious shadows forming in the garden, where the great beeches, in full moist leaf were yielding lightly to the evening whispers. Grizel, a profusion of taffeta and organdie, was taking a turn about the room, stopping here and there to show an unhealthy interest in a Carolean day bed, a farthingale chair and other bits and pieces that had belonged to my grandfather. Mother was taking great pains to arrange half a dozen pansies on the escritoire. Father, who regarded the MacWraths more as interesting curiosities than irritations, sat back in his chair to accept them as might a gourmet who has found something unrecognisable in a yellow sealed bottle of claret.

Lacking my father's tolerance, I squirmed on my seat trying to produce silence with images of MacWrath dangling on a butcher's hook. These little fancies, though not very effective, were pleasing enough in their way. Father and he continued to discuss my plans and debate the ideal way to achieve eternal damnation. I cannot say that the natural connection of these subjects, or my bespoken's odyssey through the furniture did anything for my humour.

"T'were liefer he followed divine studies, with the ministry in mind of course." MacWrath followed this with an empty glass gesture that I knew with my eyes shut. Well, no harm in getting up and I noted with some satisfaction the clerical beak whitening in hope, then regaining its natural hue as I rose towards the decanter and began to examine with maddening care the regimental crest cut in its flank. If his thoughts were at that moment unspiritual, they blended imperially with the facial purple. The decanter was weighty and I marvelled as I looked through it at the opposite wall; it had a clear quality that almost suggested transparency. And the stopper, I could see, fitted into the neck with a closeness that might have passed for snugness.

"Inspired craftsmanship, made when I was a lad I should fancy," said the minister, not giving up easily. "Compare that piece you have in your hand there with the trumpery rubbish they turn out these godless days." But before I could enjoy the nibble or cast another bait, Grizel's 'not

6

worth a farthing voice' sliced across our exchange with the captivating charm of a carving knife: she was saying,

"Naturally, we would want to have these chairs recovered Mistress Bryson." Then my mother, equally sharp,

"I would have you know Miss MacWrath that I made these covers myself." And I could see Father adding another jewel to his MacWrath collection while Grizel bubbled,

"Did you really? Oh! That must have been when you were much younger."

The male MacWrath was now evidently dismayed beyond simple thirst, but from the creaking cushion beneath him, it seemed the anguish came from his angular buttocks and not from his daughter's social gaucheries. He shifted his position marginally, but not his theme,

"Aye, mmm, uhuh, aye, you must know, a holy life calls for great sacrifice, great poverty, indifference to earthly comforts and dining sparsely," said he, seemingly just aware of unsuspected beauty in sunlight fading through an inverted crystal drinking cup.

"I would not survive such hardships, Mr. MacWrath," said I, satisfied with my foray into regimental history. "I'm not as worthy as yourself, sir."

"Maybe not; maybe not. You will just have to develop that quality during your medical studies, my boy. Yet when you have climbed the ladder, you will doubtless be well endowed with worldly goods. The only course will be to learn how not to enjoy them," sighed the cleric, mortifying his impatience with a lengthy homily.

"A good wife would ensure that, Father," twittered his daughter, fresh from her inventory.

"Indeed she would," declared her comfortably widowed father putting down his goblet in exasperation.

"Have some Madeira, Mr. MacWrath," said Father.

"Ought I to? Ah well, a wee stoup of wine would not insult a man of God," said the minister.

Our pleasures for the day were wound up by Grizel squalling *Will ye no' come back again?* over Mother's harp with a passion that might well have explained why he hadn't.

While my place in eternity was being arranged by this fraudulent prophet, my place in Edinburgh University was being arranged by John Thomson, the former Professor of Military Surgery. A droll puckered joker, as sharp as a cat's whisker, he could predict your own behaviour before you had thought of it yourself. This Celtic second sight had made him take five years to choose a house; it had stopped him from choosing a wife, and it led him to see fatal flaws in a career that everyone else thought established. He had spent the entire war dining with the officers

7

of the Royal Scots at Edinburgh Castle, emerging when it was all over, to justify his title by sawing off a few legs in Belgium. But in the middle of the triumphant parades he recognised that things military were going out of fashion, and he could see that sliding under the table and getting measured up for new uniforms were not the thing for a man without a private income. So he discovered one night that he had always had a lifelong interest in Surgical Pathology. Rearranging his beliefs, his conversation, his appearance, his companions and his interests, he left the Town Council no alternative choice for Professor of this new subject in which he was so specially qualified.

Such a facility for direction made all subsequent arrangements simple; there was a great deal of scribbling, sanding and sealing. Beattie from the schoolhouse was persuaded, possibly against his better judgment, to depatch a faintly misleading account of my scholastic merits. Mr MacWrath undertook to guarantee my purity and humility. My father undertook to foot the bills. Letters returned from the college bursar. He did not refer to my particular genius or fitness for entry to the Medical faculty, nor did he seem to care that I was a classical prodigy, on the brink of sainthood. He did have a lot to say about Professor Thomson and his important friends and begged that he might be remembered to him and was our humble and obedient servant and if he could creep any lower, Professor Thomson had only to say the word. Uncle John did not waste any more words there, but he told me that Alexander Monroe, the Professor of Anatomy, had grave difficulty in understanding his own subject, which seemed a curious obstacle to teaching it. So we had to send off yet another letter to Robert Knox— the king of the Edinburgh Anatomists.

Now you may imagine that this was a rather casual way to choose a profession, but what else could I do. My tastes prepared me for galloping around our land, but we had none. Father forbade the Army and the Navy, and Mr MacWrath's selective Calvinism did not inspire me to the cloth. The Law, in the person of our local solicitor, Mr Dunsome, was regarded by the divine as glib lies and money spinning cant. The stage was even worse though Thomson was frequently heard to say, "If you have a liking for dramatics, you could do no better than a senior staff appointment at Edinburgh Royal Infirmary."

All that was as it might be, but I had to do something, and a physician's life in the Big City did not seem to me to be too arduous compared with, say, that of a surgeon-apothecary in the country. I had watched Father whipping up his trap from one stricken home to another. I had noticed that people spoke to him only when sick, and if they were well, then only about when they had been sick. I had seen him give solace when I knew that he needed it more. I had watched him listen endlessly to old grannies who had nothing wrong but thought they had, and to the not so old who had everything wrong but thought they had not. I felt there was something more to being a doctor—fame for example. I felt I belonged more naturally in a close carriage in Edinburgh. I also had a suspicion, though I suppressed the thought at once, that it required a special talent to take on my father's role and merely ambition to take on the one I was imagining for myself.

Events thereafter moved fast and before I knew what I was about I was standing on the doorstep saying goodbye to our assembled family and family to be. Mother cried and pressed upon me some clean linen and a hamper full of meat and pickles. Father shook my hand. My brother and sister squabbled so long over who was to shake my hand first that neither did so in the end. Grizel stood about in the background in a morning dress she had made for herself with rather more than the recommended amount of material from an illustration in *La Belle Assemblée*. She now tripped forward to bid me God speed to the city.

"I'll marry you when you are a professor, my love," she carolled. Well, thought I to myself, that gives me twenty years to break the engagement.

"But no," she went on, looking pointedly at my cheery face, "I'll marry you before then and I shall help you in all your struggles. Ah, Father," she sighed, "the good Lord works in mysterious ways, does He not indeed?"

The Reverend MacWrath, with his taste for theatricals, made me feel I was going off to join the East India Company rather than eight miles up the road to Edinburgh. He turned his palms to heaven and called upon the Lord to lead me triumphant from the paths of lechery, self indulgence and a host of other attractive distractions. I could still hear his ringing declamation as the curving road took me out of sight of my home. I walked briskly past the turning corn and fields of potato shaws half frightened at what I had let myself in for, and at the absence of actual thought that had gone into my choice of occupation. The September sunshine highlighted the leafy yellows from the Pentlands across to Musselburgh, and although it was still warm I shivered. Here I was going to be a doctor because I could not think of anything else to do. My first inclination had come from watching my father go grey in a pursuit that frightened me. However, no footpads appeared on my way, to convert my foolish anxiety into genuine terror and I reached the Cameron Toll about eleven o'clock. There, a sporting gentleman on a large bay entire, directed me up the road to the University buildings where I had to matriculate.

Edinburgh to a wee country laddie is both fabulous and disappointing. I listened in vain for the learned thoughts of David Hume and Adam Smith. Instead I heard the noise of the water carriers in their grey duffle greatcoats as they shuffled and laughed up the Potter Row. I heard the Newhaven fishwives enticing you to look into deep oyster creels with their musical wail of "caller ou ou ou ou", or other street hawkers, tempting you with less musical noises towards barrow loads of rotting fruit, or buckets of hot peas and beans, and others still, offering brushes to clear up the mess afterwards. Though to be sure it would have taken a thousand brushes in continual use to make any impression on the gutters, already brimful with the illegal contents of a thousand chamberpots. It seemed that you saw the Flowers of Edinburgh with your nose. I found out later that the alleys off the High Street were even worse and that it was not unusual to find the odd horizontal child or adult who was not just asleep.

I carried on my way through the offal, the carters, the vagrants and occasional gentlemen, and found the University buildings easily enough, just round the corner from a bowling-green. What was not so easy to discover was which door to use, for all available entrances were obscured by a swarm of builders' labourers, faced with the impossible task of erecting a sparkling new University while tearing down the old, without interrupting the flow of knowledge. I picked the least imposing entrance only to find that it would not open in either direction. The most imposing, which I had first avoided, opened in both directions and swung shut too quickly, knocking me flat on to the black and white chequered floor in front of a College servitor, who looked beyond me with the unruffled indifference of a camel contemplating eternity.

Once inside I found that matriculation gave my self esteem another mortal blow. The bursar wore city black, relieved only by a cream collar and a patronising smile that gave his whey face a suggestion of surprised disgust. He was pleased enough when I reminded him that my father would settle the accounts, for this meant that he escaped the tedious business of financing yet another promising beggar. He could not have known that I had read his obsequious letter to the important Professor Thomson.

"The Annus Medicus commences on October 3rd," he announced. "You will find the course laid out in this." He handed me a sheet of paper with high nosed condescension. I looked at the sheet in dismay. In it I read that I had to do Anatomy, Physiology and Chemistry for my first winter session. It was a fairly daunting prospect. I further saw that Anatomy was dropped in the summer, but taken up again the following winter. I wondered if this had something to do with the rumours about Professor Monroe. The bursar was smirking at me, and I speculated what his response might be to a quill up his black nostril. Instead I said,

"Can you tell me, sir, why we do not do Anatomy in the summer session as well?" The bursar withered me with another pedigreed glance. He said,

"Because, my good fellow, the bodies—you know—the dissecting specimens—can be used only in the winter. If you will permit me to observe, by April even medical students find working with them distasteful."

I was surprised to find later that he could look even more unpleasant when I asked the way to Dr Knox's establishment. His leer vanished.

"Oh, you'll find that quite easily," he said with a sour grimace. "It's down there," he added vaguely, pointing East and West at the same time. He then spun on his heel and walked off to encourage someone else.

Fortunately both directions brought me to where I wanted to go. Knox's school lay at the south end of Surgeons' Square, flanked by what I recognised from my father's maudlin descriptions to be The Royal Society of Medicine and the Surgeons' Hall. All very handsome— square stones, Grecian pillars and heavy oaken doors.

I looked over Knox's house before venturing up to the portal, and I also looked in vain for the tirlin pin to tell them I was there. There was no pin but there was a long chain which I hoped was attached to a bell somewhere. I pulled it and to my horror found that it was attached to a pack of hounds. There now started a fierce and ravenous howling that swarmed right up to the other side of the door. My reason exploded. I decided to run away. I then decided not to run away. I thought of my bag of meat as a bait. I thought of myself as a fox and renounced my hunting interests. A thousand other mad thoughts jostled their way through my head to no conclusion. After a heavy rattling of chains, three suspicious faces suddenly appeared around the door. Two belonged to the biggest dogs I have ever seen. The third belonged to a bearded lackey, whose whole strength was spent just holding the brutes off my throat. I did not find speaking easy. All three growled at me, dragging and scuffling on the ends of the leather thongs, fortunately in opposing directions.

From inside a surprisingly smooth voice said,

"what is it, Jock? No, no, I don't think this is the man we were expecting. It's the wrong door anyway. You can take the dogs away."

I looked sideways at the straining leashes, not sure who was to take whom. I found my voice and repeated my introduction. Knox, for it could be no one else, took my hand and led me through a large hall into his study. He settled me into a high-backed chair and took his station before a wide grate of burning logs.

"Well, sir, what can Robert Knox do for you?"

"You will have heard from Professor Thomson Sir".

"Ahah—the chairmaker," he observed sardonically, leaving me for an instant to wonder if Thomson had added carpentry to his many other disciplines. "Yes I have heard from him."

"My father has written as well sir. I have the letter here." He took it and read it carefully, giving me time to observe at leisure his quite arresting appearance. A pair of gold-rimmed pince-nez perched in a deep notch on an elongated nose; smooth scalp glistening through unruly fluffs of white hair; face heavily pocked; a black patch across his left eye completing the appearance of a man not to cross lightly. His shoulders were broad, but tapered to the slender fingers, which in the left hand tapered to a heavy leather purse. I liked the look of him but found him faintly frightening.

Now he smiled confidently down at me for he had always known why I was there.

"So you want to join my extra-mural class in Anatomy," he said at last. "Well, I think you could be squeezed in. We're very popular you know. Two sets of lectures daily, one at eight, one at six—different groups of course, with practical surgical demonstrations too. You'll have to work hard."

He stopped to introduce some snuff below the pince-nez. He went on, "your father says he will be paying the fee. It's payable in advance, you know. Four pounds a session, and you'll see that we have a Summer session as well as a Winter one."

"My father will instruct his bankers as soon as I let him know you have accepted me, sir," I said.

Knox's face clouded briefly. "I was hoping to have had it in coin now, but no matter. We have an introductory lecture on October 3rd at eleven o'clock of the morning. You may pick up your card of admission there; I would counsel you to register with the academic library today; there will be fewer students about." While he was speaking I worked out the significance of October 3rd.

"But Professor Monroe gives his opening address that day also, sir." I was aghast.

"Well, well," he smiled, "so he does, but if you will just consult the University sheet you will see that my lecture is first." He tilted his gaze at me with smug irony. "That is a subtle choice, for it will give you an opportunity to set your standards here before you go to hear what the Professor has to offer."

2

The most important thing after matriculation was to find a watertight roof; in fact some sybarites gave it first priority—and for me it had been a day of firsts. I had walked to Edinburgh for the first time. I had matriculated for the first time. I had met Dr Robert Knox for the first time. I was hungry for the first time and might have run home had I the strength to get there or to explain myself when I had. A substitute was the thing and I began my search with a random interest that rapidly developed into a florid obsession. Even Grizel began to bewitch me, bubbling away in a pot of carrots and thyme.

Good landladies, though I did not then realise it, are like precious stones—picked up by the few and sought after by the many. I in fact started my treasure hunting in the anteroom while I was awaiting the bursar's pleasure. The trails to be followed were hidden amongst a collection of other notices, where established students passed off their unwanted rubbish as unrepeatable bargains. The clues stood out from this scribbled optimism as much by their professional neatness as by the unbelievable luxury offered for just ten shillings a week. There was Minnie Haddock telling everyone in her fine italic that her victuals were better than any in the Fleshmarket Close, or Bertha Fleece, who was willing to throw down the gauntlet to anyone over the whiteness of her sheets.

You might think that these were the best available. You would be wrong. The reputations of the best spread quickly by word of mouth, but not so quickly as the students who believed in them. Only the second-rate appeared on the notice board.

In my innocence I thought to try Bertha Fleece, the duelist of the Potter Row, and rattled the risp at her front door, which she opened, at once revealing a sepia hall—all of two feet wide and possibly twice as long. This was convenient for she was shaped like a crooked sabre. Her complexion of hide and her lips held onto her face by a purse string, she now shuffled towards me on slippered ramrods. She had the appearance of a woman who has either watched her husband succumb to the drink or perhaps driven him there. I stood my ground and stated my business, at which she gave a money catching smile and began an immediate stream of lucrative deceit in a Highland lilt that would have charmed a hanging judge into a reprieve.

"Ah, sir," she said, "I haf chust the nicest room that would be fery suiting to the likes of yourself."

"Does it have a view?" I asked hopefully.

"A view, sir," she riposted, stung to the brink of a challenge. "A view, sir, you haf not seen the likes before: if you would be pulling yourself on tiptoe up to the skylight now you would get a fine wee keek at Arthur's Seat that would be worth twice the rent to a chentleman such ass yourself."

"Good," said I, all dignity, "I'll come and see it at once."

"Ah, sir, it iss not convenient to have the viewing at the moment," said she in a flourish of wrinkles.

"Then, madam, I await your convenience."

"But, sir, you would be waiting the long while. You see I haf chust this fery morning let it out to someone else—but you'll be pleased to know, sir, he iss a scholar not unlike your good self."

I sighed and asked if by chance she had heard of Mistress Haddock. She was shocked.

"Don't you be going anywhere near Minnie Haddock." she warned. "She iss chust a dirty wee trollop," with which parting caution she withdrew into her scabbard. And when I ignored her recommendations it appeared that Mistress Haddock held the same or very similar opinions about her rival, and she had just let her last room as well.

I now began the long cheerless grind of looking for a likely hovel amongst the thousands of other unlikely hovels up and down the closes off the High Street. I climbed up stairs and I climbed down stairs, collecting abuse, rebuffs and advice, but no offer of lodgings. My ears told me that none were available; my legs told me I had better find one soon. I wanted to go home.

And so I came at last to Robertson's Wynd, a narrow grimy thoroughfare swarming with grimy children. The houses seemed to consist entirely of stair wells. How anyone lived in them at all I could not conceive, but judging from the children I was the only one to be so affected.

It must have been the hundredth door I knocked at, two flights up, where a matted slattern answered my knock and eyed me with ill disguised suspicion and given the neighbours I had passed on the way up, this was probably reasonable. I tried to see past the flare of her soiled kirtle into a hall that was if anything even more narrow than the one I had failed to rent so long ago. Seeing the direction of my gaze she filled in all the available observation holes with herself.

"Whit dae ye want," she snarled, gripping her broomstick a bit more tightly. I smiled with synthetic sincerity.

"I am seeking lodgings, madam," said I.

"Hae ye ony siller?"

"I can pay, yes."

"It'll be ten shillin's a week, and ye'll find yer ain candles and yer denner."

When we had reached an agreement she began to smile a bit and the result was quite horrible, but she said,

"Aye, ye'll mak a fine lawyer." I started at this.

"But I am studying to be a doctor."

"A doctor," she shouted, "weel the rent will be fifteen shillin's then—a dirty crowd of brutes ye are tae."   "But, madam . . ."

"Dinna 'but madam' me," she growled, "lawyers are, what would ye say—clean and of some yase forbye. But a doctor—if ye're no weel, it's better ye dinna see ane. Heh, heh, heh."

I gathered up my belongings and stamped out in a rage and after another futile hour I arrived back at Robertson's Wynd and struck rather despondently at the same rotting door.

Looking, if anything, filthier, the old witch pulled it open. She grasped the situation at once.

"Ye're back," said she, her powers of observation as sharp as her nose.

"I'll take your room," said I sullenly.

"Will you then," she said. "Weel, the rent is noo twenty shillin's a week."

"What?"

"Aye. The worth of siller is droppin' every day."

"You have me dead to rights," I said.

Suddenly I was aware of another voice behind her.

"Becky, is it not hard ye're bein on the young gossoon there?" The voice could say no more for lack of breath—its owner, a crumpled old roué of about forty and completely toad-shaped. His mouth was a toothless sack, his nostrils snuff caverns, his eyes providing the water for the whisky in his cheeks. He had that shifty jovial look that makes you turn the other way in a tavern and feel for your purse. However at that time I had barely been in a tavern. He went on,

"Barney O'Loan at your service."

Such amiability in so hearty a setting was not to be resisted. I stepped forward to shake his hand, and felt a mouthful of resentful teeth closing on my ankle.

"Aargh," I bellowed and fell back. A scruffy wall-eyed mongrel was disappearing out the door. Mrs O'Loan was not pleased.

"Attack my bloody dug would you." said she. "Afore Ah ken where Ah am ye'll be tearin' him up for an experiment."

What I should have said was, "You silly bitch, it's him that'll be

15

tearing me up." What I ended up saying was, "please forgive me, madam. I had no idea you had such a nice animal in the house."

She gave me a queer look.

"Ye're no' referrin' tae ma husband?"

"No no, no, madam," I said hastily.

Mr O'Loan could not be insulted and he did not think I was referring to him, because he came around his wife, all smiles, and took my bag. A digestive look came across his face, and his nose twitched.

"Sure there must be beef in this bag, I'm thinkin'" said he all a-quiver. He turned to his wife and nodded, "Becky, we must be invitin' this young gentleman to supper."

The cordial grimace on Becky's face stretched even further, and it was soon all settled, the time, the place and she even went so far as to promise to wipe the platters clean.

He took me up to my room—a wee corridor off the stair well, leading into an empty grate. I gazed about in dismay. It certainly was not much for the price. The floor of coarsely knotted pine, through which I could see, acted as the ceiling for the room below. Mine boasted a cracked ewer on a sloping dresser, and a bed, managing with three legs and a block of wood. It looked worse in the failing light. No candle was provided, but there was an empty crusie lamp hanging from the mildewed ceiling. The scene was not inviting. I sat down with a weighty gesture of despair and found myself on the floor beside the now two-legged bed.

A fat cough recalled me to the cheerless outside world. It was himself breathing heavily. Much air but not a word crossed his lips and he watched me free myself from a ragged fustian blanket.

"I was thinkin'," he gasped at last between spasms, "that we might take a little turn out to procure a dhrop for the supper."

"A drop of what?" I asked, all suspicious but his cheerful humour seemed to spread over his whole body.

"As though a fine gentleman like yourself would not be takin' my meanin'. Ross's tavern was the place I had in mind."

It certainly couldn't be worse than where I was at the moment.

"All right, I'll come," I said, none too graciously.

As Ross's tavern was not a gracious place, my surliness did not matter much. We stepped on to a thick carpet of sawdust, which collected the overflow from the tankards, barrels and stomachs. It was low, and the illumination solely dependent on windows which were dirty. Mr O'Loan seemed completely at home. He knew the tavern; he knew the landlord; he knew what he liked to drink, and they knew what he liked to drink. His bidding to the landlord had a jaunty familiarity that sought to disarm in advance a not impossible refusal.

"Would you fill these jugs for me, Wattie, and I'll have a dhrop of what's good for me and for me friend here."

Two brimming tankards were set up, and I took them over to a quiet corner.

"We'll be settlin' later, Wattie," said he, turning away with surprising acceleration before Wattie could disagree. Mr O'Loan settled himself in layers comfortably on a large stool, before addressing himself to the tankard. After a long draught he addressed himself to me.

"It's like this, sorr," he said. "I get this terrible pain when I bend me back." He was prepared to demonstrate too and cleared his legs from under the table ready for the performance.

Now what on earth do you tell a man who has no waist when he tells you he can't bend? But he was going on,

"To let you understand, sorr," he pointed to his vast thigh now, "the pain runs down me leg here." I was certain it was not the only thing that ran down that leg. I tried to look like a medical sage.

"I beg leave to wonder, Mr O'Loan, if you might not be a trifle large for your size. Such must have a stiffening effect upon your spinal column." I was rather pleased with this little speech. It sounded almost professional, and I hadn't even attended my first Anatomy lecture.

"Ah, that'll be right, sorr. Ye've struck the answer there. Of that divil a doubt. But this pain," he continued, "is not content with me leg. It goes on into me fute."

"Well, sir, I would incline to the belief that the pain is in the extremity; that is to say, it's in the foot," I finished lamely.

"Would you think that now? In the foot, ye say; well, well, well. Is it not you that has the brains, doctor?"

He fell silent awhile, and emptied the tankard, pondering my professional deliberations. Around us grumbled a hundred furtive conversations. In the flickering fire light I viewed their source—red noses, tam o'shanters and churchwarden pipes and I, the next professor of whatever, pleased at being consulted in such a den. O'Loan was giving voice to fresh thoughts.

"Jaisus. I have this terrible thirst, too, doctor."

I wasn't going to be stopped now that my advice was being so freely sought. He was not to know that I had not yet acquired a complete list for the causes of his condition. I put my fingers together as I had seen my father do often, and tried to recall the Latin word for thirst. It didn't matter; such erudition would be lost on Mr O'Loan. I began sagely,

"Ah, thirst. Yes. This is a large subject, and I would recommend that you . . ."

He put a hand on my leg and halted my oratory with a fatty gurgle.

"It's not a diagnosis I'm after, doctor. It's another mouthful of the

17

porther beer I had in mind. As ye can see, I have some difficulty in getting up. So you fill up the tankards now, and God bliss ye." When I returned with the drinks, he changed the subject to his own previous activities in the city, which had been hair-raising certainly and illegal probably. His increasing girth had put an end to everything except breathlessness and reminiscence. He entertained me with a string of incredible stories, of which he was always the main character, about churchyards and anatomists, and the resurrection men who kept them supplied with dissecting specimens. The stories fascinated him enough to make him forget his back, weight, his foot and his thirst.

Finally he tired of his recital, and wheezed and struggled to his feet, as ungainly as an old armoured knight waiting for the hoist to his warhorse. He gestured me ahead of him.

"I'll take those jugs now, Wattie;" he shouted to mine host, "the doctor will pay."

And pay I did, not only that night but the next morning. My head expanded and contracted irregularly, and it was worse when I moved. Still, I had to get up for this was the great day. I set off from my new lodgings, giving myself plenty of time (I needed it) to get to Surgeons' Square, and also to fancy how Dr Knox might dispense his pearls. Certainly they would be polished and rare. He would see to that.

Mr O'Loan, although given to drawing the long bow, had certainly coloured in my background knowledge of the Edinburgh medical scene. These classes in Anatomy that flowered outside the University walls, the so-called Extra-mural Schools, owed their rapid growth to the ineptitude of the Intra-mural Schools. There had been a series of them. John Bell was the first to see a market for anatomical teaching. His school had bloomed for a while because it was good, and collapsed before the combined wrath of the professors because it was too good.

Another John—Barclay—had taken over the school, which now continued under the care of Robert Knox. Nor was this the only one, for another Robert—this time Liston—established a rival school in the same Square. As far as teaching was concerned there was no rivalry, for Professor Monroe bored so many students to death. But when it came to acquiring dissecting specimens—well, that was quite another thing. These specimens just had to be found if the students were to find their way through the confused tangle of essential structures that coiled in Latin from one unpronounceable bone to another.

Legally acquired bodies were scarce. They came in the main from the gallows in the Grassmarket. As John Bell was wont to say, "to get a half acceptable practical course in Anatomy in the University, you would need three good murders a year, not to mention the apprehension of the culprits."

The anatomists occasionally managed to buy the odd corpse from needy relatives, but these were casual sales. By far the greatest numbers were stolen from freshly dug graves by bands of dedicated body-snatchers who were drawn from the riff-raff of Edinburgh, the same scum of the earth who had fought the French.

I didn't need Barney O'Loan to tell me that people went to enormous lengths to protect their dead. The richest remained intact in their family vaults. The less rich placed heavy wrought-iron grills, or mort-safes, across their recent departed. As money became scarcer, the poorer paid the still poorer to stand guard, which they did after a fashion, until they fell drunk. The very poorest did the watching themselves, or just did not care.

The snatchers also went to great lengths to defeat the guards, and to steal only the body, which in law was not a hanging offence—but stealing the shroud was. And if they did manage to seize a prize they had to stop competitors from stealing it from them. Theirs was a hard life. I could see why Mr O'Loan had taken to the bottle. I could also see that I was near Surgeons' Square, and my speculation ended as I found myself part of a stream of students straggling up to Knox's house, armed with manuscripts, paper, quills and ink.

As we entered the lecture theatre I could hear Jock and his ferocious pets pit-patting about on the other side of a happily powerful door. The lecture room was built in the style of a Grecian amphitheatre, and John Thomson's remarks about the stage floated back to me. I tried to work out how two hundred students could be squeezed into such a room. If the rumours were true, this was so.

We diffidently chose our places on the hard benches as far apart from each other as we could. The only figure that showed any emotion in the room was a skeleton, wired up like father's leg, and suspended from a curved stand. It grinned at us humourlessly. There was an air of conspiracy about the room. We did not speak to each other. We did not look at each other. We just took a warm comfort in each other's breathing, said nothing, looked at the stage and waited.

Suddenly the spell was broken. The door was flung back on its hinges, and a lordly young man of about 21 strolled in. He was dressed in what might be called "the extreme of fashion". An exquisite cravat; a chestnut tailcoat, nankeen breeches, so fitting, I was sure he would not be able to sit down. He kicked the door shut with the heel of one of his calf boots, and quizzed us through a lorgnette.

"Hullo,", he said, "so this is what a collection of medical students looks like. Haw, haw, haw." He took a prominent place in the front row and I was wrong about the nankeen breeches. He then crossed his legs, placed down his cane with great care placed his corn coloured head back with equal care and closed his eyes as if to sleep. We eyed him in silent wonder.

If we had needed any common bond before, the arrival of this gorgeous man gave us a shared feeling of social inferiority. We began to murmur amongst ourselves. I discovered that the dark-eyed fellow on my right was Aeneas McBeen, and his father was the minister at Inveresk. His eyes were fierce, suggesting a fervour not wholly religious.

On my left sat an even more startling figure. A stack of careless hair made his head twice as large as it was. He said his name was somebody Darwin, and that he didn't know why he had bothered to start this course. It had been something to do with pleasing his father. Looking at him, I could only agree. He had an untameable air that did not seem as though it would ever be squeezed into the strait-jacket of a conforming profession.

Beside him sat the only man who had been talking when the dandy entered. He was a good-natured smiler, with the honeyed liquid of Dublin on his tongue, and though this was not instantly apparent, he turned out also to be brilliant, for his tastes ran far beyond his favourite black beer to a genuine interest in the heart and blood vessels. His name was Dominic Corrigan. He was the only one who seemed to be laughing in the room.

He was still laughing when the arrival of Dr Knox reduced us all to silence. Knox was looking more cavalier than when I had first met him. He took us all in with his only eye, and began his address. "Gentlemen, you are free to do anything you choose in my lecture theatre. You may smoke, you may take snuff, you may sleep, you may get up to anything you fancy, but you will not talk. I am the only one allowed to speak in this room." He paused to assess the effect of his opening remarks, then went on,

"My aim," he said, "is to teach you some Anatomy and Surgery, and to help dispel the clouds of obscurantism that emanate from that canting humbug who calls himself Professor of Anatomy—Alexander Monroe—Tertius." He spat out the Latin ordinal as he might a piece of bad meat.

He told us that his basic course was for two years, and that we would be sitting for M.D. examination after three. You could not deny the man had presence. He would not deny it either.

"You will learn your surgical skill on real bodies, acquired freshly and frequently winter and summer. You will learn to recognise those vital nerves and essential vessels and irreplaceable ducts, the section of which in the operating room can lead only to disaster and possibly to the court."

He dropped the high-flown delivery and became almost conversational for a while. Then he told us that Monroe, being a mere physician, was not in the habit of operating at all.

"He is a sophist, practised in that realm of science called evasion; a peddler of cordials and nostrums, a concoctor of witch's brews and potions; a dabbler with his finger in every pie, and indeed better for humanity that it stay there than stray into a surgical wound. How can such a man have the effrontery to teach Anatomy to aspiring surgeons?" His eloquence increased as he warmed to his favourite hate, the University. A deeply felt passion gripped him as he described the iniquitous clique of professors led by no less than Professory Gregory, he of the powders in my father's bag, to have John Bell excluded from the Royal Infirmary. According to the one-eyed Knox, Gregory had stuck posters on the Infirmary doors warning Bell's surgical patients that they were about to succumb to the knife of a charlatan and mountebank. He also published a scurrilous article in the *Caledonian Mercury,* in which he confidently stated that if a man or his family were sick, he would get better treatment from a mad dog than he would from calling in John Bell. They were not uplifting legends.

"And he signed himself Jonathon Dawplucker," thundered Knox in rare fury. "A well chosen nom de plume for a trafficker in bombast who feathered his own cap as well as his nest." All this was delivered in a fine ringing voice, which suited his style marvellously. We were quite partisan now in our laughter, and he himself, obviously delighted with the effects of his lecture, told us that the real thing would start at eight sharp the next morning. He also wished us well in our afternoon lecture with the Professor.

"So," said the dandy, while we were shuffling towards the door, "it is clear that this sewies of lectures is going to be wather intewesting, what, haw, haw, haw."

I felt rather diffident at being addressed by such a man, but he seemed pleased enough to chat with me, so I walked along with him.

"I wather fancy a little stiffener after all that. It would set us up in pwime and plummy order for the afternoon, what. What do you say? Will you join me, sir? Haw, haw, haw!"

He re-arranged his already flawless necktie while we sauntered across Surgeons' Square. He was certainly a most confident man, and some years older than the rest of us. His smooth prattle carried on.

"So you are one of the local boys I take it, Well, you can no doubt keep me up to scwatch with all the funny twaditions." He laughed easily at this, and I could not take offence when he said, "I find your town

21

vewwy quaint alweady, you know. I have had the stwangest expewiences. Do you know, I was walking along Queen Stweet, would you believe it, just last Sunday. And I had to laugh at something quite funny. Possibly it was the misewable looking worshippers on their way to Divine Service, I shouldn't doubt. Well, one of them had the effwontery to addwess me. He said, 'Do you wealise, young man, that laughing is forbidden in the open stweets on the Sabbath. You wun the wisk of being convened.' I discovered that vewwy afternoon that by that he meant to have me flung into the pwison, and flung out of Scotland. Now what do you make of that, eh, what? Haw, haw, haw!" I didn't know what to say. It was all so reminiscent of the Rev. MacWrath. By this time we were almost near the door of my first tavern of the night before. My new friend was still talking.

"As for the language, you know, I cannot make out more than one in thwee words of what the locals are saying. As for the common people, I wonder if they understand each other at all. Pwesumably they do. Ah, here, we seem to have awived," he said, kicking open the door of Ross's Ale House which looked even bleaker in the daylight than it had the night before. He scrutinised the occupants through his gold lorgnette, grimaced, and moved to a table by the window alcove. Wattie, the landlord, had deteriorated overnight—like his house. My new acquaintance was quite unabashed. He struck the table with the ferrule of his polished stick, quite certain that the tapman would come in answer to its call, and he did.

"Ah, my good fellow," he began, "a measure of bishop for me and for my fwiend ...? I opened my mouth to speak, but the landlord spoke instead, in the tones of a rutting bull. I saw my new companion recoil from the noise.

"We'll hae nane o' that; nae talk o' bishops, we are guid Christians here, ye ken." He snapped his mouth shut like a gin trap, and would have been happier to see us go than to take our money.

My friend was not at all put out.

"Hey ho," he smiled, "Edinburgh is worth a conversion. What does one dwink in this confounded hostelwy, eh, what?"

"Ye can hae a chopin o' sma' beer," rejoined the tetchy landlord. "Well then, let us have two chopins of sma' beer here pwomptly," he replied, guffawing loudly. What a scuwilous fellow," he mused, while the man went off to draw the ale.

"Well," he glanced quizzically at me. "My name's Deelatwumpe. Quentin Deelatwumpe. And yours?"

I told him.

"Bwyson," he repeated, "well, Mr Bwyson, what bwought you into this noble pwofession?" I took a sip of beer, and found it remarkably pleasant, considering I had vowed just that morning never to touch it again. I said something to that effect.

"Ahah," declared Mr Deelatrumpe sententiously, "similia similibus cuwantur. In case you haven't come acwoss the term before, it means "a hair of the dog'—haw, haw, haw!"

"I know my Latin," said I peevishly. "In fact, I suppose that's why I am doing medicine at all. My father is a doctor, and I could not think of anything else to do."

He slapped his thigh heartily, and emptied his glass with a flourish. "Well, damn me, that's honest, haw, haw, haw! My weasons are qwite diffewent, you know." He called for more ale, and told me he had been in the Army, the 17th Lancers—a regiment of light cavalry. He had a buoyant way with him, and I could easily see him prancing down Rotten Row, passing his life in a never ending succession of simple cavalry manoeuvres, card games, gossip and illicit trysts in other peoples bedrooms.

"I understand they're getting a new colonel—a fellow called Bingham, heir to Lord Lucan—some Iwish earl, I hear. Anyway I'm no longer a light cavalwyman. I am going to be a physician, charging the sick instead of charging at them, haw, haw, haw!"

I could not fathom what had prompted such a cavalier exchange of London gallantries for Professor Monroe and the rest of them, or for that matter the heroic dead on the battlefield for the pathetic dissection specimens in Knox's rooms. I was not to know he had never seen a battle and had never intended to.

He clearly wasn't going to tell me either, though I did find out, and possibly quicker than he would have liked, from the tousle-headed Darwin, who came from the same part of Shropshire. Mr Deelatrumpe was the younger son of a tumble-down squire near Oswestry.

"He rides madly to the hounds," said Darwin candidly. "They put on great style in the county but I don't think there's a brass farthing to rub together in the whole family. Now I know there was some scandal over a game of cards. They did not actually throw him out of the Lancers but it was generally understood he would not carry on in the service."

To take up the study of medicine as a cure for family disgrace, was a strange reversal of accepted landed practice. A normal recourse for a younger son in trouble was to join the Army. If the 17th Lancers had already flung him out, then his natural escape route had been closed. Poor Quentin Deelatrumpe.

However I knew none of this when I first met him, as he told me only what he wanted me to know. I was certain I hadn't seen his like in the district before. He got to his feet casually, and said,

"Well, that was an expewience. I feel I must go and lie down before heawing Pwofessor Monwoe this afternoon." He stepped out across the sawdust, as if King George IV were waiting to knight him at the door.

King George IV was not at the door, but there was somebody of similar magnitude at the bar counter—none other than Mr O'Loan, my new landlord. A large goblet of brandy stood before him, with rather greater steadiness than he was managing himself. As I went over to him I could see he was not sure which one of me he ought to speak to. He nodded his head amiably.

"The top of the mornin' to ye, doctor. Ach, in the name of God, this brandy at 12 o'clock does me no good at all, at all." He reached for his glass to confirm this statement.

"Do you often drink at this time, Mr O'Loan?" I asked him solicitously.

"Aw, naw, naw, naw," he said airily, "just once a day."

3

The moment I saw Professor Monroe shuffling on to the podium for his opening address, I recognised in a flash that we were in for a ghastly afternoon, but probably no worse than I had learned to suffer in the Reverend MacWrath's bible class every Sunday at home.

You see, it is the Scottish tradition not to educate you merely for life, but for a life of improving torment. Sophists argue that in so poor a country, improvement is the only course, and it is one guarded jealously by the men of the cloth. There are exceptions. Lairds and their friends, for example, being improved already, can only degenerate, and in any case they control the distribution of manses, glebes and livings, and if pheasant is to be eaten off silver platters to the greater glory of God it is at the big house that it will be found. For the rest of us, the clergy manage to pass off this bleak spiritual contract as a divine concession due entirely to their special arrangements with Heaven.

"Build up a large enough credit of misery when you're young," they thunder, "and we can promise that the Lord, in His mercy, will compound it for you when you're old." But there are advantages—a certain comfort to be drawn from the certain discomfort of everybody else, and in return for this life of penance they promise you immunity from damnation on the Day of Judgment, even if the resurrection men happen to disturb your last sleep. It is a grim faith.

So, in addition to being well prepared for eternity, I was also well prepared for Professor Monroe, but not that well prepared.

Monroe was the third in a line of Anatomy professors that had started with his grandfather, Monroe Primus, in 1720. Sadly, the family brains had been used up by the time Tertius was born, but this was discovered only after the Town Council had confirmed his occupation of the Chair of Anatomy for life. His incompetence was proverbial. Some blamed Monroe for this, but the more knowing blamed the Town Council. It was not that he was lazy. He did not take the term "occupation of the Chair" as literally as did some of his colleagues. In fact they often said of him that he did not sit still long enough to think of anything at all. Certainly he busied himself in a thousand energetic projects that ended in a confusion worthy of the thoughts that prompted them in the first place.

I gazed in horror at this apathetic scarecrow, who was regarding us with the weary bafflement of a cow in a cloud of summer flies. This was the University's counterblast to Robert Knox. He peered at us through his straggly eyebrows. His white hair hung in untidy strands over a cravat, arranged around his neck like an old dishcloth. If his shirt had been white then it was no longer, and he could not make up his mind which foot to stand on. His one firm action was to keep his left hand in his pocket. He looked woodenly at our class, bowed deeply, and began,

"Gentlemen," he said, "Anatomy is the basis of everything. That is to say it is—ah—fundamental to the good practice of Medicine and Surgery. We all find it a difficult subject," he continued, "that is to say, students and teachers alike find it extremely—ah—difficult." He droned on in this manner for a while, and I began to wonder how he managed to keep awake. It was the benches that kept us awake. They were designed to point us at all times towards the Professor, and their construction was such that if we fell asleep in them we would fall out of them on the shoulders of the man in front. There was a skeleton beside him, which showed remarkable animation, considering everything. To my delight I saw that it was not articulated as well as my father's noble limb. Monroe was going on, and with almost a spark of passion, for he was coming on to his favourite hate—the Extra-mural Schools.

"There are in this great world of teaching, however, some mountebanks who shall remain nameless, but who, for the sake of argument, we will call John Bell, or Robert Knox, or John Barclay, or indeed Robert Liston."

"You must know that John Barclay was a student of Divinity in the University of St Andrews. I wonder that the very churchly fabric of that town did not influence him for the betterment of his soul. The Cathedral itself should have led him into paths of righteousness, and away from the teaching of Anatomy.

"The Cathedral, as you will know, was designed by Hubert of Falaise, noted not only for his architectural skills, but also for his humped back. Now humped, or hunched back is due to an exaggeration of the normal posterior curvature of the thoracic spine where the posterior surface is convex and the ah—the ah—anterior surface is—ah—concave. Not that this deformity in any way hampered his career. Indeed it is said he developed his theories on the extended arch in the main gateway from the arrangement of the bones in his own back—ah—a clever—ah— development. Now not all architects have had the good fortune to be crippled. Indeed most of them have straight backs, though the term "straight" is an anatomical misnomer for "normally curved" and if I might say normal in this context means . . .."

The subject of backs held him briefly before leading naturally on to baboons' wrists, ponies' stifles and tailors' knees, from which he found his way to an execution in the Grassmarket, which had provided him with his latest dissecting specimen. Somehow from there he moved on to the subject of shoeing of post-horses, while the class grew more restless, and Quentin Deelatrumpe was moved to say,

"I do believe that Pwofessor Monwoe has missed his twue vocation as a blacksmith and fawwier." If Monroe heard him, he was quite unmoved and did not even unpocket his hand.

Fifteen minutes later he led us into his dissecting room. This was a long low-ceilinged affair, almost like a wide passage, whitewashed to reflect the light that came from its many windows. A marble-topped table with a sheet over it stood in the centre of the room, and a decrepit attendant stood equally motionless in the corner. In time we learned that this was Willie Briar, and in no time at all we dubbed him Marble Willie after the style of Mortar Willie, the genial half-wit who carried packages between the apothecaries' shops and the Infirmary. We clustered round the table to watch the performance. Because of the lack of bodies we were not actually allowed to cut anything ourselves. This was done by the Professor or some of his favourite students, who hoped that this unpaid admiration for the Chair might one day be rewarded with a paid appointment in the Royal Infirmary.

Regional dissections of a foot or a hand were necessary to demonstrate subtle anatomical points, and their more memorable demonstrations were preserved in large jars, labelled like pickles. These stood on shelves along the dissecting room to encourage the bright and instruct the dull.

As Knox had already told us, we had to spend much of our first few years operating on the dead, thus learning how to carry out the same procedures on the living. Speed was the essence, for we had to recognise in an instant what we might cut and what we might not, while the patient was screaming and doing his best to remove the operating site and its obscuring blood from under the surgeon's scalpel.

Willie Briar indolently twitched the sheet away from our specimen, revealing a spare body, wrinkled and puckered like a rotting beetroot. His arms lay behind his back, where his bonds had held him through his last public appearance in the Grassmarket. With thirty students crowding round, there was little fear that we would learn anything.

I could see the rope-shaped groove round his neck, and I wondered away to myself what noble Judge had condemned him to the gallows and for what. I recalled Thomson's story of Lord Eskgrove passing the death sentence. He was reputed to have said, or Sir Walter Scott said he said,

"I do not know of what religious persuasion you are, or, if as I suspect, you are of no persuasion at all, but there are plenty of religious gentlemen around who would be pleased to show you the way to eternal life."

I felt sick and wanted to run away, but I was hedged in by a wall of eager novice surgeons. Monroe had started speaking again, and was discussing, would you imagine it, the special glazing carried out in his dissecting rooms by Wilsons of Leith. He was saying,

"All the best glaziers are to be found in Leith, and the reason for that is . . ." I began to consider various professional escape routes. Physically I was trapped but my mind was not. I began to think again about the Law, but all I could think about was Lord Eskgrove and his black cap, and I dismissed the possibility. I even considered the Church; after all the Rev. Gideon did not fare too badly. He passed his life in a furnace of invective against all other weaknesses except that of gluttony. And it was only because he burned away all his fat thundering against the other deadly sins, that he managed to maintain any credibility as a spiritual advisor at all. I had now come to thinking what if he was one of the religious gentlemen pleased to show you the way to eternal life: the final walk from the Calton Goal, the hostile mob, the scaffold, the noose, the hangman and this clerical fraud to open the Gates of Heaven.

"May the Lord comfort you through this coming ordeal, my son," he would say, "and I'll just have a wee nibble at this cheese here to give me strength to get down the gibbet steps."

I heard a voice in my ear.

"Smells of spiwits," said the voice.

"What does?" I asked, thinking that Deelatrumpe meant the Professor.

"The body," he said, "they've pweserved the body in alcohol. That's how Collingwood kept Nelson intact after Twafalgar, so that he'd last until his state funewal. He pickled the body in Navy wum in an oaken coffin, I think made out of some ship's mast or other. Or perhaps it was bwandy, since he was an Admiwal. I pwesume he looked just like that when they bwought him home, poor fellow, haw, haw, haw!"

"And now," said the Professor, like a cook about to reveal her new pie, "this is where we begin our study of the upper limb. That is to say, where we commence our interest in the subject of the upper extremity. There will be twenty lectures to the first year students, with demonstrations, and it will go on for twenty weeks—that is, for five months. Come closer now," he said, and began to slit through the skin with a fluency that had marked none of his other manoeuvres. At this level, his fluency stopped. He fumbled with muscles, couldn't identify nerves, and if the precise relationship of the brachial plexus to the axillary artery was clear to him, it escaped everybody else. As for surgical demonstration, a dead patient would have decomposed even further before Professor Monroe reached any conclusion. Perhaps it was just as well that he was a physician.

We settled into our routine of dissection and lectures easily enough, and that part of the course dominated our studies. Our hundred students or so began to separate off into little cliques, and my particular one was the unlikely group of myself, Quentin Deelatrumpe and Aeneas McBeen, the minister's son from Inveresk.

Aeneas worried about everything, and swung from one extreme to another with an ease that must have appalled his father. He either drank all week, or not at all, and he either lusted after the trading fair ones, or anxiously scanned his palms for any signs of sprouting retributive hair. But on the crest he was a cheery companion, and an easy-going object for Quentin Deelatrumpe's army witticisms. Quentin latched on to the name Aeneas immediately and dropped the "e" at once from his subsequent pronunciation. On the fringe of our group were the two class geniuses, Corrigan and Darwin. Darwin told us reluctantly his name was Charles, which sent Quentin into agonies of laughter.

"So we've got a weady-made Charlie in our midst. What pwodigious luck, haw, haw, haw!"

Our keen Charlie spent as much time rooting about the Borough Muir as he did in Monroe's lecture room. He never took to Knox, who kept stressing the surgical aim of all his dissections, and Monroe's fumbling displays were too unprofessional for his liking.

We had hardly heard of the humerus before Charlie came back from one of his moorland tramps with the same bone of a fox, a dog and a rabbit. He would then bombard the Professor with keen questions which Monroe invariably failed to answer.

"If we were always meant to walk upright, sir, why does the upper end of the fox's humerus resemble our own?"

"What was that?" said the Professor, shaken briefly from his customary lassitude. Darwin repeated his question.

"Ah, my boy, a fox you say. Aye, an evil and dangerous animal the fox, the cause of much depredation around our farms still. A cunning beast he is too; in fact, the very word vulpine has come into our language meaning just that."

"But", persisted Charlie, "to call the fox evil is to put a Christian value on its behaviour. Surely Holy Scripture would deny that right to a fox."

I thought Monroe must choke or failing that, might be persuaded to exercise his own humerus on Charlie's head. I misjudged him. He just changed the subject.

"Holy Scripture, you say. Are you aware, Sir, that King James the

VIth and Ist personally translated the first seven and a half verses of Genesis and on paper too that was milled by the Water of Leith?"

"But we were discussing the fox's humerus, Sir." sighed Darwin patiently.

"That was never in dispute Mr Darwin." said the Professor with sudden conviction. "You should know by now that the bone in question lies in the upper part of the fox's forelimb between the radius and the scapula. In the fox we call it the foreleg and not the arm as we do in the human."

"My question was not about its position, Sir."

"Indeed not? Aye, well then, you had best learn to pose your questions more lucidly, Mr Darwin, had you not, eh—heh?"

Charlie put up with these exchanges for a while—but not for long.

The remainder of my year was as unremarkable as myself; there might have been one or two hundred. I don't know for sure. Some were hoping to take a diploma from the Royal College of Surgeons, and others, like me, were at the University. Whatever, we all met at Robert Knox's, and if we didn't meet there, we met in Ross's tavern.

Medical students were not the only ones we met at Knox's, for we also ran into divines, architects and country gentlemen, who found that Knox's lectures satisfied the grand national interest in scientific discovery. They might also have found a certain exhilaration, because although we all suspected where the bodies came from, no-one actually said so.

It was common to see black-avised villains lurking about Surgeons' Square at dusk, with large sacks on their back, in deep conversation with Knox or Liston. I well remember hearing Knox outside his home remonstrating with a large ginger beast of a man, in a stove-pipe hat and a greasy black coat. Knox was saying,

"Five guineas is my highest bid—not another penny. Do you imagine I am a Rothschild of Paris, a dealer in bottomless sacks of gold?"

"Ah well," said the stove pipe, fleering evilly," gies her back and I'll see what Liston offers me."

"Damn your eyes. I'll make it six."

We learned that these scenes were quite frequent. Opposing armies of snatchers would fight pitched battles in the middle of Surgeons' Square, much to the amusement of passers by, and to the embarrassment of their clients, who paid them handsomely to keep the peace and not to leave their merchandise on the pavement.

From the start Deelatrumpe displayed a lively interest in the body snatchers. In this connection his lofty bearing was distinctly of benefit. After all it was quite the thing for sprigs of fashion to swagger through life in a swarm of jockeys and prize-fighters—so why not body-snatchers as well. Quentin never passed them without a word, and they may well have recognised in him a fellow miscreant, though one with a better tailor.

When Monroe's first stirring lecture was over, I went off in search of a suitable text so that I might while away the evenings in productive study. I went to the Lothian Book Shop in St Andrews Square, and boldly pushed through the pebble-glass door.

An ancient man in a white wig and knee breeches came over from behind a large desk, and asked me what my needs might be. I told him.

"I thought you looked like a doctor," said he. "Well, what might I suggest for you, sir? Aha," he cried, emptying half a shelf, "you will require *Lizar's System of Anatomical Plates;* these are only in five folio volumes." I tried them for weight, and I was sure I could hardly carry them or remember their contents, far less pay for them.

The bookseller fussed about me, trying to assess the width of my pocket book. He now displayed on his counter what must have been his dearest merchandise.

"What about these?" I asked, pointing to a smaller *System of Dissection*.

"Charles Bell," said the veteran bookseller, "Charles Bell, yes—a good man, but might I be so bold as to state that a medical man like yourself will still require *Lizar's System*. Student dissection is an up and coming interest now—except, of course, in Professor Monroe's class, but I assume you will be attending that of Dr Knox as well. Dare I presume that you desire these also, sir?" He saw my eyes on Pemberton's *Study of Physik* and Arbuckle's *Materia Medica*.

"Not today," I said, hoping my reply would pass for firmness and not penury.

As I stood trembling over the cost of my new purchases, a noise behind made us both turn, and I saw two people coming beneath the low lintel of the door. The man seemed to be made of a number of loose parts that did not naturally belong together, but his companion was as neatly assembled as he was not. I assumed she must be his daughter, and I remembered that I had seen her before in one of the Garbeige House carriages just that August. She wore a light blue pelisse and bonnet, and a light smile that made me regret anew my bespoken in Dalkeith.

A change came over the aged bookseller, who now pushed me out of the shop, but I could still hear him say in needlessly truckling tones,

"Why Professor Home, sir, and Miss Lucy! Yes, your new volume is on our shelves now, sir. No, it is not selling prodigiously, sir, but give it time, sir, give it time, sir."

My regret over Miss MacWrath and opportunities taken turned at
once to regret over Miss Home and opportunities missed. Such thoughts
can lead either to melancholy poetry or desperate action. I decided on
the latter and pushed my way back into the shop to the ill disguised
irritation of the man who had just taken £3 from me so happily just ten
minutes ago. He turned a peevish and quizzical face in my direction.
Now was the time for boldness and invention.

"I was wondering if you have Professor Home's new textbook in
stock?" I fabricated the title in a soft mumble.

"You mean surely *In the Footsteps of Hippocrates,* corrected the
wigged bookseller, gladdened again at the prospect of despatching
another albatross.

"Yes, yes, that's the one".

"Well, sir, we happen to have its illustrious author with us just at this
moment," said the bookseller, pulling the Professor towards me, half
deferential, half insistent, as if uncertain which obeisance would bring
him the greater profit.

"Not *the* Professor Home!" I held the bookcase for support, suitably
aghast at my proximity to so great a man, although to be fair I could not
recall him from John Thomson's anthology of academic buffoons. He
was speaking to me now.

"Where did you hear of my treatise, Mr—ah—ah," asked the
Professor. "That is to say, who told you of it, sir?" That caught me, but
only briefly.

"My father, sir—a physician in Dalkeith." There was no point in
being wholly accurate about the apothecary bit. "Indeed he is the
visiting physician to Garbeige House." The Professor's face was
enlightened. He turned to his daughter,

"Ah, Lucy, that will be the man that dealt with our friends—the
Fairley-Dunns—when Sir Donald ran into that goose. They thought
very highly of him. Well, well, so that's your father." The bookseller was
doing a little minuet in glee, clearly delighted that there would be at least
three fewer books to dust. I saw the Professor's interest was beginning to
flag, so I rashly pulled out a sovereign and he brightened up again.

"You will come to pay us a visit, Mr—ah—ah—Bryson," said he
graciously. "Number 12 Charlotte Square, any afternoon between
three and four. My regards to your father, sir. Come, Lucy." I thought I
caught a smile from her as he dislocated his way through the doorway.

"Shall I wrap the book, sir?" The bookseller drew me from my reverie.

"No, not for the moment," said I pocketing my sovereign. "I have
enough to carry just now. I shall collect it next week."

Despite my burdens I skipped back across the North Bridge, highly
pleased with my good fortune and with the clever way I had manipulated

an introduction to Lucy Home. As it was, the October shadows were drawing in as I made my way back to my lodgings in Robertson's Wynd. I let myself in carefully through the entrance for I thought I could hear Mr O'Loan's thirsty breathing not far off.

In the sanctuary of my room my sweet triumph began to turn sour. I found my water ewer. It was not however full of water for Mrs O'Loan's tracerwork chamberpot had proved porous; indeed, it had emptied quicker than it filled. I took the jug over to my craquelured window where it did not seem gentleman-like to shout as I turned it upside down to augment the Flowers of Edinburgh below. Mrs O'Loan was her usual model of charm and grace when I went to ask for water.

"Ah've nane left." she snapped, "The pump's at the head of the wynd." I thanked her with a deep bow that Mr Deelatrumpe might have been proud of before setting with as much dignity as was allowed to a gentleman about to carry his own water from a public well and in an occasional chamber pot too. To make matters worse, her husband thrust another empty bucket in my hand with a wheedling, breathless smile that promised only further unrefusable requests to follow. I resolved in future on direct access to the streets through the window without recourse to the privvy two floors up.

When I splashed back, my unwieldy landlord gave me the cheerful news of a letter, just brought in by the Dalkeith carrier. It was lying on my sloping dresser.

I broke the seal; it was from my intended—who else could write in such coy terms after the scene surrounding our betrothal? She tittled and tattled about her loneliness and how she hoped my drive to fame was prospering. She then turned to more literary things. Had I read *The Man of Feeling* recently, she begged to know? The begging to know was farcical for she had tormented our evenings, reading it to the entire family just last year and the year before that too. A dreadful book—it traced the decline of a melancholy youth, Harley by name, who pined for but dared not approach an ethereal being called Miss Walton, and when not dreaming about her, he sighed over sunlit meadows, cried over moonlit forests, gave away a purseful of sovereigns to a blind beggar who fled at the sight of so much gold, and when in the last chapter Miss Walton said she would have him, he died. It was not my favourite book but lest I forget, Grizel had rewritten the entire manuscript with some improving embellishments of her own devising. As with a scorpion, the sting came in the tail. "Father," it ran, "has important business to attend to in the city. We will stage from Dalkeith on the 21st inst. and will be visited at the Crown Hotel in Princes Street."

I had to take a seat—even the unpredictable pine structure beside my bed—and I held her communication as far off as was possible without actually dropping it. Why me, I wondered modestly? I could only ascribe her limpet adhesiveness to the unlikelihood of other suitors, for it was certain that for many years to come my practice would have no hope of supporting her in the manner to which she planned to become accustomed. More to the point, though, how was I to hide her many talents from my student colleagues when she and her febrile sire visited me?

4

Quentin came to my rescue quite heroically by lending me his visiting card tray followed by his house.

"Come and have supper on Wednesday week. Quite by chance I'm entertaining two wuffians who would bweak their hearts to meet your charming lady-to-be and her father."

"I trust they will be suitably charmed, Quentin," said I morosely.

"Anas must join us too" went on Quentin jovially, "with his father of the cloth, he and Mr MacWrath must have many happy expewiences in common to endure."

Supper parties were all the rage in Edinburgh now, where good food and plenty of it were the mode, for people thought nothing of washing down devilled kidneys, jugged hare, a few slices of teal or widgeon and some suckling roast, with a bottle or two of claret—for breakfast. Supper was a rather heavier meal. Well, at least the MacWraths would be happy on that score.

I waited with sullen anticipation for the Dalkeith Stage in the convenient doorway of a spirit dealer. Up lumbered the diligence an hour late, into a bedlam of porters, beggars and barking dogs and began to disgorge its contents—a red-faced coachman, five heavy boxes, three officers of the Royals, and finally Mr MacWrath and Grizel. She squeezed out the door into the square, like the wife of a mill owner's clerk aping a duchess. She wore a ridiculous pink bonnet festooned with feathers and gaudy ribbons, and she rocked me on my feet with a kiss on both cheeks.

"Gallim and his daugher come unto Babylon, my son," shouted the minister.

Under the pretext of solicitude for her exhaustion after such a journey I insisted, nay commanded, that she rest at her hotel before we ventured to Quentin's for supper. My gallantry quite overcame her natural aggression and she did my bidding. When she was settled, her father disappeared on his urgent business and I disappeared to collect Aeneas. He, however, had decided not to accept Quentin's invitation on the grounds that he might strangle Mr MacWrath if he met him.

When I arrived to assemble my party for the evening, they tumbled into my hansome cab and declared themselves ravenous. They were still declaring it when we knocked on the door of Quentin's residence at 19

Hanover Street around eight of the evening. The door was opened by Quentin himself, who was in full evening fig and smiling over a huge lace cravat that covered most of his jaw and stopped his mouth from freely moving. He bent his lips low over Grizel's hand, his feet instep to heel, slobbered briefly, then laid his hand across his heart before taking the minister's hand in further welcome. This deflection of his attention took what might have been a critical eye of the rising half of Grizel's curtsey.

What took my eye even more, and I suspect Mr MacWrath's as well, judging by his widening eyelids, was an undulant creature with black eyes, black hair to her waist, a smile full of innuendo and a decolletage that made you think of a hot summer afternoon in a secluded spot.

"Meet my sister—Mrs Cudleigh," said Quentin urbanely.

Greetings and doffings over, we began to move to join the company. I could see that the furniture was in the new style popularised by Sheraton, light and slim, and it suited the domed hall to a marvel. Quentin found enthusiasm to crow over his domestic fitments—

"Fwesh water flowing out of a main pipe. Quite extwaordinawy," he laughed.

We edged into the drawing-room, where a large chandelier shone like sunlight on a long Grecian couch, a brace of drum tables and light striped arm-chairs. It also shone on two men who were heating their coat-tails before a wide marble fireplace. They looked towards us.

"De Serte," shouted Quentin in high humour. "I would like to intwoduce you to Mr Bwyson—a fellow student of mine—his affianced and her father. Haw, haw, haw!"

"Major the Honourable Robert de Serte," said the stranger, offering his hand with the expansive candour of an imposter, "late of the 15th Hussars—my card, sir."

His face was a stormy sunset, a portrait in old brandy. I could see right up to the top of his nostrils, and his voice forced its way past the grit and phlegm of a thousand segars. He must have been about forty-five years old and could easily have passed for fifty if the light were right. He was the sort of man you see in borrowed pinks on a borrowed mare, helping himself to large draughts from someone else's bottle, while he takes over the combined roles of whipper in and master. Indeed with little extra adornment he might have played the fox as well, and very possibly had. He turned to Grizel, bending as low as his arthritic spine permitted. Quentin was bubbling on in the background.

"We had a pwofitable time at the waces today," he said, "quite cleaned out the turf Shylocks. Bob certainly knows what to do with the gallopers, by Jove."

Their younger companion was introduced as Tom Cockle.

"Tip your flipper, Tom," laughed Quentin genially. Tom was tall and he shifted uneasily from foot to foot, and when he smiled, which he seemed to do nothing but, his whole face glimmered with dishonesty like that of Holy Willie Fisher caught with one hand in the Mauchline parish collection box and the other on some part of Lizzie's lass. His horizontal forehead made me think of a monkey in green velvet. It also made me wonder what our fellow student Darwin would have to say about him, and how Monroe might have set about answering his questions like, "Professor Monroe, this man's skull clearly has little room for anything after the bone has been accommodated. Why do you imagine he can speak?" But speak he could.

"Hullo, sir," he said quite happily. But he preferred to use his tongue as a funnel for the punch. Quentin conjured forth glasses of negus which he hesitated to offer the minister and his daughter, affecting surprise that they took some, and showing genuine surprise when asked to refill them in so short a time. The conversation limped as conversations do when people have not consumed enough alcohol to imagine themselves the soul of wit. Quentin explained that his sister, Mrs Cudleigh, was widowed and had come to look after him and to make sure he kept up his medical studies.

Mr MacWrath, who had been strangely withdrawn in the cab, became actively bashful to the point of silence in the drawing room; whether worn out by continuing God's work in the city or over-ridden by this cavalry swagger, it was hard to be certain. There was, however, no such uncertainty about Miss Grizel, who was making up for his paralysis with a scornful parade around Quentin's new furniture.

"Chairs without stretchers rarely last long enough to be considered antique. Continued sitting upon them splays the legs! I believe," she announced gravely. Well she should know.

"I do declare supper is about to awive," said Quentin. "Dwink up evewyone and we shall see what our fair cook has achieved." He led us across to the dining-room which lay on the other side of the hall, and where in the gentle light of a silver candelabra I could sense the quality of a long mahogany table supported at either end by a pillar with four claws, and all arranged for seven gluttons. The wood gleamed, the crystal sparkled and so, briefly, did the company. We started with oysters, washed down with a light Muscadet.

"A coquettish little white. Haw, haw, haw! Don't you think?" Quentin looked around the table. "But there's something better, a little more mature, I fancy, to tickle our thwoats with the woast." I saw a sextet of bottles, doubtless heavy with yet more aged wine, breathing gently on the sideboard and when I looked up again Mrs Cudleigh had placed a monstrous joint on the sideboard and Quentin was slitting it apart with relish.

"Quite the young surgeon, eh, Tom?" said the Major.

"Ah, ah, ugh," said young Tom.

"I do hope you appwove my taste in the wed gwape, sir." Quentin nodded to Mr MacWrath. "Chassagne-Montwachet—1817. Upon my word, a wawity! You usually get a white from that stable. Haw, haw, haw!"

Before the first platefuls had vanished several glasses had vanished as well, and with it any inhibitions of the tongue. The minister said with a longing look at the sideboard that he had never tasted such beef nor indeed such roast potatoes. The Major waded through his entire contribution to the downfall of Napoleon. Quentin called him a capital fellow.

"Aint he, Tom, aint he just," he added, winking at his speechless companion and nodding in agreement and appreciation of his own whimsy.

"May I have some more wine, Mr Deelatrumpe?" said Grizel, attempting a dazzling smile. She was beginning to flush now in a way that had caused me to despair in Dalkeith. She now began to turn her snobbish sensibility on the Major and she said, with killing condescension.

"Have you read *The Man of Feeling,* sir—when you are not defending the king, that is?"

"The *Man of What,* ma'am?"

Grizel explained at length. The Major had not and said he was not a reading sort of fellow and dipped deeply into his goblet. Quentin broached the last bottle of Montrachet and summoned the pudding. Grizel continued like a cat with a mouse that would not play.

"How did you find the Waterloo campaign, Major?" she cooed.

"I was not at—I was not present at the battlefield," he replied with the air of one who had worn out two horses in a vain attempt to get there in time, and whose dislike of boasting made him reluctant to elaborate.

"Oh," said Grizel innocently, "were you in the Quatre Bras action?" No escape. "Well, not exactly ma'am. I . . ."

"Let me help you to some flummery, Miss MacWrath," said the buxom Mrs Cudleigh. Grizel wanted blood, not pudding.

"Do tell me, you were a personal aide, seconded to Marshal Blücher? You must have been lying wounded in some dark forest, covered in gore, clutching a vital message to the Duke."

"This flummery is quite excellent," gasped the minister.

"I was in London at the time, ma'am," growled the fearless gladiator.

"In London! How terrible it must have been for you to miss all that . . . that chivalry."

"I had to, ma'am. Orders you know." This was a tarnished excuse, for it was common knowledge that Belgium had swarmed with officers posted to London who would have died rather than miss the chance of being killed under Wellington. MacWrath, with his natural deference to a voice that sounded as though it might have a living or two at its disposal, came unexpectedly to the aid of the florid Major. Stopping from time to time to wipe the milk pudding from his coat, he began a long tale about some geese that had warned the Romans of unfriendly Goths who were creeping up to their back door. Grizel said that the Major was not a goose. The Major said nothing and turned his attentions to Mrs Cudleigh who was passing across to him a salver of sugared almonds.

"Would the ladies care to retire now?" said Quentin, flashing a warning eye at his top heavy friend; she now half rose, presenting a barely captive frontage to the minister.

"Must we?" said Grizel peevishly. "I would esteem a little port."

"Surely, no need for them to leave us," said the minister, mesmerised by the vision across the table. "They liven up our tittle-tattle—the ladies, that is. The scriptures do not insist on segregation at meat. Would you not agree Mr ah—Deelatrumpe?"

"Oh, indeed," said Quentin with some resignation. Grizel asked me why I was looking so glum, and popped a sugared almond between her teeth before rounding on Tom Cockle. As I watched her I began to quake at what Fate had in store for me—I could see a wedding and flowers and strong drink and fellows slapping me on the back and, damn their eyes if they didn't envy me. I would make a foolish speech, look delighted, and undertake with my signature to finance this fell shrew through marriage and probably widowhood as well.

"Tell me, Mr Cockle," she said in her countess visiting the almshouse voice, "do you ride horse too?"

"Don't ride 'em, ma'am. Use 'em to make shoes," replied Tom uplifted by the Honourable Robert's discomfiture, into his longest speech of the night. "These fellows invited me to talk about boots."

"About boots?" squealed my betrothed. "Tell me more." Tom's oratory dried up. Quentin said,

"We have been planning a universal boot—Wobert and I, that is. Tom's father is a tanner. He will supply the hide, you see. I with my knowledge of Anatomy will design the boot. Wobert has another task, but we will not go into that. Haw, haw, haw!"

It was my turn to be interested now, and since Quentin was not saying any more I asked the Major who was still suffering his fit of the sullens— so tragical that even Mr MacWrath seemed stirred by his feeling for a colleague in fraud to ignore his blancmange and to beg the Major to tell us all about the boot. Glass by glass the paladin regained his scarlet good humour and Quentin, never put out for long, rocked back on his chair and put his feet on the table. He stretched for the decanter with a smile as Grizel tipped up her third glass of port. I suppose, in view of my own first steps towards the altar, it was absurd to be surprised, but I started none the less as her left hand began to toy with a nut near Quentin's right boot. Meanwhile it was the universal boot that caught the imagination of everyone else.

"Do you mean," I asked naively, "that these boots have no left or right to them?"

"Why, damn me, that's the whole point," said the Honourable Robert confidently.

"What are you going to do about the big toe?"

"Quite simple," said Quentin at the table head. "We'll make the tips square."

"So that there will be a gap for the big toe on both sides of each boot," said the Major.

"But that means that each boot will be huge. You could get my landlord into them." I might have added my bespoken as well.

"Not quite so big as that," smiled the Major, "but it will be more spacious certainly than Army regulations have hitherto demanded. However, I am a personal friend of Fitzroy Somerset—or at least of a friend of his."

"But the soles," I went on in wonder. "What are you going to do about the soles. They are different, you know."

"It's not wequiwed to tell that to a man who gets his footwear at Hoby's," said Quentin.

"Quite, quite," quacked the gallant adventurer, restored in his spirits. "Of course the sole will have to be cut a fraction larger than normal to accommodate either instep, but Quentin will see to that. He knows all about Anatomy, don't he? In any case," he went on contemptuously, "soldiers don't have to be comfortable—they just have to look smart."

"Well, so much for the cwabshells!" shouted Quentin. "Tell them about the leggings."

"Yes, what about the calves? They are different, you know," I said.

"Upon my word, sir, right again," said the Major. "But the right is the same as the left if you turn it round, isn't it? But that don't matter. We're going to curtain these legs about in soft leather that'll cling to the soldier's fetlock—I mean ankle—like a sock on a bit of prime blood. There will of course be a small concession in terms of military precision, but just think what a gift to the quartermaster this will be. They can order by the thousand instead of in matching pairs. A vast step forward in Army commissioning."

"Do you intend to gift this to the nation as did Malachi to Ahab?" asked Mr MacWrath.

"We will share our discovery of course, and if our country sees fit to reward us with some trifling—ah—sum we would be churlish to refuse—do you not so think?"

"Oh, indeed," said the cleric with fervour.

"What a shame," said Grizel. "I do so love a well turned calf—like this one, for example," and she slid her hand down Quentin's hessians to Mrs Cudleigh's evident disapproval. Her father slobbered up yet another plate of flummery.

"Does it mean that this footwear is to be used by officers as well? I hope it will not be used by this one," declared the minister's daughter, sliding her hand up Quentin's boot again.

"Tak yer hand off Mr Deelatrumpe's leg!" Mrs Cudleigh suddenly stood up across the table, slapped Grizel across the ear, and pulled her coiffure asunder. Grizel, briefly stunned, retaliated with a sharp left that would not have disgraced Jem Belcher. Mrs Cudleigh fell back shrieking.

"I say, ladies. Have done there. I say, Jenny—Miss MacWath—this won't do, you know," said the hussar helplessly. Jenny danced about as Grizel's first found its mark again.

"Strangely possessive for a sister," quoth the minister shaking his head and fumbling with his plate, such a marked Scots tongue too."

The evening broke up in uproar. Grizel swept out, dragging her father behind her. "Allow me to assemble your fol-de-rols, ma'am," said Major de Serte.

"You had best see your good lady to her hotel," said Quentin casually to me, "and I twust you will not all come again."

It was only when Grizel and her sire had disappeared up the Dalkeith road that I felt safe to knock again on Quentin's door. A shared brandy made the MacWrath's visit seem as though it had never happened, and before I had to give way to my curiosity Quentin had to give way to his desire to tell me why he was wasting time with de Serte and Cockle in the shoe trade. As ever, the reason was money: they hoped to make their fortune off the boot. The Major, with his long war service in London, had many friends of large influence and small scruples, amongst whom were a handful of colonels of some regiments or another. These men not only purchased their rank with their own money, they purchased their men's uniforms with the Government's money. This latter was known as off reckonings and if the Colonels bought no uniforms or cheap uniforms or claimed extra for men who did not exist at all, or did all three, then it was clear that a considerable amount of these off reckonings would find their way into Coutts' Bank in a Colonel's name.

These dauntless swindlers were known as the Clothing Colonels and so widespread was this practice that had these well tailored phantoms marched into battle, Waterloo would have happened in 1810 unless the French had been at it as well. It was a remarkable plan that deserved to succeed so much that it could only fail, especially with that trio in charge. But I had no more time to think of it, for my mind was wholly occupied with my own ignorance.

5

The weeks merged into one long dissection. When the sight of pickled corpses or the thought of Grizel became too much for me, I would trail up Arthur's seat to get a wee keek back at the town. At other times I would disport myself in Charlotte Square, idly comparing its elegant stonework with the damp boulders I lived amongst and hoping that Lucy might appear at their front door and I could say: 'Why—hullo, Miss Home. Just fancy, here I am, walking about this square whose name escapes me, and quite by chance wearing a new brass buttoned coat that my father does not yet know about, and whom do I meet but you?' Then would follow an afternoon of masculine witticisms and persuasive handsomeness and . . .

But Lucy never appeared and it took me a long time to pluck up the courage to pull the bell chain at her front door.

By December Professor Monroe's only specimen was becoming no longer recognisable. Marble Willie was to be seen shuffling about even more slowly than usual. This was to be taken as a clear omen that no further bodies would be coming under his care before Christmas. Indeed the last felon hanged had paused in the Grassmarket for the ceremony before going on to the College of Surgeons. When Monroe heard this he almost had apoplexy.

The news of this robbery found its way to Monroe's lackey just as casually as young cuts and dashers find their way home after a night's wassail—zig-zag fashion and without any impression of direction. The morning it happened I had been trailing Quentin in the same fashion and had run him to earth in Monroe's museum where I found him at work, surrounded by drawings, sections and elevations of an average foot as well as the disarticulated bones of the lower limb. He was obviously taking the project of his universal boot very seriously.

Monroe was beside him, shambling about, giving him advice, and I would imagine driving him to distraction. He must have thought that Quentin was absorbed with the scientific aspects of Anatomy and Quentin, I am sure, did not say anything about his commercial interest in it.

I left them to it and pretended to be examining the jars of pickled dissections. I heard Monroe saying, "A most interesting study the

43

foot. If you just pick up that calcaneum there and articulate it with the talus—like that—you've got the posterior pillar of the instep."

"But sir," said Quentin in embarrassment, "that's not a bone. It's a piece of plaster that fell fwom the cornice this morning." Monroe tried to brazen it out.

"Oh, a piece of plaster," he muttered, "a clever trade, a plasterer's. There are very few of them in Edinburgh can do a frieze like that," he gestured at his roof. "And funnily enough, like glaziers, the best plasterers are found in Leith."

At this point he was saved from further mortification by Marble Willie, who came over with a face as mortified as his master's. The pair of them disappeared into Monroe's office, where Marble Willie must have been passing on the story of the theft. It was reasonable that Monroe should be irate. His students were being stolen by Dr Knox, and now his rightful bodies were being stolen by the Royal College of Surgeons. A terrible noise now started in his office, a furious solo tirade backed up by banged chairs, thumped tables and flying books. The door flung open. Monroe was in full flood.

"I'll write to them—a letter—damn them. Who's the Secretary? They've stolen my body. They have transgressed the regulations. You will take my letter to them at once". And so on. Marble Willie just kept nodding impassively.

There are, of course, as you must know, no wegulations," said Quentin as we left the museum, "there are just enterpwising people, and the others".

A week later, since no reply had come, the Professor decided to present himself in person at the Surgeons' Hall, and his rage had by no means cooled either. He stormed through the front door, where the College Secretary, Mr Collick, prepared to come to an amicable arrangement, whereby the Professor was soothed with honey and the Royal College kept the body, which they had already begun to anatomise in any case.

The Secretary was a small flattened man, greyed both by waiting for a senior appointment and with soothing the tempers of men more stupid but more important than himself. He adopted the humble approach accepting total blame for everything. His duties were onerous.

He took Monroe full tilt like a farmer humouring a prize bull.

"My dear Professor Monroe," he said grovellingly, "there you are, sir. There you are."

"Aye here I am".

"There you are sir; there you are!" repeated Collick.

"You've said that."

"To what do we owe the extreme pleasure of your visit?" went on

Collick all unruffled. That he must have already read Monroe's violent explanatory note he did not think to mention. Monroe spluttered and choked and raged about helplessly.

"A letter, you say," went on the abject Secretary, "about a body, you say. Dear, dear, dear, how could I have been so careless as not to receive it when a man so senior and so involved in furthering anatomical knowledge as your good self had taken the time to write it personally and to me too. I shall go and find it this minute. My dear sir, if you would come into our Library I would be honoured indeed if you would take a little wine."

He led the Professor into his pen, an oaken book-lined room, commemorating in oils and marble its illustrious sons, and occasional rebels, blackballed when alive but proudly admitted when safely silenced under a flattering tombstone. He set Monroe down and called a lackey to pour him some fine claret from a crystal decanter (bought with the funds raised from the sale of slave surgeon diplomas), prattling the while of Monroe's breathtaking contribution to science and mankind, and nay, the entire world. By the time the decanter was emptied, the trifling theft of the University specimen was now seen in its true light in the gentle wash of praise, toadying and alcohol.

"Rest assured, my dear Professor," said the fawning Mr Collick as he now ushered Monroe to the front door. "We will take every precaution in the future to ensure that another of your rightful specimens does not find its way to our humble institution. Rest assured indeed, sir."

"The old fool," he doubtless added to himself when Monroe had gone. "He wouldn't have known what to do with it anyway. Ah well, where can we obtain the next one from?"

Although Collick's professional assessment would be right, we were still obliged to watch Monroe, the Physician, demonstrate what Monroe, the Surgeon, ought to have been able to do but could not. The Physician could talk at length about all the nerves and blood-vessels and tendon sheats that glowed so colourfully on Lizar's plates. The Surgeon could only mutilate them.

By January he had abandoned the winter dissection as uninformative, and produced an aged cattle dog, for which fifteen years chasing lively calves finally proved too much. The same fifteen years had also turned the beast into a leathery collection of muscle and bone that obliterated completely any anatomical resemblance to a human patient.

The class assembled as usual at half-past nine, the Professor wandering about abstractedly. Willie Briar uncovered his latest find, and there, instead of our felon, was the old cattle dog. Monroe came out of his abstraction, bowed with his customary old-world courtesy, and began his customary fumbling address.

"Gentlemen," he said, "I am going to demonstrate the reduction of a hernia to you—on a dog; by which I mean, I will restore the hernial sac to—ah—its original—location." He walked up to the table.

"This dog," he nodded, "is, as you know, a collie. Now the collie is a breed that flourishes . . ." He traced its ancestry back to a Pictish boarhound.

"He's wong, you know." Quentin said loudly to anyone who cared to hear. "The collie is not a hunting dog. Haw, haw, haw!"

It did not matter what we thought about him. We had to stand and gaze reverently at his display. I prayed that I would never have a hernia. Monroe kept up his commentary as he fumbled about with the dog's nether regions. Every so often he had to stop to confirm that the parts under his fingers corresponded to the words in his mouth. Frequently, they did not, and he breathed and sweated heavily until they did.

"You must first find the hernial sac, then define the margins of the orifice from which it has protruded. Then with one deft movement you push it back whence it came—like that!" He gave a sudden thrust, which did nothing to the sac, bud did bring a frown of exasperation to his forehead. He groped in silence for a few moments, then tried again. This time he reduced the dog which slipped through Willie's frail grasp on to the floor.

"You know," said Aeneas, "Willie's tasks here are not what one would call burdensome, are they? I'll wager that Monroe only tolerates him because he plans to slit him up on that dissecting slab one day—he can't have long to go now by the looks of him. I wonder if a little blood-letting might be recommended. What do you say—three or four ounces?"

Before we could speculate further on his future, the man in question idled up to the scene of the accident, and with much snuffling, restored the collie to the table. The Professor tried for another half hour, and then declared the hernia incurable. "I think that will do for today, gentlemen," he said, bending deeply towards the floor. "The hernia would be—ah—em—strangulated by now."

"As well the poor bwute is dead," Deelatrumpe observed languidly. "He could not possibly have wecovered fwom a pwocedure like that. Haw, haw, haw!"

"Professor Monroe".

"Why damn me; it's our Charlie," chirruped Quentin, "speak out, Charlie. The Pwofessor's bwain is deep inside his head."

Darwin took Quentin's advice. "Professor Monroe", he repeated, "if I might venture to observe, sir; I have the impression that in dogs and other creatures that walk on four legs, the pelvis and legs are too close together to allow the bowel any space to rupture outwards."

Monroe's flooding cheeks promised a not-to-be-missed burst of passion. The enthusiastic Charles continued, innocent and unaware.

"Could it be, sir, that the hernia you were seeking to reduce was, in fact, a heavily matted scrotum?"

Forty pairs of eyes followed the Professor's purpling face on its way down to refute Darwin's insolent suggestion. He groped and muttered, now scarlet, now white. Of a sudden, he could contain his facial changes no longer. He straightened, or as near as he could manage, and in a voice more explicit than ominous, he roared,

"Mr Briar! Mr Briar, you have brought me the wrong dog. Where is he? There you are, you wretch. What do you mean by this? You've brought the wrong dog—d'ye see? The wrong dog. There is no hernia here—just—just ah . . ."

Darwin blushed, Quentin snickered ironically. Marble Willie shuffled half-heartedly to beyond striking distance of his master and now began an explanatory babble. I would have gladly suffered five more professorial herniae to witness Willie's discomforture. It was delicious.

"Ah didna ken which dug ye wanted, Professor." was his first sally.

"You lying ruffian."

"And forbye. Ah had tae collect thae cases o' Burrgundy at Cockburn's this verra morning."

"My wine is it now?"

Willie's voice dropped to a whisper. He said, "Farmer Flint left only one dug, sir."

"He what? Only one dog? He promised me three. He's as big a liar as you. I shall have him. I shall have the law on him. Swindle me out of my dogs. I paid him for three. You will take a letter to him at once. Tell him I'll have him in the Calton Gaol and you can tell him that unless he starts rotating his grain fields, I shall report that as well. Steal my specimens— oh the scoundrel." He stamped away into his study where we could hear him sharing his anger with the door, his desk, the chair and his grovelling mortuary keeper. We could also see that the morning teaching session was at an end.

It was after this agreeable little scene that I decided the time had come to take Professor Home at his word that he would welcome a visit. I sallied forth from the O'Loan mansion around two of the clock, in a green frock coat, rather shy in the latest rage of narrow pantaloons hooped under my shoes. Fortunately himself was still sleeping off the twelve o'clock brandy, and not around to offer his special brand of insolent flattery. The sun shone weakly. and I walked slowly across the

North Bridge so that my armpits might not overwhelm my lavish application of Windsor soap. I sauntered about George Street until the long hand of my watch and I both moved around to twelve.

Number twelve was, as they say, a house to itself, sharing nothing with its neighbours except the Palladian facades of their masonry and their occupants and possibly a certain stately pride. There was no audible response to my efforts, but shortly the door was opened by a grey-haired butler, his face on the brink of laughter, and a voice straight from the tomb. He took my name and led me through a spacious hall up a broad polished wood staircase, dominated by ancestral frowns in oils and large gilt frames. I could feel their disapproval now. What must it have been like last century. The waggish butler noticed the affect they were having on me.

"Yon's the maister's mither," He pointed at a black-eyed witch in a lace cap, gazing out sternly from an ethereal rural background. "Ah kent her when Ah was a laddie, and Ah'm nane the better for it." He chortled in playful reminiscence. At the stair head he took me in to a large drawing-room, which looked down past heavy velvet curtains on to the clattering square beneath. There was a harp in one corner and a long Broadwood forte-piano in old rosewood by the shaded window. Mrs Home bustled about in welcome. She was a large woman of the type favoured by Peter Paul Rubens. She introduced me to her auburn haired daughter, who seemed to have been entertaining an aged relative by the fire. As I was presented to the aunt, I had no doubt at all that this was a sister of "the maister's mither" who had evidently inherited the same coven-in-the-moonlight glare and, it seemed, the same lace cap. Her attention was taken up by an open backgammon board in walnut and ivory, and from time to time she sipped a glass of Chalybeate water which, from the look on her face, was taken for health and not for pleasure.

"The Fairley-Dunns have a high regard for your father," said Lucy's mother, leading us across to where a young maid in a black dress had assembled equipment for making tea with leaf and oil of Bergamot.

"We, of course, only know your home town as visitors for we go there most summers. You must tell us what it's like to live there. That will do nicely," she added, as the little maid disappeared. She settled into an armchair, and Lucy on a couch, and I told them as much about Dalkeith as I thought I safely might. They both said they preferred living in the country to the town, "but alas my husband's practice keeps him here." sighed Mrs Home.

"Do you play backgammon? What's his name, Lucy?" creaked her grand-aunt, appearing behind me with eerie suddenness.

"Mr Bryson."

"What's that?" shouted the dowager, leaning into her ear trumpet. "Bison—I thought that was some sort of cow beast," she barked.

"Don't fret, Aunt Gertrude, there's all evening—we will risk a game with you later," said the Professor's wife.

"And I'll see if I can take a shilling off you next time," said Lucy.

"Humph," the old gamester, thwarted in sport made do with a cup of tea which she took off to her lair. Mrs Home smiled,

"She's ninety-five, you know. My husband says that she's outlived all the diseases that might have killed her." We drank more tea and Lucy sang *Caller Herrin* at the Broadwood.

My visit was a great success—at least enough to have a repetition suggested by Lucy, and I went back to my dismal lodgings, pleased that they had not asked things about Dalkeith that I couldn't have faced telling them, and I crushed those nasty thoughts by a concentration on my studies that I had never believed possible before I met the Professor's daughter.

During our first year then, we learned the necessaries of Anatomy and its surgical importance from the urbane Dr Knox, whose classes swelled as those of the Professor dwindled. We saw the ureters coursing out of the kidney and down into the pelvis to the bladder. He showed us how to cut for a stone—lithotomy, he called it—and he told us of the friar who first devised the procedure. He practised removing stones from all manner of impossible hiding places in the bladder and in the ureter.

"William Cheselden," he said, "took fifty-four seconds to remove a stone." He then asked us to check his time on our pocket watches.

"Speed is of the essence, gentlemen," he stressed over and over again. "And remember, you must never operate on any patient if there is the remotest possibility that they may recover without your intervention."

It all seemed fearfully complicated, still his teaching was beginning to have some good effect, and I was at last feeling at home, amongst the dead tissues at least. But when it came to operating, I would have given a dead patient a much more confident prognosis than a living one—in my hands at any rate.

Knox was without doubt the best preceptor of Practical Anatomy in Edinburgh, yet he did not have surgical beds in the Royal Infirmary. The descendants of the Dawplucker clique that had driven John Bell out of his mind, had seen to it that their own reputation would not suffer by comparison with Knox's in their own hospital. Dr Knox was therefore obliged to operate on his cases in the patients' homes, and selected students were permitted to accompany him on these errands of mercy,

49

for he did not charge unless it was clear to him that his patients could pay. He operated in bursts on small groups of people in the same street.

One sharp February day he took us into the High School Wynd, almost under the very nose of the Royal Infirmary that had spurned him; us, being half a dozen chosen students—chosen because, as late-comers, we were in the front row. There were also two overweight footmen with whisky noses, who were needed to prevent the patient from leaving the table before the surgeon had finished. There was a third footman of a smaller build, who carried the instruments.

We made our way over to No. 3 High School Wynd on foot. Knox arrived in a chaise, followed by his muscular henchmen. Our arrival caused some commotion, certainly enough to make the children stop rolling their hoops in the offal outside the house. As he entered, we formed up in a train behind him, almost pushing him through the far wall when the door was closed. When I saw the moth-eaten trestle in the bed alcove, the uneven floor and the shaky table, I had to admit that the O'Loan slum was a palace in comparison. What would the patient make of Quentin's graceful habitation?

Our patient waited impassively, as well he might, for he had only one leg. His name was Tom Burrowdoon, a retired mole-catcher, who had already given away the first half of his left leg to Robert Liston— possibly in the same room too, for Liston had no surgical beds in the Royal Infirmary either. Mrs Burrowdoon, a squat little dumpling, bustled about because there was really little else she could do. She had a large bucket of water set out by the table for all surgical purposes, I presumed. A sharp draught behind me told me that the door was open. I could see the same children from outside, peeping in with great curiosity. Behind them a crowd had already gathered. Mistress Burrowdoon rushed at the door.

"Awa' ye gang," she shrilled, "or Ah'll skelp yer wee bums."

They shut the door at once, and opened it again almost immediately. Mr Burrowdoon was now removed to the table by the two large assistants, and I could see that the skin around the stump of his short leg had fallen away in oedematous red shreds, revealing a truncated femoral shaft. This Dr Knox proposed to shorten, and to re-cover with skin.

To Knox's eternal credit, he eschewed the surgical braggadocio of his dissecting room; with simple courtesy he put the poor man at his ease—a formidable task considering what lay in store for him. But he succeeded, and he thanked the dumpling wife for the water and the use of her table.

It required no sharp observation to see that the patient was becoming uneasy as saws, bistouries and clamps were produced from the surgical bag. The whisky-nosed footmen gave a look of envy as they poured a quantity of raw spirit down the mole-catcher's throat. This may have done a little to alleviate his anxiety; it also flushed his exertions. and the raw stump began to bleed.

"Are we ready to proceed, my good man?" said the Doctor, handing him a leather plug to clench in his bare gums.

"Aye, sir."

The next movements dazzled the uninitiated by their sheer speed. The two giants took control of the victim. One fell on his chest, and the other fell on his one and a half legs. A large crowd of inquisitive sightseers, which had grown even larger by now, was kept at bay by the instrument bag footman.

Knox pounced on the bare stump, and exposed the bone with his scalpel, then sawed through the broken end as a forester might cut a small twig.

"The stump's off," shouted the instrument bag footman to the crowd, who raised a gusty cheer.

"Twenty-thwee seconds," said Quentin, snapping shut his watch.

Continuing at the same high speed, Knox washed the bleeding hole with rose water and egg white, then secured the skin flaps across the shortened bone with silk stitches. No seamstress ever worked so neat a union, or so mobile a fabric.

Only a faint moisture on his forehead betrayed his exertions. In contrast, his elephantine assistants slobbered, grunted and swabbed their foreheads freely. The instrument bag footman, with his foot wedged against the door, kept up his running commentary.

Both the patient and his wife fainted. It was, as I learned, a fairly common occurrence, but they both recovered sufficiently for Mistress Burrowdoon to jest,

'Ye can cut oot ma tongue, sir. That would please ma guid man. Hey, hey, hey."

Amid further scenes of helpless gratitude, we left No. 3 and headed for No. 10 High School Wynd, where on the fourth floor an old man was waiting for the good doctor to remove his cataract, and so restore his vision. The black-patched Knox strode the street, the crowd separating for his passage like the Red Sea for the Israelites. His cohorts came behind him, and we were flanked by skipping children.

"Cool opewator," said Quentin. "But I hear that Liston does a full amputation even quicker. In fact, I am informed by usually weliable sources that at his last, he not only took off the leg, but also two fingers of his assistant and the tail of his own fwock-coat. What do you make of that, eh, what! Haw, haw, haw!"

I had no time to make anything of that, because our little party had arrived at No. 10 and we began to ascend the narrow spiral staircase.

The house was, if anything, more squalid than the first. Three ragged children got in everybody's way, their mother ran after them screaming, and made any movement for anyone through the room impossible. Her father, with the cataracts, lay on the bed and her husband glowered at us from the black fireplace.

Knox worked his charm on everyone as he had done before. The children stopped shouting, the mother stopped screaming, the father stopped glowering. Only the old man was unchanged, and had to be carried over to the kitchen table by the two surgical juggernauts, who then held him fast.

We formed our respectful semicircle again, and Knox began.

"Observe the cataract, gentlemen," he said. "You see the grey reflex in the pupil, where it should be black? You see, if I bring a candle before the eye, the pupil closes. This tells me that there is no paralysis retinae. Now there are two possible approaches," he went on. "Daviel favours the open approach. That is, he cuts the eye around the front. This clearly has its problems, even if the patient has consumed enough brandy." We nodded, and continued to nod, happy to agree with anything he said.

"When you touch the eye, it naturally turns upwards. You see? He demonstrated, and our patient's eye vanished upwards as he had predicted. "Daviel employed this reflex by plunging his knife right cross the cornea with the sharp edge pointing downwards. You see?" He imitated the action with a scalpel. "The upward movement of the eye which follows automatically then finished the dissection for him. You see how that would happen?" We saw, and agreed that brandy was not enough.

"I prefer to depress the cataract—effectively knocking it backwards into the eye. Some surgeons achieve this with a sharp needle which they thrust through the corneal margin and through the pupil. It must be evident to you, time is not on their side if they have driven their needle in the wrong direction. You would agree? My sole instrument is a large and lively thumb." His own, held up for our approval, clearly had both these qualities.

He now settled himself on a chair below the patient, nodding to his two thickset servants. They performed their double act, one on the legs and one on the chest, while Knox quickly flicked his thumb hard against the lower part of the eye. Our patient roared and closed his eyelids, the only movement permitted by the two hulks a-top him. Knox stood back and faced us.

"You must beware;" said he, "too lively and too large a thumb can rupture the cataract and indeed the eye. Now as you can well imagine, this procedure is not unnaturally, very popular with itinerant quacks, whose greatest qualification lies in their unbridled freedom of movement. They mutter their spells, perform their mystic passes, collect

52

their fee and change their residence before any complications might make their patients reluctant to settle their account."

He now called us to cluster round more closely and separated the eyelids again.

"See—the pupil is now black where once it was grey. The vision will be blurred but let's try . . . Now my good man," said Knox, "do you enjoy what you see?"

The old father burst into tears. So did his daugher, and I do believe his surly son-in-law may have been wiping his own eye as well. Anguished stammers of gratitude, and Knox pleased and genuinely humble. This was what medicine was all about.

"Ye'll stay for a dram, Doctor," said the younger man. Knox said he would, and while he was waiting, continued his instruction to us. "If you consult your Bible," he said, "the Gospel according to St John, Chapter 9, you will read that Jesus restored the sight of a blind man. There are interesting factors in that case. The Bible says the man was blind from birth, but I think we may discount this. Jesus, you will recall, was said to have spat on the ground and made clay of the spittal, and He anointed the eyes of the blind man with the clay. And said unto him, 'Go wash in the pool of Siloam'. He went his way therefore and washed, and came seeing. Now," he turned to us, "He placed the clay on the blind man's eye, a very reasonable thing to do in a hot climate, and, I might add, he may have just put a wee bit extra pressure from the thumb. That's all that was needed, as you have just seen, and lo and behold we have another miracle."

"May God forgive you your blasphemy," said Aeneas harshly. Knox heard him and spun on his heel.

"I hope the Lord will do just that; but when I suggest how Christ wrought His miracles, I seek to cast no aspersions on the very great good that He did. If you read further in Chapter 9 you will see that the Pharisees tried most sedulously to persuade the man that Jesus was not only a sinner, but a charlatan as well. Then he answered and said, 'Whether He be a sinner or no, I know not; one thing I know, that whereas I was blind, now I see.' I am only seeking," he said, "to draw a parallel between then and now. If for Pharisees you read the staff of the Royal Infirmary, or, probably worse, the University Council, and for Christ read innovating surgeon, then surely the parallel is exact." He took the whisky and toasted the little house most courteously.

"Thank you, mother," he said, bowing to the young woman. "That's it done now, Your father's eye is as good as new—or as near as makes no difference." He smiled, bowed again, and led away his entourage.

Aeneas was not to be silenced however, still spitting brimstone behind Knox's back.

"Aeneas," I laughed, "if I could not see you I would take you for the Reverend MacWrath."

"You might need a miracle by the same to restore your vision to you," he grunted sourly.

"No, Aeneas. That won't do. The only miracle he would contemplate would be to turn me into a roast suckling pig."

"A suitable choice," was the tart reply.

6

The Royal Medical Society started like many another Royal Society, in an alehouse. I think the year was 1737, certainly it was within the last century, or as near as makes no difference. At any rate some medical students who met in this drinking den every day thought it would be reasonable to add a touch of respectability to at least one of the days, which they called The Medical Society.

Taverns are great places for medical theorising. That our anatomical skills had not yet progressed beyond the shoulder, did not stop us airing yet another profound notion that needed only a little research to confirm. We did not know enough at the time to realise that we knew so little. In any case the company was so good that it didn't really matter, and many's the promising hypothesis that came to the end of its useful life in the foot of an empty whisky quaich. Anyway, the Society flourished. Each week one of them gave a weighty dissertation on any medical subject he chose, while the others imbibed and prepared nasty questions. It is a form of professional entertainment that has never been abandoned. Professor Thomson was right about many things, including the dramatic talents of his colleagues who sat through these dissertations only because it guaranteed them a hearing when they chose to walk the boards themselves.

As the idea caught on, the Society expanded. It became more respectable, and had to accommodate its growing reputation, so it took premises in Surgeons' Square just before the turn of the century. This was the house my father had described next to Knox's. So far had it grown beyond its bacchanalian origins, or was it so little that the king, George III, saw fit to grant it a Royal Charter. This brought panting to its doors the more august of the Edinburgh professional hierarchy, who saw in their patronage not only captive audiences, but knighthoods and baronetcies as well. The success of the Society was thus assured.

For the students it was an education in how to survive, not just disease but their colleagues' opinions. It allowed them to hear the cut and thrust of debate, to match their new learning against the older learning of their mentors. They might also try to recognise some medical Chiefs from the character sketches that were in wide circulation.

And if they failed to recognise their Chiefs, they might also fail to recognise meetings as those that had been advertised. All it needed was one professor to cast doubt on another professor's favourite theories, and the evening might end in the destruction of the programme to the ill disguised glee of the undergraduates.

If some smiling rival, rash enough or powerful enough, were to halt Professor Gregory's rhetoric with a playful:

"I'm having grave doubts about your mixture sir, I have just carried out a survey on some fifty patients, and I have been struck by the number who find their symptoms worsening upon its administration. I would hazard that you have permitted too powerful a concentration of ginger, some might say injudicious, and from this has flowed a series of further complaints that might have been avoided, had your prescription not been ingested in the first place". Gregory's eyes bulging, face red. "So much so, that I fear you have committed the cardinal blunder of ascribing recovery to your preparation, when the good Lord had already set the patient on the road to health—a classical example of post hoc, ergo propter hoc. It is an easy, logical mistake." Snuff to the nostril and a cambric flourish.

For such amusing little scenes, the possibilities were boundless. Gregory, succumbing to acute phrenitis; smirking faces; students' hands over mouths; colleagues' hands over bellies; the more imaginative, seeing visions of Gregory's revenge when staff appointments were being considered. Gleeful little cameos of a great professor stirred to wrath.

Or when Professor Monroe appeared before the Royal Society, one hand in pocket as usual, the other clutching a large jar which he brandished aloft.

"In my hand, gentlemen," he announced with his customary gravity, "I am holding the largest male organ in Christendom."

"Which hand, sir," whispered a voice loudly.

Quite often the provocations came from the Professors themselves. The most quarrelsome of them was James Hamilton—a man learned in the art of Obstetrics and Midwifery, and in the behind-the-scenes fencing necessary to keep his position secure. He travelled by sedan chair, and quarrelled with everybody. He quarrelled with the Town Guard. He quarrelled with the President of the Royal College of Surgeons. He quarrelled once publicly with Professor Gregory, who ended the argument by beating him about the shoulders with his walking stick—an assault that cost him a hundred guineas. Gregory himself laughed it off and said he'd pay the same again just to do it again.

Hamilton suffered a sharper, if less violent reply when he ill-advisedly told the redoubtable Robert Liston before the Medical Society that some knives he had devised were useless.

"The only use I can think of for Liston's knives," he said airily, "is for cutting cheese."

Liston rose to his feet, cool as you please, and said sweetly,

"I can well understand that Professor Hamilton experiences surgical confusion with my knives. I would imagine that cutting cheese is about the only possible use he could put them to."

So it was with the full expectancy of academic brawls and learned pettiness that we foregathered for the January meeting. In deference to the ten student founders, we met in the founding Inn at Gladstoneland, where we poured down several mutchkins of Younger's Edinburgh ale against the cold.

"Keep smiling, Anas," said Quentin, emptying his tankard with a bold flourish. "Tonight we're off to dwink at the fountains of knowledge, eh what! Haw, haw, haw!"

"You sound as though you've already been at another fountain," said Aeneas acidly—poor Aeneas, his mood was on the wane again, his wits addled by the brimstone in his soul.

"Now, now, a fellow must wet his thwoat fwom time to time. I say," he babbled on, "I heard a vewwy amusing tale about Pwofessor Monwoe. I think he was actually adwessing this Society. Anyway wumour has it that he came out with his hand in his pocket, and in his other hand he . . ."

"I've already heard it and it's disgusting," said McBeen.

Quentin raised his eyebrows tolerantly, and shouted for another flowing bowl: I drank deeply with him for in my pocket was another love poem from the Reverend Gideon's fierce daughter.

Also from time to time on our way up to Surgeons' Square, we had to stop to wet the pavement, and when we finally arrived we were on the tail of a great hubbub of arrivals. Throngs of drunken students were exchanging club-footed witticisms with habitués of the Square. Every so often a smart cabriolet would disgorge a smart physician or a smart surgeon into the mob, before being high-stepped away by the coachman in great style to await the pleasure of their owners.

"That's Robert Liston," said Aeneas in my ear.

He pointed out a large man in a bottle-green coat, with an orange stick in his mouth and at his lapel in place of a flower, dangled a bunch of ligatures. I had heard about Liston's running battle with the Royal Infirmary. He stepped into the hall of the Royal Society of Medicine, a powerful figure of a man, judging from the firm set to his mouth—a man to be feared. If the stories were true, he had put to good use the experiences he had acquired as a Surgical Clerk in the Infirmary. He had begun to build himself a great name amongst the Edinburgh poor, and the Royal Infirmary surgeons, fearing for their private practice had conspired to have him removed. Their conspiracy finally succeeded when the Hospital Managers sent him a letter forbidding him to enter the Hospital. They said that Liston's presence was "not compatible with the smooth working of the Department of Surgery." We followed him at a respectful distance. He strolled into the hall and sat down somewhere in the middle, laying his booted feet on the seat in front of him.

The hall was high and vaulted, and much dominated by the mahogany girders considered necessary for this spread of higher learning. We sat on hard benches of an inferior wood, gently tiered to demonstrate to every lecturer, with hideous accuracy, the precise effect their words were having. Around the walls long mahogany panelling reflected back the glow of gas burners—that is, until they went out—suddenly.

Groans and shouts and gropings in the dark gave way to roars of laughter and bawdy songs. A serving man with a loose sleeve where his arm ought to have been, was summoned with a fluttering taper, which failed to ignite the gas burners. The taper went out, to a frolicsome chorus. Off went the caretaker, and returned with the lighted taper, guarding the flame carefully. The students made blowing-out noises. But now it turned out that there were no candles. When there were, the one-armed caretaker had a terrible time lighting them. Thereafter it was merriment unbridled—I was sure it was going to be a good evening.

While we waited for something else to happen, we looked around for famous names.

"That's Professor Russell," said Aeneas.

He pointed to a wrinkled old man in a red wig, who was yawning, on the front bench, in a state of senile torpor. Beyond him I could make out another growth of red hair, probably natural to its black coated owner, and in dire need of mowing. It became evident later on in the evening that this was Daniel Hatchett, one of the more newly appointed Infirmary Chiefs, old enough to take fright at any innovation and young enough to do what he was told by the somnolent Russell. He was the ideal friend for such a man. I guessed that the small man on the same bench was Hamilton, the pugnacious gentleman accoucheur, but at the moment he seemed to be drowsing quietly, like a terrier in the sunshine beside a well gnawed bone.

About half-past seven the proceedings at last got under way. They were opened by the Society President, David Iveagh, a final year medical student. He was sandy-haired and edgy, and pushed by ambition to posture before people he probably didn't like, to gain a position he probably didn't want. I was fairly certain he would rather have been idling in front of a fire, but we all move in mysterious ways. He reminded us of the august history of the Society, told us a humorous tale to put us all in good heart, and then introduced the first speaker— Alexander Ball, a young physician with an interest in physiology. Ball, even when lecturing to students, had the air of a man who expected ridicule and mockery—not the defiant air of the professional martyr—but rather the resigned air of a questing mind set in a timid frame and beneath a curtain of straggly hair he looked more like a forte-pianist than a doctor.

If his manner was backward, his subject was startling. He described in some detail experiments carried out by a young Shropshire veterinarian called Hickman who had quietened a cow sufficiently to put a knife in her side without getting a cloven hoof in his face. He had achieved this by tying a bag round her head until she became insensible from breathing in her own expired air. Ball then went on to describe how he had applied the same technique to open a cold abscess in the neck of a young man.

"When he awoke, he asked me when I was going to start? I must say though," Ball admitted, "he did take on a disturbing blue colour. It would still seem to me that if this approach could be developed, it would not only make surgical operations more tolerable, it would—ah—also make them more certain by allowing considerations other than mere speed." He blinked unhappily, awaiting the inevitable.

It is not that anyone took Ball seriously, for he was always recommending grotesque lines of treatment. Why only last year, in the *Medical and Surgical Journal,* he claimed to have cured erysipelas of the arm by feeding his patient some mould he had found growing in a pot of strawberry preserve. Professor Home demolished him that time when Ball would not admit that local inflammations can be treated only with local applications.

"Are there any questions?" asked Mr Iveagh. I could see some activity over beside Professor Russell—surely not initiated by him: it was, but he did not get up himself. He leaned over to mutter something in Hatchett's ear, the mingled red hairs briefly giving the impression of one large head. Hatchett then began to nod in vigorous agreement—too vigorous, I thought and jerked to his feet like a crow startled off a feast of dead rabbit by the sight of a live one.

He began with counterfeit bonhomie and thanked Dr Ball for his most interesting address and said:

"That's the first time I have heard a cow described as having a face, but then we all have to conduct our practice as best as we can. Still, I must confess, your experiments cause me some distress. You realise that if your patient had died it might have been a case for the black cap." He paused here to admire the effect of his remarks, then continued. "This notion, of making patients unaware of their operations—if it were possible—in my opinion denies them what indeed can be an enriching experience."

"And painful," called Liston, from the audience. Hatchett sweetened by the sound of his own voice, ignored him.

"Before we know it, you will be using some other gas, perhaps out of those burners up there that are not working; perhaps that oxide of nitrogen used by Sir Humphrey Davy in his frivolous inductions of hilarity—'a wee whiff sir and we'll have your leg off without your knowing it' Leaving aside the implications of operating amidst laughter Sir, the whole idea is unnatural."

"So is removing the leg," called Liston again.

"Kindly address your remarks through the chair Mr Liston," said Iveagh shortening his promotional climb with a winning display of teeth to the assembly of professors.

As Hatchett sat down amidst mirthful shouting, a surgeon as decrepit as Russell struggled to his feet. He wore a naval rig, that had no doubt seen him through the Trafalgar action. Rum had given a timbre to his voice—like someone heavy limping over gravel; furthermore it had combined with the sea air to stain his countenance to the purple of the Provost's robes.

"Mister Chairman, in my experience," he quavered, "I have formed a remarkably high opinion of the value of fresh air in the treatment of established disease, and in the prevention of non-established disease. Fresh air is almost the only prescription in my pharmacopoeia. Disease should be left to itself or to fresh air. In veriest fact I would venture so far as to say I have always been a firm believer in doing nothing at all. There was considerably less chance of making things worse than before, and it gave me a little extra time for . . . a . . . to myself." He paused to regain his vertical posture. "I have seen a lot of surgery. The lads on the warships nevah flinched when we performed our necessary operations. A leather plug to bite on, and a bellyful of rum was all that was needed. So I say damn to all bags over the mouths of patients and cows and damn to all change." He fell back, gasping and spluttering, while the applause rose to a roar. The public always loves a bluff hero, especially when he gives them what they want to hear and there is no chance whatever of serving on his ship.

My father had told me all I wanted to know about the effect of cannon-fire on flesh. What the seaman lying in pieces in the cockpit of the Bellerophon must have felt when this decaying clown advanced on them with knife and tar barrel was beyond the average imagination. Still his breath might well have soothed them if his words did not.

Now it was Professor Home's turn and I wondered what his daughter would think of him as he declaimed, "Speaking as a physician, I am of the conviction that any manoeuvre that may give the surgeon any more time in which to deploy his fiendish instruments is to be deplored."

Ball retired to a back bench and we laughed a while more before Iveagh brough us to order with James Syme, who was to tell us in the second paper of his experiences with amputation low in the leg. Syme was a dapper little man, with a mind as enquiring as Monroe's was shut. He ran an extra-mural class in Anatomy with Robert Liston, whom he also assisted in his private surgery, and with him he had suffered the wrath of the Royal Infirmary for the ineffable crime of being too successful too young. Nor had his interests been solely medical. While still a student he had discovered that india-rubber dissolved in naphtha could make canvas waterproof. Having discovered this fact, he abandoned it, only to hear that a Glasgow chemist called Charles Mackintosh had started to manufacture overcoats with it that kept out the rain.

Without Ball's hesitancy, he certainly convinced us that a foot amputation at the lower end of the tibia allowed a labourer much more chance of continuing to walk than did the orthodox section higher up the leg. From his steady description he had obviously many cases to back his claim.

"The incision should go from malleolus to malleolus, and the saw cut should angle backwards just above the lower articular surface of the tibia." He did a quick sketch on the blackboard. "In my hands," he went on confidently, "I have found the operative morbidity is low, and moreover it allows the labouring man to take up his tasks again more quickly and more easily than does the amputation at present practised. Thank you gentlemen."

Liston clapped noisily, but the little group around Russell muttered and buzzed like furious bees as the drone Hatchett rose to defend the beliefs of the Queen in the red wig.

"Mr—ah—Syme, is it?" he began sententiously, "we have practised mid thigh amputation in Edinburgh for many years—nay, many decades—with great success. I repeat, with modesty, great success. Professor Russell will bear me out."

"Um—oh—yes, yes. Quite, quite definitely." Russell, nodding head, wig awry, eyes closed as if deep in thought. Like this when awake, dared he sleep lest he die? "We can see no reason to change our methods now,"

"Heah, heah," called the naval surgeon.

"Well said," trolled the Russell puppets.

Syme waited until the ribaldry settled, then he said quietly,

"Mr Hatchett, you are a man of great skill and honesty. It would do you great credit if you were to think for yourself occasionally." End of Hatchett, face a-flame, hair a-flame, mortified as Syme laid him open on the raw. "You should never defend publicly, Mr Hatchett, a position that you do not really believe in," he finished.

Russell opened his eyes like an old satyr awaking suddenly in the sunshine, and struggled up to defend his sixty-five professional years of mental stasis.

"Bigod, he can stand as well," said Quentin. "Haw, haw, haw!"

The Professor spoke on the subject, around the subject, and indeed off the subject, summing up with an emotional,

"Because you are young, sir, you now think that you are a brilliant surgeon. But there are situations that—that call for maturity and judgment, and a hand guided by experience." Syme did not even have to answer this, for up sprang, in one bound as they say, the bottle-green Liston, his voice as big as himself,

"Maturity, judgment, experience. These words have a fine noble ring to them. But too often they are used as a cloak for yesterday's men doing yesterday's operations, and I suspect the only maturity is in the wine that gives colour to their cheeks, and a certain shake to their experienced hands."

Iveagh called for silence. He knocked on the desk with his hammer. The Professor began to use arguments that were not strictly scientific.

"You, sir, are a poltroon and a scoundrel, and indeed I shall now make every endeavour to make sure that the managers of the Royal Infirmary never appoint either you or that young butcher there to the staff!"

"That's a dangewous wemark to make publicly," observed the languid Deelatrumpe. Liston knew this also, for his manner grew calm as Russell's grew stormy and disarmingly, he said,

"I have no doubt, Professor Russell, that you have been making these endeavours already—long before tonight."

It was hard not to be drawn into the noise. So I shouted with the rest of them. The programme had been exploded again. Iveagh abandoned his hammer as useless, and announced to the heedless mob that he had decided to cancel the last paper. After the reception of the first two, I could not think that the last speaker would be sorry. Professor Russell swept out with his cavalcade as fast as dignity permitted, the very model of offended majesty.

"See how the conquewing hewo goes! Haw, haw, haw!" said Quentin sardonically. Liston, on the other hand, sauntered out with his friend and invited some senior students to help him,

"Empty a bottle or two at home."

We, the uninvited, found our way back to Ross's where we swallowed a few more jugs before going our separate ways. Although Ross's beer gave a certain haze to my thoughts, I am sure that total abstention could not have done anything to dispel the confustion I now suffered.

Academic revels were all very funny at the time, but in fact we had been laughing at ourselves.

I tried to think about success, and did not like what I thought. It seemed that success did not mean only hard work and penury. Above all it meant the Lord's own luck, and playing toady to all powerful professors, who through a fit of ill temper could destroy in a second the achievement of years of grovelling. And supposing there had been no professorial fit of the sullens, these same years of grovelling then prepared you to demand just that from your own thread-bare juniors; you elevated poverty (other people's) to the level of a cardinal virtue. You became more concerned with destroying rival reputations than with expanding medical knowledge, and if you did all this with panache you could be hated enough by your colleagues to have a statue raised in your memory, when to everyone's relief you had gone. After you finally gave in to gout and port, august College spokesmen would make fulsome speeches at fulsome dinners financed by failed examination candidates. In private they would be more thirsty at their own expense and more honest at yours.

These and a bevy of other disordered ruminations foundered about my fuddled brain. The same brain that was guiding my stumbling feet. By what pathway did the brain control the feet? God, I didn't know. Did anyone know? I didn't care.

I found No. 3 Robertson's Wynd just in time to avoid some ordure making its way to the gutters below. What a foul lodging-house it was. But I had no money to stay anywhere else. The spiral stairs seemed unnecessarily spiral, and seemed to go on for ever. They were also uneven. I cursed and blundered up into my room, knocking over the minute tallow which my allowance permitted. Where were my dirty shirts? I had to tie up a bundle ready for the Dalkeith carrier, who would pick them up at seven of the morning. I wrapped them up, and lay down. As soon as I lay down the roof spun around. When I stood up the floor did the same. I lay down again on my crippled bed, then I stood up again and vomited out of the window.

I slept late the next day and dreamed of Lucy Home. The dream became a nightmare as a larger figure in the shape of Grizel MacWrath appalled me into consciousness. If I succeeded in my ambition to enter the Edinburgh medical hierarchy it would land me up the aisle with the portly Grizel. If I abandoned my ambition and settled in my father's practice, Lucy Home would never look at me, and Grizel, with her spreading wrinkles, might well say that she always wanted to marry a country doctor anyway. My excesses of yesternight gave my mind a leisurely graciousness. I found to my surprise that I could even feel sorry for the adhesive Grizel, but not as sorry as I felt for myself.

Such a dilemma was soluble only by John Thomson. I decided not to listen to the delights of Professor Monroe that morning, and I went to seek out the sage himself as soon as I was steady on my feet. His office lay in the main University building, up two flights of stairs. It was a large room with polished floorboards and a spacious view of the Infirmary. An equally spacious rear window afforded him, and indeed reminded him, of his fight against Napoleon in Edinburgh Castle.

"Professor Thomson is no here," said a lank-haired clerk. "He said he was away to the College of Surgeons."

I strode off to the College.

"No, sir," said another clerk. "Professor Thomson hasnae been seen here this morning."

"Where do you think he might be then?"

"Oh, I would imagine that he's at the University."

I actually found him quite by chance, apparently reading *The Mercury,* in a little seat by the bowling green. As I debated whether to waken him, his eyelids flickered and shut, then flickered again into recognition—like a fat Tom cat bracing itself against an unavoidable reveillé.

"Oh dear," said he, "I've an urgent meeting at the College of Physicians," and he pulled from his pocket an inlaid Breguet watch shaped like a small cannonball, a parting gift from his fellow Castle-bound warriors in 1815. "Professor Home tells me there has been an epidemic of crippled feet in the Castle garrison. I must confess I did see them mounting guard the other day and I shouldn't wonder if it's not something to do with ill fitting boots. But bless me," he laughed, crinkling up his face, "if Home doesn't insist on a full examination. He's got it into his head that there has been an outbreak of scrofulous caries and he's planning to apply counter-irritation with moxae—you know, heated lengths of churchwarden stems."

I didn't know but I let him go on.

"Does he know, I wonder, how many men they keep up at the Castle? I told him to look at their boots but he won't listen to me; come to think of it, he won't listen to anyone."

He mused into his watchface. Could he be savouring a little cameo, with Home on his knees before a regiment of hot feet? I could clearly see the Professor of Physik weakening half-way along the first rank, and I wasn't going to cut short his labour, or for that matter put my own neck on the block by telling him that I already knew the diagnosis anyway. Uncle John came out of his military reverie.

"Ah well," he sighed, "Too late, I fancy, to help him now. Tell me, then, what can I do for your father's son?"

I outlined to him my dilemma. He listened, his brows furrowed but his eyes open and straight ahead, his belly rising and falling gently.

"There might be a lot to be said for marrying Miss MacWrath," he said, "but she has no dowry." Here he paused to think again. "Never let it be said that I am short of an answer," said he. "What you must do is to collect a bad reputation. That's it. Go to a brothel, and I'll make sure the rumour comes to me, for my students are a bad lot and are always in such places. From me you can rest assured that the rumour will find its way straight into the manse at Dalkeith. Your name will be most satisfactorily ruined—where it matters most. Count on me."

"Uncle John, what can I say?" I was almost in tears.

"Say nothing. And get into that brothel as quick as you can and sully your fair name as quick as you can get your breeks off."

I decided to waste no time and sought out Aeneas McBeen, who was the only one of my acquaintances who seemed to know exactly where such premises were to be found. He was in Monroe's dissecting rooms, unravelling the sciatic nerve of a goat.

"So you've succumbed to the desires of the flesh," he sneered piously.

"Not exactly, Aeneas. I don't want to do anything at the brothel, I just want to get a bad reputation," He withdrew his forceps from the goat's leg and said,

"Humbug." and who was I to say he was wrong? At any rate we arranged the tryst for that very evening. The ill fame of the house he took me to was a byword in old Edinburgh. We met in Ross's, and set off about eight o'clock past St Giles, past John Knox's house, as if to remind us of the squalor of our mission, and I was beginning to regret the decision to go, but reassured myself that I would just observe and enjoy myself without getting the pox. It was a squally evening, blowing gusts of rain around the rooftops, which disappeared into the mist like the Pentland Hills. We ducked down a close, which must remain nameless, and stopped at number "4". Aeneas looked up and down sharply before knocking. It's a curious thing, but in any normal part of the town people nod to and greet each other cordially, but if you don't know what the place is you can always tell a brothel because nobody recognises anybody else outside or in. At least, that's what I thought. A large woman closed the door behind us, and said to Aeneas,

"Good evening, Mr Monroe." I took it this was the madame. She was beaming and bejewelled, and the folds of her dress fell in a saltire across her bulging bosom, which merged without faltering into a similarly shaped belly. She bared a set of Waterloo teeth in what might pass for a smile.

"Good evening, Mrs Peddleclap," said Aeneas.

"You will be wanting a drink first, Mr Monroe, for it's a long while since you've been here," said she cordially. I laughed coarsely at his nom de guerre.

"Aye." Aeneas' speech became shorter as his embarrassment increased. Mrs Peddleclap waddled off, to arrange our refreshments. We sat at a small table in an alcove, and Aeneas recovered his good humour over a large goblet of whisky. I mentioned naively that everyone seemed to be wearing exceptionally large beards. He laughed.

"That's their disguise. The place is crawling with incognitos. That man behind the black silk mask over there thinks that nobody knows that he is Lord Fitzhalter." He gestured to his nose. "That neb of his is a byword in the Law Courts. They say he just brings a spare black cap with him here. And that huge moustache, do you see? Look there, by the pillar. That is meant to conceal Colonel Venneson from his fellow officers who spend more time here than they do at the Castle. In fact they all come together in false faces and moustaches and beards and cut each other dead. It's really quite amusing, like when our session clerk fell out with the grave-digger. They snubbed each other for over a year, aye so they did."

His discourse was broken by the return of the madame, who said, "Mary is not available tonight, but Lizzie's a braw lassie." Aeneas scowled and followed her.

I sat in my alcove with the fast emptying jug of whisky, and watched the comings and goings through the richly tapestried hall with interest. I tried to guess how many from the faculty of Medicine hid their reputation and tastes beneath convincing wigs, moustaches and masks. Very soon I was regretting my wish not to be disturbed. Only my fear of the pox kept me in my seat. I thought back to Mr MacWrath's warnings on the subject of sin, and how it was manifest upon the countenance of those unfortunate women. Looking at them in the half light I had to admit that he was wrong—or seemed to be. I have no doubt that my fears would have vanished with another measure of whisky, but they were not allowed to.

Suddenly I heard a fierce caterwauling from behind a nearby door. Sounds of what I took to be a whip, female giggles, and the dominant voice seemed to be running around the room. My attention left the wanderings up and down the hall, riveting on the goings on behind that door. I tried to catch the sounds, but the heavy wood blurred the detail. I could barely contain my curiosity. My glass toppled off the table, prompted into space by my careless hand. A crash, and the door opened, and out into the light of the candelabra burst the Reverend Gideon MacWrath, minister of the parish of Dalkeith. His eyes blazed, his lips were working, and his features glowered unmistakably through a ludicrously sparse beard and moustache. He was adjusting his buttons as he strode into the light. He saw me and stopped.

"You," he said.

"Mr MacWrath!" He sat down at my table.

"The will of the Lord lies heavy on the shoulders of those who seek to obey His words," said he buckling up his belly band. "I have come here to raise these fallen creatures into the lap of God," he shouted.

I restrained any obvious comments about his own lap, so stunned was I by the sight here of a man whose sole weakness I had believed to be his stomach. He was going on, with some passion too,

"There is in that room a creature. Mary Paterson is her name. Mrs Peddleclap was told about her by some wretch by the name of Hare, who lives up at the West Port. The Devil is at work in her, and I must cast him out. It is a powerful, heavy task. I tried to reason with her and she laughed. I tried to mortify her flesh, and she displayed herself. There was nothing else to do." He called for whisky.

"There she comes now. There, across the hall, that girl with breasts like grapefruits. I will bring her to the ways of righteousness yet," he roared, and fixed me with his baleful eyes, as it it were intended to cauterise the sin from my mind. As Mary Paterson disappeared he began to bring himself under control, and questioned me about my presence at Mrs Peddleclap's establishment.

How could I tell him the truth? In any case, the truth would have helped only if it had reached him from John Thomson, not from his own eyes. The fradulent lecher, I thought, trying to pass off his lust as zeal, and now daring to catechise me. I searched my fuddled brain for a plausible answer, but none would come. Fortunately, none was needed for he took my silence for scientific modesty.

"Of course, laddie, it's clear you're in the quest of some important information for a thesis, or perhaps you plan to address the Medical Society on this or related subjects. Never fear, we'll talk of this episode with good humour, when we're alone, of course, over the port when the ladies have gone, and you're my son-in-law. Hah, hah, hah. But that's all in the future, laddie. Now I must away." He paused to adjust his buttons once more, and marched off, altering the position of the hairy appliance on his face as he went. I had to confess it improved him and it would be my port, too, damn him.

My mission had been a disaster. There was nothing for it but to return to my squalid dwelling. I tried to brush away the whisky with mint paste but succeeded only in lodging a bristle between two teeth. On trying to dislodge it I knocked my powdered coral off the dresser and cracked my tortoiseshell tongue-scraper in a vain attempt to scoop up the powder from O'Loan's furrowed floor. I abandoned further efforts and when I searched for a shirt the next day, I knew that my mother would be collecting a bundle of clean linen ready for the washing.

7

Professor Monroe's first term of Anatomy rotted away in the rising April sunshine. At this point our course turned from a study of the dead to a study of the sick in general, and to James Home, Professor of Physik and Materia Medica in particular—whose daughter made Grizel seem like a grenadier. Like so much else of our institution, it was based on formal lectures, where the Professor would either captivate his class with his glittering eloquence, or hold them captive till the appointed hour was over.

Professor Home sadly belonged to the latter breed. His lecture course was obligatory, so we had a magnificent opportunity to witness the slovenly lack of discipline and general apathy that characterised his teaching method. He was in bits and pieces just as I remembered from my abbreviated view of him in the bookshop.

When he stood up for us, there was a lot of him to be seen. His lips were thick, and his nose full and bending in two planes. His frock-coat looked like an old sack, and the wearing of it did nothing to rid it of its creases, nor did he pay much attention to fitting buttons into button-holes. The pervasive aura of weariness was blown away without warning from time to time by a convulsive tick that took over his whole frame. And if he happened to be in contact with anything when the tick overcame him, then it had little chance of survival.

He had been justly famous on the subject of Materia Medica, where his eccentric ways passed for genius, but following Gregory into the Chair of Physik had exposed him to a comparison that he could not survive. Senior students told incessant tales of his antics at College dinners, where it seemed that he always waited until the guest speaker was in full spate before leaving the hall, lest he reached the high watermark himself. His dramatic exits would be prefaced by a sudden backward movement of his chair. To complete the charade of self-concealment he would tiptoe out, bent double the while, clutching at his absent buttons. The large doors he just could not close gently. Minutes later he would return performing the entire manoeuvre in reverse, and explaining to everyone in a stage whisper that he had just had to leave the room.

So we knew what we had to expect, and did not hurry to the Lecture Room, delaying as long as politeness permitted in the College quadrangle. It struck me as I entered that every lecture room I had been in had been decorated in the same way. The process of thinking must have been set into action by the sight of all that mahogany. The Professor was slumped in a chair in the front, before the tiered seats. He was clearly used to late entrances and made the best of the time available to him.

When we had also sat down, a College flunkey prodded him respectfully to warn him of our presence.

"Quite spwightly, ain't he," said Quentin.

Sprightly or not, he did manage to rise to his feet and start his murmuring discourse. "Gentlemen," he declared, "the purpose of this series of lectures and demonstrations, is to teach you the rudiments of Practical Physik. You will learn the principles of medicine and the principles of therapeutic intervention. Moreover, you will learn the fundamentals of medical observation, and the basics of conducting a medical practice."

"And no doubt we will learn the foregwound and backwound of each as well," said Quentin in his best parade square style.

He droned on over the next ten weeks, taking us through the essentials of his art. We learned the indications for copious blood letting, for blistering, for fierce purging, and for tartar emetics. He developed his theories on fevers, and how he believed that gastroenteritis was the cause of all pathology. His finest achievement was to knock over a pile of books, a jar of leeches and a pickled lung during one lecture.

Senior students told us that John Abercrombie disagreed with him. He believed each organ could suffer its own malady. More senior students told us that John Abercrombie took apprentices still, ran virtually a private medical school of his own, and had a large and successful practice.

Home told us that in the fifteenth century, physicians used to burn juniper and other aromatic substances to keep contagions at bay and to assist the natural healing process.

"Fortunately nowadays," said he, "nobody believes these quaint fictions, that is to say—these beliefs do not enjoy general credence, for now we know that nature has no natural healing process." He felt that all disease had to be arrested actively. This was following in the Gregory tradition of vigorous therapy.

"Antiphlogistic means are what are needed, gentlemen," he said. "We must employ a regimen that weakens the patient. We must not let him eat, we must apply leeches all over the body—everywhere." It was at this point that the leeches ended up on the ground—like spoiled cherries around his feet.

Robert Knox told us, during his continuing lectures, that John

Abercrombie thought blood letting was a dangerous remedy to inflict upon already weakened patients.

The Professor moved on to another of his beloved convictions, "As to the duration of disease, gentlemen, sickness takes many forms, but you can discern the trends and herein lies your art. Patients may be relaxed or constricted, that is to say they may be sthenic or asthenic, or indeed others might refer to these as tonic and atonic, and if you care for the term, stimulus or contra-stimulus. Now what would you consider a reasonable approach and treatment?" the question was really addressed to himself. "My view is that tonic states must be opposed. Resisted if you like with opium sedation, and, of course, blood letting. Atonic states must be whipped out of their flabbiness. I would suggest strychnine which you know is an extract of nux vomica or aconite. The choice is wide."

Senior students told us that he over-treated his patients, and that John Abercrombie should have been appointed the Professor of Physik when Professor Gregory retired. Well, they may have been right, and after my first few lectures I did not disagree with them, but Professor Home was our professor and we had to listen to him.

A flash of sunshine, however, occasionally seduced us away from this fount of instruction—to lose any surplus coins on deceitful horses at the Leith races, to chill ourselves into a stupor in the sea at Trinity or Portobello or, as we did one Wednesday after luncheon, to smack a feather stuffed ball round Leith golf links. For transport, our hussar borrowed an open cart from one of his tumbledown friends and, for Dominic Corrigan and me, he borrowed from Professor Monroe two old clubs, each shaped like a flat pie with a long handle. He, of course, had his own.

It was the best class of practical therapeutics I have attended. The sun was almost as warm as it looked and we held our ground with some difficulty against what the locals laughingly call a "wee breeze". Quentin stood four holes up on us at the twelfth tee and his guffaw increased alarmingly. It was at this point the expedition began to go wrong— really because of six idiots ahead of us. Their red coats indicated membership of the Gentlemen Golfers and they were sauntering about the twelfth green, reminiscing and missing the hole. Dominic, swinging with determination, smashed his ball into their midst.

"Would you look at that now!" he crowed, "Is it not dropping on their heads like manna from the sky?" The gentlemen had other views and stopped reminiscing. I saw the largest step off the green waving his club. Five seconds later Dominic's ball lay at our feet.

This was too much for Dominic's fragile temper. He strode down the links and demanded in the name of the Holy Mother to know what they were about. Quentin and I followed to watch the fun. The words, high at first, degenerated into a low exchange.

"You have insulted my friend here!" threatened Quentin.

"And what do you propose, sir?" sneered the large Gentleman Golfer.

"I have seen a man called out for less," I thought Quentin was sailing a bit close-hauled and so it proved.

"I am not averse to a swap of anything that takes your fancy. What is your weapon, sir?" said the big man.

"I would not go to such lengths", said Quentin, suddenly appalled.

"Hold, sir," said the big man. "Have I not made your acquaintance before?"

"I do not imagine so, sir," replied Quentin coolly, "but I do have a twin bwother who I am told shows a wemarkable wesemblance to me."

"It was you, sir," said the large golfer, squaring up to Quentin. "At Leith Sands last October. You attempted to nip the hamstrings of my prize filly, Natural Surprise, sired by Parson's Pleasure out of Corn Rigs. You almost cost me one hundred guineas. You and a red faced villain whom I could recognise as a candidate for the Calton Jail."

"Have a care, sir," said Quentin. "You are talking of my good friend and colleague, Pwofessor Monwoe, who was cawwying out some studies of compawative anatomy." I thought the sportsman was about to burst. He purpled and pulled at his neckcloth for more air.

"Professor Monroe, sir. Professor Monroe, I would have you to know is my cousin. How dare you defame the son of my mother's sister. That red faced scoundrel had a military swagger to him; a broken down gamester, a deserter and you try to pass him off as Professor Monroe. Are you a student in the Medical faculty sir?" He advanced in a threatening attitude.

"No, I am a student of divinity," said Quentin with the face of a man doubling his stake on a pair of threes.

"Divinity is it? God help the church. As for you", he raised his brows, curved down his lips and thrust his tilted face within breathing distance of ours.

"I will remember you all—you will come to bad ends; I shall see to it; I shall have words with the Professor of Theology who is related to my wife's second cousin by marriage; I shall. . . ."

"It's time to go," said Quentin sharply. "Come on, lads." He bowed deeply and whisked us away to our cart, and it was only when we were safely up the Edinburgh road that I began to balance the advantages of Quentin's friendship against the increasing certainty of professional disgrace.

There was little time to debate this riddle further for Professor Home, as the practical part of our training took us to the hospital where his failing charges were obliged, as were we, to accept his therapeutic theories. They lay on low trestle beds in long, dark wards. Unkempt slatterns looked after the wards with the same care that they applied to themselves. They were an evil filthy bunch, but fortunately were not allowed to look after the patients for, in combination with Professor Home, they would have formed a fatal weapon.

The care of the actual patients was in the hands of the Physician's Clerks, senior students selected every month from the ranks of Home's class. When working in his charge I had the wit to see that there was more to being a successful hospital physician than merely being driven in a fine carriage from one grateful fee to another. He had to flaunt his feeble nostrums in the teeth of incurable illness, pretending to a boldness he could hardly feel. He had to devise ways of telling the truth to those who could take the truth, and to those who could not take the truth— well, it could be delayed until they were too ill to care. I no longer marvelled that these men had to replace what was drained out of them with burgundy or port or whatever helped them forget our mortality.

The ward was always full at the best of times. During the worst of times, when epidemic spotted fevers raged over the town, like a moorland fire, they started with extra beds up the centre of the wards, then in the corridors, and it was not long before they infiltrated and finally took over the surgical wing of the Hospital as well. The surgeons then rushed to arms over their stolen beds, and heated words passed between them and the physicians, wherever they could find a room free of patients to argue in.

Nothing prompts awareness of mortality so much as a plague. These outbreaks of fever chose the hot weather for some unexplained reason— as though they were part of the seasons, like falling leaves, and when they struck it was with a swiftness that could change a swarming slum into lodgings for rotting corpses.

Cholera particularly came stealing in from the heavy sour cloud of poisoned air in mine workings and in the narrow wynds of the Old Town. Without warning, bowels would turn to liquid which at first was thrown on to the children's playgrounds below, then, as feebleness took over, was left to run over beds, over floors and over whatever else might be in the way.

As it was difficult to treat the afflicted, attempts were necessary to limit the spread of these epidemic fevers, and the very range of methods was proof that none was wholly effective. In less enlightened times physicians recommended that witches might be set on fire, or doctors sometimes ran about with spiked helmets, frightening away the contagion with aromatic fumes. A common method, considered successful for a while, was to massacre all available Jews in a city, particularly efficacious being the elimination of those with the largest collection of debtors' bonds. Enlightenment led us to encourage people to escape the poisoned air, to wash at the public wells and to drink as much water as they could. But despite our efforts the pestilence came and went as it chose, marking its passage in death and tears.

To those privileged enough to be admitted to our hospital we gave counter-irritation in the form of hot baths or blisters over the spine and belly. We forced them to take brandy and opium and calomel and capsicum, which they would vomit back at us. During the crises we always ran out of leeches, which were necessary to lay around the temples for headache. And I had to master the exact indications for these remedies by the light of my single candle in Robertson's Wynd, secretly terrified that I would be needing them myself before the week was out.

There were lighter moments though. I recall now it must have been about the second week of my first cholera epidemic. Down the ward, picking her way between the sodden trestle beds, came a ward skivvy, clutching a bowl of foul green bilious fluid.

"Bigod, there must be a gallon of vomit in there," Quentin stared in horrified amazement.

"That's no' vomit," snapped the shrew, "that's soup."

The lighter moments were not many, however, and to make it worse Mr O'Loan brought another letter from Dalkeith which announced Grizel's intention of coming to the Assembly Ball, and her hope that I would fill up her card to dance with Professor This and Professor That, and of course that charming Mr Deelatrumpe.

I survived that letter and the epidemic, and we continued our study of Physik with Professor Home. He took us to his clinic in the Old Town Dispensary, where free inoculations against smallpox and medicine were handed out to the needy and indigent, who eked out life in the tenements and warrens of the High Street.

Free care for the needy was a benevolent feature of the Edinburgh medical scene. The Royal Infirmary itself provided attention for the suffering from many parishes far afield of Edinburgh. There was a Dispensary in the New Town as well, carrying the crusade against disease across the North Bridge.

Apart from these official services, unofficial ones sprouted everywhere. James Syme opened at Minto House, at his own expense, a surgical hospital, where his reputation continued to threaten his colleagues at the Royal. Labouring men would rather risk the Syme amputation, with the chance of walking out on almost two legs, than step back into history with Professor Russell and come out with one leg, or worse still, not come out at all, as was more likely.

Professor Home worked hard at his Dispensary. We watched him dealing with his patients, and listened to their gossip as they waited for the great man. Although students end up with a certain suspicion of all professors, the townsfolk by the same token placed them next to God, and some, like Gregory, thought it should be a peg beyond. Any doctor old enough, grey enough and pompous enough, they addressed as Professor—or rather Perfessor. You could hear them any time you wandered through the communal Waiting Room.

"Eh wis at the Infirrmarry and had my sight ta'en away by Perfessor Black. He's a richt gentlemen, yon yin, heh, heh, heh!" Or the one-legged man saying,

"Did ye everr see the likes o' that? That wis Perfessor Jamieson done that." And he tottered round to demonstrate his absolute mobility.

Or the man with the sunken cheeks, who said of the Royal Infirmary, "They've no interest in you in there unless you're dyin'."

All these professors available, and we had to end up with James Home. However he did teach us how to take a history, how to elicit the essential facts of an illness from the flood of information that we all feel necessary when describing our sickness to someone else. When Mrs Malarky said that she had had her sore back "a good wee whilie", that could mean anything from half an hour to twenty years, and she might well use it to mean either in the same conversation. We learned that, "To let you understand, doctor," was the prelude to a monologue that would let you do anything but.

The exchange of intimate information between doctor and patient, however, could give rise to very subtle tongue in cheek. The physician who asked a spherical Edinburgh wifie with high nosed superiority,

"Well, who are you, my good woman?" had only himself to blame when she replied,

"Fine, thanks, Hoo's yersel'?"

We were also taught how to percuss, to strike the chest like a drum to see if it was full of air, which was normal, or full of fluid, which was not and to make sure there was not too much air, which was worse.

"This technique," he admitted grudgingly one morning, "is not of Scottish origin. I would go so far as to say, it is not of English either—it comes from one of those German places. The credit must go to an innkeeper's son—by the name of—by the name of—ah—well, no matter. As a boy he used to find the level of wine in his father's casks by tapping them up and down. When he became a physician he applied the principles to the chest. You will not normally hear me approving of such innovations but I would recommend this one to your notice—your attention might be another way of putting it."

"Extend the fingers," he commanded, sitting at the centre of our semicircle. "Then flex them at the first interphalangeal joint. When you

have arranged your finger in this way, strike the chest wall like a drum—
you must do it with a certain abandon and éclat."

We struck, and heard nothing—at least nothing useful. He went on
with his dissertation,

"If the chest is solid, you will get a dull sound, like that of a drum filled
with water, or, if you care, a barrel full of fluid. But if the lungs are
normal, you will hear a sound like the striking of a drum filled with air."

He showed us another recent technique for actually listening to the
chest. A new device called a stethoscope and invented by a Frenchman
Laennec.

"It ill becomes me to speak well of the French," he said, upending a
tray of glass bottles, "but this is probably one of the most important
contributions to medicine."

He bent over a cyanotic, wheezing coal-heaver, with a rolled tube of
paper. Placing one end over the chest, he put the other to his ear, giving
every evidence of hearing significant sounds through it. After a little he
straightened up and said,

"Up this tube you will hear the heart in action, beating if you prefer,
and you will discern air going in and out of the lungs, that is to say—
ah—breathing." He bent back over the coal-heaver, and listened
intently to the struggling chest, and I began to think he had dropped off
to sleep. The man rumbled and fought for breath. We stood back
respectfully. The Professor, bent double, listened intently through his
Laennec's tube. Suddenly he stood up straight again, narrowly avoiding
a beaker of water. "You know," he said, "you must be careful what you
say in front of patients. I well remember being called to see a fellah, had a
large estate down East Lothian. After I had taken his history and all the
usual necessaries, I took his pulse and looked at my watch; a way of
timing the heart which has become quite acceptable. I had not wound
my pulse watch, and when I saw it had stopped I said, 'My God!' and
snorted or made some similar noise before proceeding with my
consultation.

"Well do you know, that man changed unrecognisably from that day?
He gave up riding to hounds, he gave up hare coursing, he gave up otter
hunting, he gave up port. Nothing could convince him that it was my
watch and not his heart that had gone wrong. Heh, heh, heh". He
laughed in amused remembrance; it was the first time we had realised
that such an expression was possible in his features.

"Now what are we to tell McHugh here?" he asked rhetorically. "We
certainly must not permit his chest to alter his life in that way now, will
we? No indeed. A few blistering applications around the chest wall—
here—and here—and there—and he'll be good for another twenty years
undergound, won't you, McHugh?"

"Thank you, surr. Thank you." He would have said more had a fit of coughing not cut him short. The Professor shook his head.

"Ah well. What's the next problem? I suppose," he added, reverting to the miner, "a good inhalation from burning tobacco, or indeed snuff, from time to time, would help clear his breathing tubes as well." He nodded in quiet agreement with himself for a moment or two, then turned to his class,

"I think a little sherry is called for, gentlemen—nunc est bibendum". So he was human after all.

Out of the University we collected beliefs, bigotries and deep convictions. At this stage many of these were conflicting and did not constitute an education. It was only in the Ross taproom amongst our fellow students that we could extend some and discard others, baptising them all for good measure with Wattie's best ale—the sole source of revenue to these extra-mural finishing schools that doubled the value of the Edinburgh medical degree at no extra cost to the University.

Aeneas and I repaired there one Friday evening, and there sat Quentin, who had cut the afternoon lectures, and was looking like a man who had just had worse news than he could bear.

"You don't look well, Quentin," said Aeneas, mock concerned. "What can I suggest? I wonder if the exhibition of a little tartar emetic might produce a definite tonic effect. Did you know," he babbled on, innocently, "that tartar emetic is made from antimony. And the name antimony comes from anti-moine. If you were a French scholar you would realise that that means anti-monk. Its properties were discovered when four monks succumbed after eating it for breakfast."

This weak sally failed to raise the customary "Haw, haw, haw" from Quentin. He looked as though he had already had more antimony than was good for him.

He groaned, "I'm all washed up—I'm queered, don't you know?" He looked it too.

"Come on then. Tell us all." We sat down to hear Quentin's tale.

The story came out in a rush; in essence it meant the total financial collapse of the Universal Boot project. The Major, it seemed, had the same talent for disaster as Quentin, and had chosen amongst his first contacts two Clothing Colonels so well clad as to be already under suspicion for misappropriation of Government funds. They were now also queered, and there was going to be an enquiry.

"The Major's on the wun. He's lying low somewhere in Somerset I think,"

"And Tom Cockle?"

"I don't know, but I don't think the wunners have got him—yet."

Quentin continued to gaze moodily into his beer a while, then turned to me.

"I'll have to leave my lodgings, you know." He furrowed his brow, clearly dismayed at the prospect. I thought he was going to cry, but he went on,

"Do you think I could move in with you? If the worst comes to the worst that is," he added, suddenly aware of what moving in with me actually meant.

"By all means, Quentin," I said graciously.

Quentin passed a bad few days, waiting from the men from Bow Street to drag him away in cuffs to Newgate, but they did not come. The days lengthened to a se'ennight then to a fortnight, and still they did not come. There came instead a letter from his accomplice—the dashing Major de Serte—indeed written in a scrawl that suggested he had been doing just that while composing it. Despite all, it was reassuring. He said there would be no scandal now. The Runners had called off their search. Come to think of it, anyone not in direct fear of apprehension could see why too, for they had quite enough on their plates trying to persuade Robert Peel they could transfer the entire underworld to the Fleet prison without any help from that police force he was forever shouting about. The letter further informed him that the Major had now emerged from his West Country lair, and he thought it wiser to retain in his hands for an unspecified period of time their joint funds.

"Thoughtful of him," said Quentin, "ain't it just—and he didn't even bother to scwibble me the vowels. Not that they'd be worth a farthing anyway."

"Vowels?" asked Aeneas.

"'I', 'O' and 'U'", said Quentin. "Vewy useful between men of honour as a substitute for the weady. Don't you know?"

Though Quentin had not the benefit of even that substitute, he rapidly regained his composure and Professor Home lost his. It all happened over the Bostonian lady philanthropist—Mrs Jocelyn Dewlapp, who burst on to the Edinburgh Medical stage one sunny April morning. Her wealth was enormous and its source a dead husband who had wrung a fortune from a huge brick factory in Massachusetts, and if her fortune was ample so was she. You could never look at her without thinking that an apple in her mouth would have set her off to perfection—but the mouth was never still for long enough to let anyone try the effect. A quizzing glass with a gold frame dangled from a golden chain that vanished into the folds around her neck.

From the gush of speech that poured from her we gathered that she had conceived the noble idea of buying her way into Paradise (not her exact wording) with an immense charity hospital where her late husband's brickmakers could succumb to their lung disorders in comfort, and with the extra workers employed for its building, there would be even more patients to enjoy the completed wards. Hospitals, bricks, architects, physicians, nostrums, opening ceremonies, her genius for filling in silence drove her friends to fear that they too might soon be in need of her new infirmary. They persuaded her that expert knowledge was necessary, that the fount of all medical wisdom was Edinburgh, and the man who formed the major part of the spray was James Home. Within four weeks, she was in the capital in humble search of a drenching.

The Professor, with his wide Lothians practice, should have had a matchless experience in handling formidable women, but Mrs Dewlapp crushed him into a state of silent terror that moved even the brutish louts in his class of practical physik to a flicker of sympathy.

"Would you imagine now the effect of that on your good health if you didn't feel too well," said Dominic in amazement as she hove into view. Quentin's sharp ear for a ridiculous blend of shape and sound was imagining something else, and before she had negotiated the double doors of Parliament House, he had restyled her Jocelyn Buttocks. And now in perfect harmony with her new sobriquet, this bountiful sphere rolled about Edinburgh in pursuit of the Professor who managed to avoid the horror of a second meeting for at least a week.

Recent history has its parallels; they tell of the old Duke of Marlborough who, after three years without uttering a single word, when told that Madame de Stael had arrived to pay him a visit, broke his self imposed silence, shrieking: "Take me away! Take me away!" Professor Home's dismay was no less moving.

As Mrs Dewlapp queened through the Royal Infirmary he slipped out through a postern gate down the wynd to the Surgeons' Hall, where no professor of Medicine had stepped before without an invitation. He was found hiding in the cloakroom by Mr Collick.

"Professor Home, sir, there you are, sir, there you are, cooed the charming secretary as Home fidgeted beneath a standful of capes.

"Aye, here I am," he grunted shortly—later explaining at his customary length just why. Telling it to the apparently discreet Collick was like shouting it from St Giles' pulpit; from then on all joined in the conspiracy to save the Professor.

When Mrs Dewlapp was sighted off the larboard quarter of John Thomson's office, the evasive surgical pathologist, convened a meeting of all available professors with the express purpose of keeping Professor Home out of Mrs Dewlapp's field of vision until hunger removed her from his.

The chase continued to the door of the Dirty Club, over which no woman bar a dollymop had stepped, even with an invitation. After a tense little scene she accepted the steward's explanation that the professor had resigned his membership. Professor Home, however, could not keep up the pace, and Mrs Dewlapp finally pressed him to the wall in the Old Town Dispensary, where he was casting pearls before our somnolent class. Flanked as he was by us and by a group of patients busily rolling bandages, and with the bulky vixen between him and the only door, any attempt to disappear would be noticed. He turned at bay like a jowly gander against a farmyard fence on Christmas Eve.

"Glad to have taken you at last, sir," shouted the benefactress in triumph, unruffled, if at all aware, that the professor was in the grip of a totally different emotion. "I have but a few questions to put to you, Professor Home, concerning my proposed charitable foundation for Boston brickworkers and their dependent relatives." And put them she did, in that curious nasal wail that passes for English across the Atlantic. She surged about him like a flabby child debating whether to cuddle or dismember a fluffy toy.

I began to feel sorry for him, so much so that I started to invent escape routes for him—an art that had proved my salvation during a hundred weary lectures. I dismissed simple vaporisation as too quick; a hot air balloon brought a brief and distant smile to my lips: but I decided that the way most likely to entertain me and deal with the weighty American at the same time was a pulley system, and with luck it could catch them together as the swell brought Mrs Dewlapp broadside on to the Professor. Within seconds I had this deftly slung from the skylight window, the Professor ascending and Jocelyn Buttocks dangling from a grappling hook below him, still putting questions which she answered herself or deemed not worthy of one. Did he think hospitals should face north or south or in both directions?

"Well, madam, I—er—ah—"

Did he not surely believe that much was to be said for not segregating men and women in separate wards? Just what the Professor thought of that heresy was evident from the way he reassembled his straying features. What were his learned views on the inhalation disease of brickworkers?

"Ah—ah—I—" It sounded even better at the top of my rope.

"Would it be reasonable, Professor, to attribute the clearing of bronchial phlegm to the vesiculative properties of blistering the chest wall or to the stimulative properties of nux vomica? Can these therapies be exhibited in hospital circumstances or in social and domestic circumstances?"

"Well, I—ah—"

I conjured them back to the floor and let my unattached thoughts toy with the delicious notion of MacWrath on a spit, being turned by his daughter—or better still, with their roles reversed.

"I would have held with the latter myself," Mrs Dewlapp was braying.

"Madam, I—ah—"

"Of course in Boston we follow the tonic atonic view but we also espouse teleological medicamenting" which she pronounced medick-ay-mentin'. And more of the same besides. The professor resembled more than ever the trapped gander and was clearly in dire need of a saviour — from anywhere—even from amongst the ranks of his students. And out of the ranks strode a saviour in the form of Quentin Deelatrumpe, now safe from the boot scandal, once more the debonair hussar, poorer perhaps but every threadbare inch of him a cavalryman.

He stepped forth and bent low before her, took her hand to his mouth and said soulfully,

"Madam, clearly the faiwest flowers flouwish in Boston soil! Haw, haw, haw."

"Why, sir," she simpered; almost but not quite speechless. "I do believe you're a gentleman, sir. I do indeed."

"What on earth is he trying for," I said to Aeneas.

"Hoping to refill his coffers, I shouldn't wonder."

Quentin continued to play the gallant as though he had never heard the name—Jocelyn Buttocks. He drawled,

"You must permit me to show you our Dispensawy, then I shall conduct you to its equivalent in the New Town, then we can see the beauties of its open architecture. Then let us wepair to Johnnie Dowie's, where we can eat oysters and dwink bwandy punch in pwoper society." The well fed lady could only accept. He wafted her away, and Home sighed gratefully as he heard her powerful twittering disappear into the distance.

Quentin benefited in several ways from his adroit rescue of the Professor. It secured for him a place in the affections of at least one of the medical hierarchy. It also secured from the Boston lady philanthropist a grant of £100 to spend in any way his perfect scientific mind thought fit.

"Whatever you could consider medically, therapeutically or spiritually beneficial to mankind, Lootenant," were her exact words. As a spiritual benefit to herself, it was understood that Quentin was to escort her to the April Ball that was to be held next week in the Assembly Rooms. My own spiritual benefit was enough for both of us, for in my pocket was folded the only letter from my chosen one that I had thumbed with frequent reading. She regretted she could not dance the new waltz with me and my handsome friend; she wept; she was even now lying abed with suspected gout and my father had forbidden walking until at least the day after the ball. Also in my pocket was an even more thumbed letter from Mrs Home inviting the dragoon and me to join their party for the great night.

8

On Friday, the evening of the Assembly Ball, we decided to raise the style of our 6 o'clock tipple by meeting at 19 Hanover Street, which Quentin, saved from instant bankrupcy by the £100, had not had to quit after all. When I rang at his door, a gorgeous confection in scarlet and gold and ermine, bade me enter with a deep bow. This of course was Quentin in the full dress uniform of a Lieutenant of Hussars. That he was no longer entitled to it worried him not at all, and he was sure that he could explain it away to Mrs Dewlapp as necessary expenditure prior to true research.

Mrs Cudleigh was lurking about behind the light cavalryman, her lips drawn up into a pout. I could easily have understood if Quentin had told me he had changed his mind about coming to the Ball.

"Jenny is wather displeased," he explained a trifle superfluously," but what can I do after all? Business is business and I don't flouwish scwubbing for my pennies any more than she does. Ain't that wight m' dear? Come Jenny don't take on so; I'll buy you some furbelows and wibbons at the mercer's, day after tomorrow, when I've cleared my head of tonight's fwolics. And Mrs Buttocks will foot the bill," he added as a final persuasion. Moved by his subtlety, the ravishing Mrs Cudleigh flung out of the room. Quentin shrugged and turned to me.

"Women-alas. Have a dwop of gin punch," He handed me a large container, and took one of the same himself.

"So Anas is not going to twip the light fantastic with us tonight. Poor Anas; no doubt he's having a fit of the Scotch glooms again. Poor Anas," he added thoughtfully, "he's fwightened to be happy for fear something goes wrong. I suppose if he's misewable all the time then he knows things can't get worse. Haw, haw, haw!"

I watched him speak, and I rather envied him his easy way. I knew I cut a pale figure beside him in my new coat and pantaloons. My lilac waistcoat and neck lace had seemed to me rather lively till I had come face to face with my dashing friend. I thought rather ruefully of the cost, and hoped that my growing taste for beer would not make my suit unwearable before changing fashions made it obsolete.

Mr O'Loan had given my confidence quite a boost as I clattered down the spiral staircase in Robertson's Wynd. He was standing sentry, as usual, in the street. He had looked me over with false admiration.

"Ah, it's yerself, dochthor. Well is it not powerful handsome that ye're lookin' tonight. Ye'll be twistin' the hearts of the young ladhies, not a doubt of it, perhaps twistin' a bit more besides, eh?" With this last, he leered and dug his elbow in my ribs. In some pain I thanked him for his flattery and hoped that Lucy would think the same.

"Not at all, not at all, dochthor," he said grandly. "When I saw ye comin' down there like Brian Boru hisself, I said, 'Barney, miboy, there's man who'd lend you a couple of bob and think nothin' of it.'" I couldn't tell him just how much I did think of it, for I had only twenty shillings in my pocket. But I gave him two of them on a long term loan (more's the fool me), pulled on my galoshes and clumped away down through the Cowgate, in rare spirits. My spirits took a plummet again, however, when I saw the mettlesome galloper and his picturesque domestic. It was impossible to feel low for long in Quentin's company. When his pocket was full and his glass half empty, you couldn't find a better companion. We tittled and tattled through another measure of gin punch, then left for the Ball in a hackney carriage.

"Mrs Buttocks will pay. Haw, haw, haw! Twelve Charlotte Square, cabby," he shouted, jumping into the vehicle. When we disembarked, Quentin skipped about the street shouting "En garde", and fenced madly and briefly with the railings, while I pulled on the bell chain.

When he opened the door, Jamie, the butler, all but collapsed with uncontrollable glee at the sight of Quentin's uniform.

"Help ma Boab," he declared, backing against the wall. "The military is upon us. Would you have me surrender now, sir? Or would you do battle with that auld wifie up there in the frame?" Certainly Lucy's grannie had gained nothing in charm. He led us into the drawing room, where were collected most of our party for the Ball.

The Professor, wearing sombre evening garb, hailed us cheerfully, and threaded his way through the throng towards us. I had enough time to cast a wary eye on our friends for the coming festivities. That tall thin youth with his back to the fire could only be Home's son Gavin. He was evidently playing the role of country sportsman up to town in a dark green and red suiting and he cocked his head, rather like a pheasant, as he listened intently to his partner. To be honest he played the role rather well. Auntie Gertrude, defying her years, was still in her lair, clutching the ivory counters and gazing around for a victim. And there were two bearded uncles who were planning to alternate between the backgammon board and some bottles of rare port that were sitting in readiness on a small walnut side table. And to get themselves in readiness for the vintage the pair of them even now were examining the dregs in their glasses and keeping a hopeful eye open for the man with the decanter.

Quentin and I nodded and smiled and sidled past this group of gambling folk to take up station within earshot of Gavin's hunting recollections.

"Bad year for the grouse," he was saying, as his father drifted back to join us.

"The Honourable Eliza Thredbair," said the Professor to the galloping lancer, "of the Philiphaugh Thredbairs, you know," he added by way of explanation.

"I see," said Quentin gravely, none the wiser, but trying hard.

Home brought us before his wife. She smiled, and her,

"How kind of you to escort Lucy to the Ball", made me feel quite the gallant. I blushed and bowed awkwardly to her daughter, who in her high waisted green sarsenet quite took the breath from my murmured chivalries. I blushed more as I bent to kiss her hand. I cursed my clumsiness. Why should easy manners belong only to bankrupt dragoons?

As the Professor gathered us all into conversation I became increasingly aware of his wife's honest good humour. She had not a nasty word to say about anyone. I was astonished that she could have survived friendship with the other University wives.

University staff life, with its subtle social gradations, gave rise to far more wifely vendettas than to brilliant academic discoveries. Despite themselves, these learned husbands would find themselves dragged into the battle. They would be called upon to court this one and snub that one, or write a damning reference on somebody else. And when it came to intra-mural bickering, the Professor of Greek was far less informed on Plato than he was of the Professor of Surgery's theft of a room in the old college he had planned to steal for himself from the Professor of History. He spent more active thought on how to get it back than on ancient translations and his wife would not speak to Mrs Professor Russell till it was restored, after which Mrs Professor Russell would not speak to her. These academic brawls gave more pleasure to acid palates through the dining season than did a kitchen full of Marjoram and sweet Basil. Yet Mrs Home rode out these squalls like a full breasted swan and from all the signs, her daughter was going to have as placid a cruise.

Of Mrs Jocelyn Dewlapp there was not a sign. We moved around and drank the fashionable new Champagne that had bubbled its way into Edinburgh after the French wars. This was at least one field where the Professor's dislike of things Gallic did not apply. I began to feel more comfortable in my lilac suit, and my cheeks glowed with wellbeing. Quentin had fallen into light conversation with the Professor, and I could hear Gavin saying,

"And there were these two foxes up the gully, running in different ways. I couldn't decide which brush to go for, hah, hah. The Honourable Eliza was listening as though her life depended on it. Quentin performed an elaborate ritual with old black Rappee out of a silver snuff-box. And everyone said,

"Thank you—uncommon civil of you," and sneezed or smiled according to their expertise and waved handkerchiefs as large as a regimental flag.

"Gavin chasing the wrong fox," said his father, with his timing wrong as ever. "Young Gavin's never out of the saddle except when he's at full gallop after a young lady." The humour was heavy. The Honourable Eliza reddened at this risqué witticism.

"That is to say," went on the Professor placidly with unconscious relevance, "he is very keen on the chase, or the hunt, if you prefer it so."

"I twust he wuns the quawwy to earth then," said Quentin, "haw, haw, haw, before the quawwy wuns him, what?" Miss Thredbair reddened further. The Professor said,

"Hah—hum—mm." Gavin said nothing. Quentin looked unabashed. The Professor said suddenly,

"I wonder why Mrs Dewlapp is taking so long, my dear?" This to his wife. "Perhaps we should ask Jamie to. . . ."

"Mrs Dewlapp!" shouted the jocular butler almost at once.

A tidal wave broke and eddied around the elegant drawing room, and the ebb revealed the lady herself, clad in a ridiculous candy of silk and lace. She was drawn in tight at the waist, and wore the cork bustle that had gone out of favour at the turn of the century. She hardly required any fraudulent means to increase the draught of her stern. The hard earned fruits of her deceased husband's labours were draped around her neck, and she wore more of the same in her hair. On a daughter it might well have been fetching, but even the shadowy light of the sconces failed to flatter the mother. However, queens are more or less beautiful. Quentin skipped to her side and bent low, murmuring fictitious gallantries, and the Professor, well aerated by his own Champagne, managed a few on his own account.

Mrs Dewlapp simpered at everybody, and drank rapidly two or three bubbling goblets before taking flight into her favourite subject, like a well-intentioned vulture. There was no escaping her talents—at least not for Home. I fell into easy discourse with Lucy. She told me she had attended a small private boarding school and an Edinburgh finishing school. She told me she liked to see operas by Paisiello, and that Mozart was a delight to play on the forte-piano. I made a mental note to learn some convincing facts about these composers before we met again. Mrs Home smiled at everybody, and Gavin took refuge in badger hunting. I half heard Gavin saying, to no-one in particular,

"Professor Monroe has given me to believe there is no scientific evidence that badgers have short legs on one side to let them manoeuvre on sloping terrain, but he has not verified it himself."

The Professor offered Mrs Dewlapp more Champagne, and his frolicsome servant put an end to the libations by announcing that the carriages had arrived.

There was a great going away to the Ball scene in Charlotte Square, the gentlemen standing chivalrously at the kerb in great protective boots, and the ladies doing their best to flutter down in heavy overcoats and iron pattens to protect their dainty footwear. We settled into two carriages and trundled back the way we had come, across the North Bridge into the dark cobbled byways of the Old Town, and up to the Assembly Rooms in George Square. There was a great feeling of occasion. A large awning was set up, and a shaft of light from within picked out the fretting horses, the gowned ladies and the strutting beaux, ragged ne'er-do-wells and town ruffians that are an indispensable part of an Assembly evening.

We exchanged our shawls and cloaks, galoshes and pattens, for numbered metal discs, and assembled in the outside hall. I had never attended such an entertainment before and proceeded rather cautiously, not quite sure how to behave with Lucy. At last the roll-call was complete, and we waited to be announced. The frisky hussar was capering about like a well oated stallion, and Mrs Dewlapp was quite prepared to play the mare, a role that came to her quite naturally. I watched them canter up to the door, leaving the rest of us walking behind. A flunkey with a mouth like a retriever announced us and we each braved our entrances in our own ways. The equestrians guffawed and whinnied. Gavin and the Honourable Eliza looked as high nosed as their youth permitted. The Professor pretended he was addressing a class of Materia Medica, while Lucy and her mother were themselves. I slid in behind, pretending I wasn't there.

Four coruscating chandeliers showed that the Professor's party was the first of the second rank of notables to arrive; they also revealed the early social hopefuls in little edgy clumps, all clinging to the walls like ivy. We, of course, were equally exposed by the same light.

"Just wegard," shouted Quentin, "I do declare they look positively wevolutionawy." Those who might have heard this shaft of wit, could not, for the musicians had fallen to tuning their instruments.

There were three fiddlers and a pianist, all in black knee breeches, bound at the calves with silver garters. Their graceful violins looked even more richly grained against their velvet coats—themselves relieved at the wrist and throat by fine-spun lace. I could see lying behind them some cylinders cut from African black wood and chased in silver.

Obviously some Highland cateran, recently made quite the mode by the acres of tartan that King George had found necessary to cover his large buttocks in 1822, would later strut about, blowing us into a frenzied whirl and himself into an acute state of whisky deprivation.

Sir Walter Scott was the man behind this Jacobite revival. By a deft sleight of conscience he managed with equal fervour to produce tearful romances about the defeat of the Young Pretender, and a grovelling rhyming salute to King George IV. This was meant to whip the loyal Scots into a lather of affection. The first verse went something like,

> "The news has flown frae mouth to mouth,
> The North for aince has bang'd the South;
> The de'il a Scotsman's die o' drouth,
>   Carle, now the King's come!"

Thirty-seven similar verses followed. They were not Sir Walter's best work.

The King not only came, but he came in Highland garb—feathered hat, kilt and sporran, his regal legs bursting out of pink tights. This tartan-clad buffoon then capered around the town, acquiring a taste for Glenlivet whisky and ptarmigan. We were going to enjoy the fruits of Sir Walter's toadying tonight. Quentin and his lady skipped up towards us. The bulky widow was squealing peremptorily.

"Lootenant Dellatrumpe, is that actually a musical instrument?"

"It looks like some tartan octopus to me Ma'am, pwobably netted in one of these bleak Highland lakes, I shouldn't wonder." Mrs Dewlapp's retort was lost in the wail of fiddles preparing to attack the quadrille. Shortly afterwards, the light dragoon and his hefty consort disappeared into the same dance and returned to us when the fiddling had died away, their withers quite wrung.

We settled into the chairs at our table, and instantly waiters fluttered around with tempting intoxicants. The hall was now beginning to fill with kenspeckles; the entrance flunkeys making sure we all heard them—"The Earl and Countess of This; Sir Somebody and Lady That; The Honourable Somebody Else; and Dr Robert Knox."

"What," snorted Home, "I thought this was to be a proper Ball—and why will he not show us his wife?" His ire bubbled away as he scented across a few tables a coquette peeping at him behind her fan. His good humour expanded. He raised a glass of gin punch, nodded to the lady, careful that his wife shouldn't see him, turned to us and said,

"I give you a toast to our splendid evening." He raised his hand to meet his wife's glass, and smashed the crystal.

"James," she sighed.

Before he could reply, Quentin leapt to his feet and said,

"Can't be helped, ma'am. A bowl of punch is in order, what. Haw, haw, haw! Waiter, clean away this cwystal!"

"Sir Walter and Lady Scott," shouted the dog-faced flunkey.

"Not the author surely," giggled Mrs Dewlapp.

"Indeed, Madam, it is," said the Professor, now recovered from his accident. "And I would warn you," he added sternly, seeing her quickening interest, "his wife is French. That is to say, she used to be before she ceased to be." Satisfied with his lucid explanation, he turned to look where everyone else was staring, and grumbled,

"I see she's wearing those same red flounces she had on last time. They are quite unbecoming. She would look better without them."

"James Home," said his wife aghast. "How could you?"

"My dear." He looked baffled. "Ah—I see. I meant that she should substitute another garment for the one that does not suit her. That is to say, she should not take off the flounces without replacing them, though not of course here. . . ."

Quentin and his partner neighed in unison. Meanwhile the Master of Ceremonies, an oily-voiced man with a trailing wispy beard that made him look like a goat, called us to a Reel.

The whole hall was now aflush with tartans—Stuart, MacPherson, Hunting Farquharson, Ancient Cameron, and not one of them older than 1815. Laughter and squeals everywhere.

"Come on; energetic young lady needed for a set here."

"Two enterprising youngsters of less than seventy would complete this set here," joked the goateed humourist.

Pushing and jostling, finally the circles of eight were prepared. Lucy and I stayed safely in our seats. Up on the dais I could see, and indeed hear, the kilted ruffian that I had feared, wrestling with his carnaptious instrument. He seemed to be talking to it, then he adjusted the length of one of the tubes, stroked it, coaxed it into silence, then smote the bag, reducing us all to silence. I now knew that it was not Wellington who had finished off the French Emperor, but the Scots Infantry Regiments and their fearsome pneumatic music. We sipped our gin punch, while the throng swirled before us, rising and falling, elegant lace ruffles or elegant lace cuffs, at the end of elegant arms held aloft. The sets were now no longer in neat circles. I thanked God for letting me sit down beside Lucy, and hoped that she was thanking God for letting her sit down beside me. In fact she was thinking about someone else, for she said suddenly,

"The late Robert Burns summed all that up in three or four lines in 'Tam o' Shanter'. The Devil was his piper you know. What was it he said?

'Amd Satan glower'd and fidg'd fu' fain,
And hotch'd and blew wi' might and main.'"

The black-haired barbarian up on the dais could easily have been Burns' model. As for the rest,

'They reel'd, they set, they cross'd, they cleekit,' and they made a great noise too. In Alloway's Kirk they began to throw off unnecessary raiment. Here they had to sweat genteelly. From time to time we could hear the temporary clansmen skirling daintily. Lucy broke into my thoughts again.

"Perhaps father was right, Mr Bryson," she said unexpectedly. "They might be happier taking off something if they get too warm. I don't know why Mother takes on so." To make herself heard above *Duncan Ban's Hairy Breeks,* she had to edge close to me, and she blushed. But she continued none the less.

"Do you find my father's lectures interesting?" What could I say but,

"Why, Miss Home, indeed they are. He captures our—ah—interest— and we all find them most—er—er—interesting."

"Do you? Ah well, I suppose when he is amongst his medical confrères he must be a very different person from what he is in the house". She sighed, "I suppose you too are set on becoming an important doctor in Edinburgh?"

I changed my reply from "do you think I ought to, Miss Home?" to "would you like me to, Miss Home?" She blushed again.

"That is your choice." I saw in a flash why women have always dominated the guild of oracles. No man has the ability to tell the truth with such evasive dishonesty and make it mean anything you want it to. At least Lucy did not have to translate her remarks into a series of synonyms as her father would have done. She continued to ask me questions.

"Have you ever thought of being a country doctor like your father?" She eyed me closely. How could she know that my father was a country doctor?

"Well, yes, Miss Home, I have, but the idea does not greatly draw me. I had thought of trying to emulate your father," I said, with a look that meant to convey modesty, ambition and a galaxy of other endearing qualities. A passing vision of Grizel MacWrath added a transient spasm of its own. Lucy was solicitous.

"Is anything the matter, Mr Bryson?"

"No no no, Miss Home."

"Why do you want to be like my father?" she queried. There was no real answer to this, for no-one in possession of his full senses would want to be like her father. But I had to say something.

"Well, I mean—I would like to be as famous as he, Miss Home."

"Yes, I suppose he is famous, and we do not see him overmuch in the house because of his fame." I could not be sure if I was meant to be pleased for her or not at this parental absence, for we would all have cheerfully kicked him against his skeleton cupboard had he not managed to trip against its veneer by himself. She shook her head.

"We have queer views on fame in our family," she reflected. "But if you insist on trying to become a professor one day, then my father might well be pleased."

And so no doubt would Miss Grizel MacWrath, thought I to myself, but a nodding head and troubled brow were enough to turn the talk to other matters, which themselves were engulfed by lone dancers returning from the finished reel. Our conversation was drowned in a sudden drumming of applause, and shouting and hallooing, as the breathless dancers warmly congratulated each other and the Piper with his shaggy head back was now pouring a large quaich of whisky down his throat. Our laughing, panting party fell into their seats and gossiped as much as their dyspnoea permitted.

I tripped a quiet measure or two with Lucy, and another with her mother. Quentin continued to shower gallantries on Mrs Dewlapp. I was sure he was hoping that he might be invited to perform some important medical role, as, say Physician in Charge of the Dewlapp Charity Hospital in Boston. He would perform his tasks to perfection, provided not too much administration was required, and a few impotent committees could meet to drink the hospital claret. Or would they have claret in America?

Sortly afterwards the hairy goat announced supper; this was fortunately timed, for another round of punch on empty stomachs would have been catastrophic.

"Mr Deelatrumpe seems to find Mrs Dewlapp very congenial," said Lucy quietly.

I could see Quentin deep in some droll exchange with the widow as we waited to fill our bellies with duck, quail, sliced beef, pigeons, mashed potatoes, oranges, figs, chestnuts and a thousand sweetmeats. The supper was, I think, a success. Afterwards the ladies disappeared on some mysterious errand. Professor Home disappeared to avoid Dr Knox, whose great height made him recognisable from any part in the Assembly Room. Quentin paused to say to me,

"I do believe this evening will pwove to be the turning point in my caweer," before he scented off after his game. He was now anticipating his sinecure in Boston.

I took the opportunity to nose out the entertainments other than dancing which were offered. At the end of the hall, a narrow corridor led into a smaller hall that housed the card room. This necessary diversion gave some excitement to those for whom wedlock had become something of a padlock rather than a transition in the delights of courtship. It was rather full.

I could see Sir Walter, no doubt gathering material for his next novel, in the midst of a covey of claret-faced lairds. And was it? Yes, indeed. Professor Monroe slumbering over a hand of whist, while a bystander played it for him, with some skill too to judge from the glum faces around the table.

There were also collections of matrons of varying size and age, trying with bone and silk, lace and powder to look like Gainsborough's portrait of The Honourable Mrs Graham. They were fanning themselves gently, and indulging in small talk. I heard one say to another,

"When I get through a whole pot of Lilyroot and Marshmallow lotion in a week, I know it's time to call in Dr Abercrombie."

"Dr Abercrombie," shrieked another, "he is so clever—he tells everyone they're getting well and never bothers his patients with any uncomfortable thoughts of death until the actual moment arrives. Is not that lovely?" Squeals and titters of agreement and rapid fluttering of a dozen fans.

A curiously uncomplicated approach to the greatest test life offered us; no-one could accuse the doctor of charlatanry or falsehood—for sure it was just a matter of timing his delivery of the truth.

My attention flickered from this decorative pageant on the floor to a valiant one that was taking place above the door in a scrolled gilt rectangle. A handful of kilted heroes of lofty brow and noble mien were advancing to slaughter a squadron of Poniatowski's Lancers, who to a man could be recognised from the eyebrows that formed both the upper and lower borders of their foreheads. Directing this preposterous enterprise from the centre of the canvas sat Colonel the Earl of Dunderhead astride a mettlesome warhorse, poised to leap instantly in all directions. The Earl had twisted fiercely away from the battle site to display his gold facings, his flying dolman, sable headgear, complexion gules and moustache rampant to their best advantage. I could not decide whether he was trying out his sabre as a pointed riding crop or preparing to disembowel his charger from the rear. My balance began to waver in face of all this impending carnage. For a passing second it seemed he was about to launch himself at me. I groped for support and found myself providing it instead. There was an urgent tug at my rising sleeve, and a more urgent voice in my ear.

"Quentin!" I said in surprise.

"Jesus. Oh, Jesus." Quentin's soft voice, was positively warm. "Jesus, you must help. Oh, my God. I'm in an awful pickle." He began to babble incoherently.

"What is the matter, Quentin?" I set him down on a chair. It seemed the best thing to do. "Well, come on then. Tell me what has happened."

"That bloody woman," he gasped.

"Yes?"

"She wants to mawwy me—no! She wants me to mawwy her. Oh, Jesus." He wrung his hands and banged his head to see if he could turn the horrible facts into a bad dream.

"I thought I was wipe for a loan or an important position in Boston. Now the important position is to be her husband. My God! Get me some bwandy, fast. What am I to do?" He began to cry.

Perplexed, I got him a bottle and a glass, and as I watched him pour one after another down his throat, a brilliant idea emerged from the punch in my brain.

"Quentin," I said sharply, "you must get drunk."

"What do you think I'm twying to do?" he snapped, almost hysterical by now.

"No, Quentin. I mean, if you get disgusting drunk and fall about and insult her, she will see what a brute you are and think herself fortunate to have escaped you. You could do it very well, I'm sure." His eyes flickered in sudden illumination.

"And I can keep my hundred pounds too—or what's left of it." He gave me a quick hug.

"What a fwiend! What a fellow! Haw, haw, haw!" He lurched off, still clutching the now empty brandy bottle. The bearded varlet in the Mackerel filibeg now picked up his alarming cluster of tubes and inflated the tartan sack which briefly bleated like a dying sheep. Then in went the elbow and off went the dance.

Quentin set about his new part with gusto and alacrity, for by the time I emerged from the card room he was already in the toils of yet another Highland canter. His face was red, his eyes rolling, and he was swaying rather more than a Highland dance demanded. Mrs Dewlapp was now gazing at him in amazement, and I thought I could detect horror in her eyes. Before I could suppress a laugh she was leading him off the floor to our table, where she pushed him on to the chair and, still fuming, took a seat as far away from him as possible. At the same time, I noticed the old Earl of Kenless being helped to his feet on the dais, clearly waiting for the piper to reach for the quaich before giving us a few words.

"What's wrong with Lieutenant Deelatrumpe," asked the Honourable Eliza, who had just returned with Gavin from a long tour of important people that had lasted all evening.

"The fellow's drunk, I'm afraid. Come away," said young Home, escorting his fair intended away from a sight that she must have witnessed a hundred times beneath the stag heads in Selkirkshire.

"Lootenant Deelatrumpe," brayed Mrs Dewlapp. "How dare you treat me like this after all we've discussed." Quentin's answer was to fall off the chair on to the floor. He then proceeded to empty his belly. We watched fascinated, as one soft wave after another of cock-a-leekie, chestnuts and brandy spread gently across the floor. It was like a large dog after a stomachful of grass and water and unaccustomed exercise.

"Oooooh." Mrs Dewlapp burst into a flood of tears that threatened to drown her. She fell into a swoon only to be instantly revived by the Professor, trying to open a bottle of smelling salts at her nose.

"We've all had a happy time tonight." quavered Lord Kenless on his platform. Mrs Dewlapp stood up and announced that she was leaving the ball at once.

"See to her Lucy," said Mrs Home. "I shall look after this poor young man."

"We had a happy time last year too," continued the Earl.

"Drunken barbarian," observed the Professor, thrusting the powerful bottle back into his coat pocket.

"No James, he's had a bad experience and when all said and done, he did save you from Mrs Dewlapp, did he not?" All the while, she was wiping his face patting his cheeks and mopping up the vomit from across his gold braiding.

"And I feel sure we will all have as happy a time when we foregather next year," concluded the Earl.

"It's evident he hasn't been following the fortunes of our little party then," said the Professor through tightened lips. "What on earth are we to do with this—this incubus?"

"We must carry him to the carriage in secret," declared his wife.

We, the Honourable Eliza included, formed a guard of honour to take him to safety, past the front door lackey and the scandal-loving fair sex, into Home's vehicle.

The carriage was never designed for such arrangements. Quentin was laid across the main seat, while the rest of us sitting bodkin found what nooks and crannies we could.

The hussar himself, at least I assumed the bleating sound came from his mouth, broke into my thoughts.

"I've a touch of the wherry go nimbles," he mumbled.

"What?" said the Professor.

Quentin spoke no more, but clutched the belly band of his regimental breeches.

"Oh—my God," said Home, suddenly comprehending, "and to think I've no commode. What can we do?" he added helplessly.

"The poor wee lamb. Stop the carriage, James," said his wife. We did,

and took Quentin outside, and a fearful performance it was. We finally
got him back into the carriage and to Charlotte Square where Lucy,
already home, was shouting in the doorway,

"Mrs Dewlapp has gone, Mamma, to Dumbreck's Hotel. She says she
will never come back here again."

"Probably as well," said Mamma coolly as we laid Quentin down on
the hall floor.

The Professor looked down at the still slumbering lancer, like a
minister seeking eternal truths in an open grave.

"You've a taste for the drink, laddie. Not a doubt of it. But you've
saved me from that woman. If that's what American womanhood is,
then thank God I'm a Scotsman with a good Scots wife."

"Amen to that," said Mrs Home, all smiles. "Now let's put this poor
soul to bed." We trundled Quentin up the stairs, and after further
refreshments, suggested by Lucy and agreed to by her mother, Jamie
trundled me down the stairs again.

"If it's after an invitation you are, to spend the nicht here," said Jamie,
a helpless bundle of mirth, "you'll hae to succumb to the liquor like your
friend, sir."

Sadly my cargo of brandy punch did not even qualify me for a cab. On
my belated return to 3 Robertson's Wynd, in those rat-infested slums
that defy gravity, any tipsy good humour left by the walk was magically
blown away by five pages of closely written verbiage from the sick room
in Dalkeith: There was another of her ridiculous verses and, pressed
between the paper, a birchen leaf of all things, to remind me of where we
had first plighted our troth. Quentin was lucky, damn him, being put to
bed by a bevy of concerned females. I had to put myself to bed, and a
sloping one at that, and I spent the rest of the night in a ghostly birch
forest pursued by a fork tailed clergyman with an escort of black harpies
towards an altar, where the largest harpie of them all was preparing a
wedding ring, shaped like a thumbscrew.

9

In the days following the Assembly Ball, we, Quentin and I that is, basked in the sunlight of Professor Home's approval. We became favoured guests at Charlotte Square, and Quentin managed, with all the hardened skill of a soldier, not to repeat his performance of the Assembly Rooms over Mrs Home's damask table drapes. Even the disdainful Gavin joined in the general feeling of benevolence. He said to us one evening after cards,

"I'm sure we could possibly arrange for you both to come as house guests for a weekend to Thredbair Hall. I will think about it some time."

"That might be quite useful," said Quentin to me later on, "but I would stake half a guinea he's keeping us in reserve for fear the pheasants don't turn up."

I could do quite happily without the Honourable Eliza, and I did detect that the feeling was reciprocated, for the summons to Philiphaugh never arrived. The Professor had clearly taken to Quentin, for he said to me one day,

"Principled young fellow, Deelatrumpe I am led to understand he resigned his commission because he disapproved of gambling."

Quentin, however, was well aware that these good impressions and the delight of Mrs Dewlapp's departure would soon wane, and unless he could produce something more than a timely inebriety then the invitations would soon cease. He was always the first to say,

"No more wine, thank you very much."

He told stories that might have come from the Headmistress of Lucy's finishing school, and he always walked home straight, without the traditional dasher's zig-zag.

Unfortunately the Professor now grew used to our presence at his lectures and, more to the point, would have recognised our absence. We therefore put on a facade of great eagerness throughout his interminable paraphrases and synonyms and recurrent jousts with the furniture.

But though the Professor was clumsy, his daughter was not, and I was delighted to find that she had not just put on her gaiety with her gown for the Ball. It could not have been an invention, else how could it have survived her fretful father. She liked to chatter. In the evenings I talked to her in a corner of their drawingroom, while she worked her sampler, a map of Scotland in black and green thread on fawn silk. When she found stitching tedious, which was often, she would set herself down at the long Broadwood forte-piano by the window. There she could charm a haunting fragile magic from its yellowing keyboard, to the delight of her mother and the bemusement of her father.

"Why on earth do you practise these endless scales, Lucy?" was a frequent and peevish question.

"It's not a scale, papa, it's Haydn. It's his Serenata, don't you know?" she replied, all tolerant.

"Mmmmh," said the Professor, exposed again.

He could usually distinguish a song by her favourite, Robert Burns, from one by her second favourite—the Irishman, Thomas Moore, and many's the time I've seen a wistful melancholy displace the customary petulence from his mouth, while his daughter sang to her own accompaniment.

She sang these Irish songs often, and one evening sang them for me especially. Her father had said he was off to a tedious meeting—his own adjective, and one that spoke volumes for it. Her mother was in conference with the cook downstairs, Gavin having already vanished earlier in the day, clutching a long sporting firearm. We were alone.

I don't know what we had been talking about, perhaps *Marmion,* perhaps her new cat. At any rate I wandered across to look through the window at the odd barouche, and the trees, lightening with leaves in the Charlotte Square Gardens. Of a sudden, the keys rippled with an open chord as from a harp. When I turned, Lucy had begun to sing *The Spinning Wheel.*

My enchantment with her lingered beyond her last refrain,

"Ere the wheel and the reel stopped their spinning and moving,
Through the grove the young lovers by moonlight are roving."

I was the shadowy form at her casement, and she my Eileen Achara. I stared at her in a fever to trap for ever a fragment of life that would one day be a fading memory.

"Play again, Lucy," I pleaded, now standing behind her. She played again, and before the strings were silent, I was in love.

Mrs Home did not object to our growing friendship. We used to go on little jaunts together with the rotund cook as duenna. In those early summer days we would climb to the top of Arthur's Seat. She brought a little pocket volume of Burns' poetry to read to me. She grew sad at the betrayed lover in *Bonnie Doon,* and she laughed earthily at Holy Willie and his "fleshly lust".

We wandered by Salisbury Crags, and took cold duck and claret from a wicker hamper, whilst from our vantage point on the warm grass we wove our separate dreams, and watched the fleecy wisps and tendrils floating and drifting in the blue sky above Berwick Law.

I escorted her and her Mamma to musical evenings given in St Cecilia's Hall in the Cowgate, where we shared a worldless longing over what she told me was the last forte piano concerto that Wolfgang Mozart ever wrote. The soloist that evening was Stephen Clarke, who daringly broke with tradition to introduce this very modern music. Despite its strangeness, from the very first bars of the plaintive Allegro I felt impelled to seek Lucy's hand, which she helpfully put in the way of being found. When the limpid theme of the Larghetto came stealing above the strings and woodwinds, I became aware of a sudden that Lucy was crying gently, and I felt my own eyes moisten. We glanced at each other, and side by side stole another hostage from eternity.

Lucy loved the Old Town. She found the New too new for her taste. She devoured the past, especially the romances spun by Sir Walter Scott, and I was careful not to laugh too openly at his "Carle now, the King is come," but she knew instinctively what I thought about it.

May gave way to June, and before I knew where we were, we were all shaking hands, shouting good-bye, and making impossible plans and promises for the summer vacation. I was stricken to the core to leave Lucy. I was sorry to leave my new friends, but leaving Mrs O'Loan and her parched husband cost me not a moment's anguish, even when she said, with unusual respect,

"We'll be expectin' ye, surr, in October."

The Dalkeith Carrier added me to his regular bag of dirty linen. If he thought that I might also have been in need of cleansing, he did not voice his thoughts, being in need of my custom and in any case he may have been silenced by esteem for the first scholar in a long while from Beattie's School to be accepted into Edinburgh University. So he just sucked on his clay pipe and abused his old horse every furlong or so.

Dalkeith at last, nothing remotely resembling Mr O'Loan between me and the front door. My mother fell on my dirty clothes and launched at me a thousand questions, which she gave me no time to answer, and she said I must be hungry. She signed to our Annie to have my bags taken into the house, and continued to shout questions at me from the ale making in the back kitchen. Father, when he returned from his rounds, shook my hand and asked my opinion about treating diabetes with extract of spring cabbage, a notion he had just read about in the *Medical and Surgical Journal*.

This and kindred subjects brought us to supper time, and when I was sanguine enough to imagine we were to escape a visitation, there was a loud knock on the door accompanied by shouts and scuffles.

"The first scholar from Dalkeith this ten years, I'm thinking," shouted the minister, barging into the hall. "Let me see you, laddie." He pushed his enthusiastic face into mine. "You have all the sinful marks of the city beneath your eyes, just as I predicted," he added sagely, his pig's bladder piety quite unshrunken by the scenes of our last conversation and his attempted redemption of Mary Paterson. Behind him, filling the doorway, was his daughter.

"Here's your man, Grizel. If he's just ridden in from Edinburgh he'll be in need of loaves and fishes for five thousand." He sniffed the air appreciatively, and led us all as near to the diningroom as politeness allowed. Mother, too amused to adhere to her original plans, allowed us to continue in the direction chosen by the divine. Within ten minutes he had emptied his first plate. Mother fussed over and beamed at her brilliant young son, whilst telling his brother and sister not to be cheeky.

"Your brother is now a very senior medical student," she told them magnificently. Grizel, occupying every inch of her chair on the opposite side of the table, fixed me with a stooping to conquer eye, and said she was so sorry that I had had to forego the Ball in Edinburgh on her account.

Yes, I agreed it was unfortunate, and with a flash of invention added, "But I'm delighted to see you've recovered—now!" That was true, and there was no point in saying that I would have been less delighted a month before. My mother, possibly mistaking my concern over time as solicitude for Grizel, said,

"You should not be thinking of capering around and dancing while you have your studies to finish. And indeed, you are not to be thinking of marriage a long while, even although Mr MacWrath has just come into an inheritance. You are still a bairn," she admonished me, forgetting I was now a very senior medical student.

Mr MacWrath had come into an inheritance. I marvelled what misguided wretch had included him in his will—it could only have been some parishioner, who on the brink of death had mistaken his fleshless look for starvation.

"An inheritance, Mr MacWrath," I said, watching him and his daughter closely. "This will surely free you to visit Edinburgh rather more often." I had to give it to him. He met my jibe without a blush, and talked at length about spiritual freedom.

"Inheritances are all very well, but your mother is right, you know," said Father. "Until you are established, marriage is not to be considered."

"Nor is indeed fornication," added the Reverend Gideon, wiping up the last smear of gravy with a needlessly large chunk of bread. "Even when you are established," he finished, with a line of crumbs giving his mouth the appearance of an archery butt.

Our plates were removed. The reverend divine now wondered what delight the good lady had prepared for pudding.

"Ah! Syllabub," he gasped, attacking his new plate with zeal. "My very favourite, and the ale was quite perfect." He sighed again.

When we had all done, Mother, like a broody hen, ushered away my youthful siblings, and her muscular daughter-in-law elect.

"To leave the men to their port," she added eyeing Grizel with a steely twist that the indiscriminate would have accepted as a loving smile.

So I was a man—fit to take part in the company of my peers. I looked at these peers, at our counterfeit prelate especially, as Father manipulated the decanter. Poor Mr MacWrath, his windy pious rhetoric had never brought me to my knees in reverence. As for my father, well, as every man nudging nineteen knows, fathers have a lot to learn, but I was sure I would help to complete his education by the end of the summer, and I came to the understandable conclusion—logical I suppose—that I was the sharpest and wittiest and best of the three men there.

The over port conversation dropped instantly into serious matters like patriotism and blood letting. It started, as conversations do, out of chance remarks. Possibly the sight of Father, sabring the underdone joint; it could well have been the Baron Larrey—he who had commanded the Field Ambulance of the Grand Armée, and whom Father, although avoiding the term hero, regarded as his only great man. Could it not have been the port itself? Certainly the Minister still had two fingers left in his glass when Father said, "I think blood letting is a dangerous and useless remedy."

"But Father," I riposted, "all physicians in Edinburgh recommend its use." I had Home in mind with his leeches and his bleeding cups. So possibly did he.

"Do they," he said drily, "all the more reason then to question its value."

This was all very baffling. It was one thing ungrateful students making mock of their teachers, but quite another to hear your father doing the same thing himself and paying your fees to have them teach you in the first place.

"Surely," the Reverend Gideon came to my rescue glibly, "there must be some justification for its wide usage then?" Father just glowered away like an old fox trying to convince his fellows that continuing to eat chickens might not be in their best interests.

"None whatsoever. Consider. If one loses a leg he bleeds to death. At what point then does conserving his blood become more important than releasing more of it?"

"Aye, there's no gainsaying that," said the Reverent Gideon, for once defeated. I now started up on my father.

"But if his blood is diseased, then it should be drawn off."

"Who are we to say that bad blood is not better than no blood at all. No, if blood is in an inflamed part it must be serving some useful purpose."

"But the pain," began the divine.

"Laudanum!" said Father, as Mr MacWrath donned his eternal punishment face.

"But the Scriptures are quite clear on the subject of pain."

"They may well be, but so am I. Man, I've seen five thousand soldiers lose one limb or another. Do you know, I found that those I had no time to bleed recovered the better with laudanum alone than did those who were unfortunate enough to receive their wounds in a smaller battle, when I had all the time in the world to bring them the benefits of medical knowledge."

"Does anyone in authority other than your good self support your views?" said the Reverend Gideon.

"Larrey does."

"Ah, the Frenchman."

"I met Larrey, you know,"

"Did you, indeed," said the Reverend, as though this information was being offered to him for the first time. The old fraud, I thought, he knows perfectly well that Father met the Baron Larrey.

Had I been as sharp as I thought I was, I would have realised that a man who dines out almost exclusively in other people's homes, has to find their conversation as tasty as their viands. He helped himself to the decanter at the same time. Had I been sharper still, I might also have realised that there was a limit to his bland accord, and the port was beginning to show him the way beyond this limit. But Father was in great voice and not to be stopped.

"Yes. I met him at Corunna. In fact I dined with him after the battle."

"You what?" The old Covenanter exploded like a spoiled bottle of Communion wine.

"Yes. We had a pleasant camp dinner, as I recall. We agreed about a lot of things—the futility of blood letting certainly. After all, swords and cannons make a much more thorough job of it. I think we may also have remarked on the foolish pass that patriotism had brought us to."

"Do you mean to say that in the middle of a war with France you discussed all these treasonable matters with a Frenchman? You would have done better to sabre him on the spot than to take his salt." Mr MacWrath was not the man to allow his love of God to come between him and his fellows, especially if they were Frenchmen. He shook a warning finger from a hand already shaking from reasons other than the impending sermon. He blared.

"The tyrant shall be overthrown, the righteous shall be triumphant. If they are not smitten by the sword, they will be smitten by the emerods, the scab and the itch."

"Take the other decanter, Mr MacWrath," said my unruffled sire. "It puts a fire somewhere into you. But you're wrong none the less. Larrey is not any damned Frenchman. The world would have been a lesser place for his death. Even the Emperor was moved to call him the most honourable man he knew. He made him a Baron of the Empire, you know for feeding staff officers' horses to his wounded soldiers. They did not like it one bit." His face creased at the thought of all those dandies soiling their riding boots with unaccustomed walking.

"From a scoundrel like Buonoparte such praise is quite worthless. Why, the man was an atheist anyway."

"Some Frenchmen might disagree with you. And by atheist do you meant that he did not believe the Scriptures, or that he was a Catholic?" I could see Father was savouring the disagreement as he might a venison collop. I sipped my port.

"It makes no difference," shouted the indignant divine. "Romish dogma is worse than the denial of God altogether. To be Romish is to be unpatriotic. They should all be put to the sword."

"Well, your own views, as you must know, came originally from France. You will recall John Calvin."

"What was that?" MacWrath fell back just far enough to keep a grip on his glass.

"And what's more," my father went on relentlessly, "your patriotic wars are usually a means of making heroes of ruffians whose talents would otherwise have led them to the gallows. And you pray for their victory to the same God who looks after the enemy? Or is he a French God?"

It was a memorable evening, what I can remember of it that is. Father had improved marvellously even since I had come home, and I was beginning to feel that there was a bit more to him than what the Duke of Wellington said next.

I had a chance sooner than I had expected to see Father's heresies in action. The whole of the Lothians at that time were in a turmoil over the colliers, who had just formed co-operatives to prevent their wages from dropping below ten shillings a week. These were disrupting the mine workings and disturbing the mine owners, who replied by importing black-leg Irish labour. I would suppose that for them there was no choice really between no potatoes in West Meath and rotten potatoes in West Lothian. The local Scots did not quite see it that way. The coal lairds saw the Irish as saviours, if somewhat filthy. The Scots colliers saw them as a threat to their living standards, and the Irish saw themselves as threatened wherever they were.

It happened one July afternoon when the trees were shadowy with leaf and nodding sleepily in a gentle heat haze that shimmered off the roads. Father and I were trotting briskly in his trap towards Loanhead, just avoiding all those other gig drivers and horsemen whose sense and direction were all wanting.

Of a sudden we heard a wild caterwauling and shouting, with some higher pitched screams of fear and pain. Silence, then boisterous laughter swelling and dying away to a grumbling murmur, which became louder as we rounded the next bend.

Father pulled up the trap, cursing at the shifty mob that milled about in front of us. Two monstrous giants blocked his way. One a great cross-grained bully, as broad as a knotted plank, and the other no smaller, swaggered and waved their fists under Father's nose. But a man who has seen the advance of the Imperial Guard, even if it was from behind a dead horse, was not to be daunted by a herd of rioting colliers. He pushed his way boldly through their ranks. Whatever they had done was at the centre of a small moving circle, that gave way before my father's resolute step. Then he saw what had happened.

"You beasts! You fiendish bloody beasts!" He glowered at them as they jostled away from his gaze like children caught with stolen apples.

On the ground lay two black-leg Irishmen, and on the ground beside them lay their ears. Between, rose regular pumping sprays of scarlet blood. They were screaming but motionless.

"Here, help me up with them," ordered my father, as though he were addressing his orderlies; and they did help him. It was the two hulking coalmen who had just defied him, that carried the two men to the verge of the road. We then set about staunching the blood flow by pressing on the holes where the ears had been.

But cool as you fancy, Father commanded two others from the crowd to sit astride the first man while he probed with his forceps to catch the bleeding vessels, around which he placed tight ligatures.

I looked as cool as I could too, but their savage and largely frustrated attempts to escape the searching instrument was almost too much for me to bear. When it was all over, he forced some laudanum down their throats—now unresisting—thanked the four Titans who put the men in our trap, and we drove off with our silent cargo. Somehow our July afternoon had now lost something of its charm.

We had no need to ask where the men stayed. The mine owners reserved a particular kind of hovel for the men who hewed their coal, and we knew exactly where they were.

"Well," said my father quietly, after a long silence, "would you bleed these fellows?" I said nothing.

"They say you should put boiling oil or tar on wounds such as these. That's something else I found out in Spain. When I ran out of tar, as I believe Paré did before me, I found a little boiled water makes for much better healing. Still," he went on, on another tack, "I suppose we ought not to blame these people. As long as they die on the battle-field they are remembered as heroes; let them come home, and someone is obliged to find them employment."

There was no time to say more, for we had arrived at a cluster of small cabins, each perhaps about twelve feet square, and patrolled by a shuffling army of little creatures, recognisable as children only by their size, not by any happy faces.

A brief glimpse at the bare interior, odd ruins of furniture and crockery, and the drab trollops so remote from their sisters of the Assembly Ball, was enough to silence me for the rest of the day. We rattled off, leaving our earless pair behind—the most recent to suffer in this happy land, in whose armies they had so gloriously fought, to rid the world of an oppressive tyrant.

I was aware of my father speaking again.

"That's the least of their problems, you know. Come the wet heat of August, they will die like flies of the spotted fever, if consumption does not carry them off before then."

"They need help, Father. They need more than a charity physician. They need their own doctors."

"You're wrong my boy. It's not lack of physicians that's their trouble, it's filth, and lack of proper food too. And don't start pitying them either," he reproved me. "They are no more lovable because they are poor, and they don't want your charity."

We drove along in total silence now. I looked soulfully at the trees and the birds, and the grain on the turn for the harvest, and yearned for the perfect world that only a nineteen-year-old can envisage, free from poverty, disease and Mr MacWrath. When I thought of it, Mr MacWrath too was always yearning for the perfect world, at least he used to thunder about it in the pulpit every Sunday morning and evening, calling loudly for victory over death. Now for him that would have to exclude cattle, else how would he get enough roast beef. He would be unemployed too, with no-one else in need of professional reproof. If the two of us had such a selective view of perfection, then so must everyone else. Perhaps imperfection was better after all. I could hear our wheels crunching over the gravel. A brace of wood-pigeons appealed to me more than philosophy, and would, for the evening at least, make me forget the gallant role I would be called upon to play for much of the summer.

But youth is nothing if not young, and I rushed to join the colours when my father asked me to help him during an epidemic of spotted fever that had been raging for the last two weeks at Easthouses; it also gave me an honourable reason for not presenting myself at the Manse.

We left the main track, and turned up a rutted path that led past the mine workings, to a straggling line of grey, bleak little houses. A curious miasma, not wholly due to the location, hung over the area, and dull, lifeless children watched us with suspicion and indifference combined. Every home was the same, and in each lay one, or two, or three bodies— living or dead I don't know, it seemed to make no difference. They were grey and wrinkled and caked in their own ordure. Only random breathing marked the dying from those who had already passed beyond our care. For those who passed as healthy, my father had an encouraging word and a phial of laudanum, to ease the anguish of their failing relatives. Further instruction about cleanliness, diet or change of clothes would have been as useless as recommending to the King that he should lose some weight for his own—nay, for the country's good.

"You see what I mean about the value of doctors," said my father as he whipped up our aging cob. "I did nothing there except hand out soporifics."

"You diagnosed their condition."

"A monkey could have done that," he snapped. "They know it themselves anyway. They've seen enough this past fortnight." He started thinking about the cause. "They all suffer the same condition. It must get to them somehow. There must be a common source—water, or perhaps the milk—but no, they don't all drink milk."

"Why did you give them laudanum?"

"Because it's safe, and allows them to die the easier." He gave a wry laugh. "That's another of my Spanish discoveries, hence the large bottles. Whatever I do for these folk, some are going to die—most of them in fact—and some are not. Why make death harder for them by useless purging, useless leeches, useless aconite? Anything I prescribe has the supreme value of being totally harmless and, I suppose, totally useless. But until I know why I give what I give, I'm not going to give it at all. I know why I give laudanum, and therefore I will continue to give it."

This sounded so sensible that I felt it must be wrong. It certainly bore no resemblance to the bold assertions of Professor Home, who seemed so sure about the tonic and the atonic causation of disease and his most stern indications for blood letting. Yet he walked about confidently too, and still managed to collide with every available piece of furniture. Mayhap his medical convictions also had been acquired by collision as well? It was a most disturbing thought, and yet he was the Professor, and yet . . .

I was further disturbed as Father swung his trap into an imposing gateway. I knew well the proud escutcheon carved on the pillars and the crumbling gryphons, bound to the archway by stone claws. The house and the estate beyond belonged to Sir Donald Fairley-Dunn; the last time we had met was over a trout I had poached. I blushed at the memory, but there was no escaping now. Our trap clattered on up the drive to Garbeige House.

Everyone knew that Sir Donald was the tenth in a long line of Lothian lairds. The first of the line, having fortunately come between James V and a wounded pig, had been rewarded with lands as far as the eye could see, and a baronetcy. Sir Donald, however, had fallen on hard times and maintained a seedy gentility in his tumble-down mansion, until an ambitious merchant called John Dunn had given him his daughter in wedlock, a stately hyphen and a coal mine.

Free now to live in the proper style, he had flung himself into blood sports. As the Master of the Temple Hunt, he hunted the fox; he also stalked deer and slew game birds, until his hunting career was cut short by a low flying goose. My father had been summoned to the house to find the front of Sir Donald's right eye to be full of blood and the ball ruptured. As there was no needle fine enough to stitch up the cornea, he had covered the eye with a firm pad, put the knight to bed and over the next few weeks presided over his partial visual return with some inert lotion or other. Sir Donald had been delighted.

"Why, man," he guffawed, "you're a gentleman, ha, ha! Not just another damned saw-bones. Ha, ha, ha!" Thereafter Father was always welcome through the front door, and it did much for his practice reputation, not to mention his income.

We drew up at the portico and rapped at a large studded door, which was answered after a suitably proud delay by a bearded retainer in a brocaded smock. Entering the arched hall, we came face to face with a large stag. It looked so real I could have sworn that the rest of it was lurking behind the oak panelling. Sir Donald was admiring his trophy like a weary falcon. He now turned his magenta cheeks in our direction.

"A relic of my hunting days," whinnied the baron-knight. He obviously remembered me, but had forgotten the trout. I breathed easily again. "Can't line a gun now," he pointed to his porcelain cornea and diverging eye.

"So this is your young cub," he added, sizing me up as a suitable quarry for the Temple. But his laugh was forced. Sir Donald was a worried man. His wife had the fever and he had heard there was trouble at Easthouses. No time was wasted crowing over stuffed game for he wanted to take both of us to see her at once.

He led us past the stag and past a tableau of the first Sir Donald outstaring a mighty boar and upstairs to a dim bedroom lit by fluttering sconces, where Lady Fairley-Dunn lay sick as though to death, her breathing rasping, her skin blotched and her hair lank. She barely seemed to be aware of our entry but her eyelids flickered a welcome when Father's shadow fell across her face.

"It's good of you to come, doctor," said she.

Father took her hand, and turned to her husband.

"Why do you shut out the light, Sir Donald?" he asked peremptorily. He strode over to the windows and pulled open the shutters.

"Well, we thought it would help," mumbled the laird.

"And the windows," Father kept on relentlessly. "The windows. We must have some fresh air."

"We thought it was dangerous," explained the laird helplessly.

Father and he opened the windows between them, then he joined me by the fire, while Father went back to give judgment on her Ladyship. He talked a while to her. He felt her wrist and looked at her tongue. He felt her forehead, listened to her breathing and examined the blotches on her skin. Still holding her hand, he turned to the knight and fired a volley of questions at him.

How long had she been like this? Had it happened suddenly or slowly? Did the rash come first or was it the fever? Had she been vomiting? Had she been eating? Had she been drinking? Were there any other symptoms? And so on.

Sir Donald did not flinch under this bombardment; he had bottom. He looked Father in the eye and answered like a man. Father looked again at the lady, then made his pronouncement.

"She will recover," he said shortly. "Give her some drops of laudanum every six hours, and draughts of water, and a little broth if she asks for it."

"Ah, Dr Bryson," Sir Donald smiled happily for the first time during our visit.

"You have brought me peace. You have brought me peace," he repeated. "Come and split a bottle with me. I will be back later, my dear." He kissed his wife before escorting us from the sick chamber past the mounted trophies and past the fabled pig that had so fortunately dared to cross tusks with the first of the line.

We took a glass of claret with him in his study, and arranged to return on the morrow. He personally escorted us to our trap and stood waving as we cantered off down the drive. Once beyond the crumbling gateway we settled into an easy trot and Father said,

"Well, that visit will buy us a few extras, I'm thinking."

"Father, how could you be so sure that she will recover?" I was still mystified.

"Two reasons, I suppose. Firstly the Fairley-Dunns don't use the village well. They take their water from up that hill there, I should imagine. Secondly, I could see that she had a looking glass under her coverlet. No woman about to quit this world would bother about how she looked, now would she?" He drew into the grass verge to let by some eager youth on a fearsome stallion and finished his wee lecture.

"Never forget," said he, "we all live in a series of postures. I would not have come back from Waterloo with my body and my reputation if I hadn't been like the rest of them. But it's all different when you are sick. Your patients will come to you with their postures gone and their guards down. Treat them as you will, make them laugh if you can, but never break that trust and you won't go far wrong." Then he whipped up the mare and she strolled off as was her custom.

There was a third reason that he was too modest and I too proud to mention and what, if pressed, he would have called experience. It rankled that he should be so reasonable, so unaggressive and so obscure. The looking glass I could understand but there was no academic harangue and the water from up the hill made no sense at all.

I settled back in the trap, now convinced that an M.D. and fluency in Latin did not make me a better man than my apothecary father. It would take twenty years and perhaps a Peninsular War and then I would be defending myself against the new Symes and the Listons with words like, "maturity, wisdom and judgement," whose resonance might finally deceive me into mistaking my own grandeur of manner for genius. Thinking about it served no useful purpose. Mother was making kail tonight—I would just think about that instead.

10

The entire summer was not taken up by therapeutics. I talked to my mother and played with my brother and sister, and I went for long solitary walks in those woods behind our home where I dreamed of Lucy. I went for less solitary walks with my future bride whose belated insistence on propriety demanded that we now move about with a chaperone. I was called upon to escort her into the social whirlpool of Dalkeith. Sir Donald gave a firework display to celebrate his wife's recovery, and Grizel declared him, "A treasure—a man of such sensibility." On Saturdays she would drag me down in a disintegrating phaeton to scatter alms, which she usually borrowed from me, amongst the mine workers of Easthouses, and of an evening would either frighten us to sleep with readings from the latest Gothic tales of dark abbeys and swarthy strangers who threatened the heroines with death, but never a fate worse than, or would squawk to her own accompaniment on the forte-piano.

Before I returned to University there was a harvest merrymaking, with a drunken fiddler and wild dancing on the village common. It was at this jollification that she told me,

"I have decided, my love, to found a society for fallen women, and my father has promised to help me. He tells me his vocation has brought him knowledge of where such women are to be found." As I watched the intoxicated musician, out of his depth with some virtuoso lunacy, I could see that the Homes and the MacWraths, like his trills and quavers, must soon collide. It was therefore with feeling I said,

"Your concern for humanity will influence the lives of many unsuspecting people, Miss MacWrath."

On my first night back at my studies in Edinburgh, I called at 12 Charlotte Square to pay my respects, and stayed to dinner. It was a cheerful meal, and as Aunt Gertrude had retired there was no rival to whist. Lucy then read to us from *Childe Harold's Pilgrimage,* after which she gave a wickedly accurate imitation of Professor Monroe sitting down again after he had risen to say it was time to go hone.

"And I am told," she rattled on, "that he still uses his grandfather's lecture notes, unaltered and says 'when I was in Leyden in 1720 and the students blow barley at him every time he does it." This was true; I had been on the firing end of a barley shooter myself. Even her father, warmed with Madeira, came near to separating into his various parts with laughter. I was sure his own little weaknesses had given rise to similar mimicry elsewhere in the house.

On my second night back in Edinburgh I called at 19 Hanover Street, where the billowy Mrs Cudleigh opened the door to me. She was clad in a low flimsy dress, and clearly unworried about any effect the sharp autumn air might be having on her chest.

She curtsied deeper than strictly necessary, and I could see that the Autumn air was having no ill effect on her chest at all. When she took me to the drawingroom, I found that Aeneas had got there before me, and was already well into a deep goblet. Poor Aeneas, I thought—he must have spent a bleak four months in the Inveresk manse. It would be like staying permanently with Mr MacWrath—a foretaste of Hell for the wicked.

I said hello to them both. Aeneas nodded sourly, but Quentin bounded up and whooped "Hello!" Haw, haw, haw!" and shook me by the hand, then replaced his hand with a goblet of depth, similar to the one held by Aeneas. He then joined us on the arm-chairs, and resumed the conversation I had interrupted.

"What were you saying about Invewesk Church, Anas?"

"Well, the church was built in 1805, as far as I recall, and the man who designed it was . . ."

Quentin was impatient.

"No, no, no. It's not the architecture I want to hear about. I'm not weally intewested in the church itself. What about the churchyard? How many gates does it have? Is it overlooked at all? Are there plenty of twees about?" And more of the same.

I could see Quentin was off on a new venture. He listened with attention to Aeneas, who tried to answer as best as he could. Though the graveyard dispositions were not a subject he had taken much note of and Quentin's interest baffled him a fraction. He looked to me to be on edge and was persuaded with difficulty to have his goblet recharged. When he thought he had satisfied Quentin's curiosity, he emptied the glass with somewhat less persuasion and rose to take his leave in some haste, I thought. But he was not to be delayed, for his look was burning and his mouth set. Quentin, all courtesy, saw him to the door, thanking him for his company and his information. Quentin laughed.

"I do declare, Anas, you're in an absolute fwoth to get away." Aeneas blushed—the deeper when Quentin's sleek cook curtsied her farewells to him. Quentin went on ironically,

"Why, damn me, you're off the see the twading ladies? Well, don't come back with the pox. Haw, haw, haw!"

With Aeneas gone, Quentin turned to more serious matters. His coffers were again empty, the Universal Boot scheme having collapsed like the South Sea Bubble, Mrs Dewlapp's hundred pounds almost gone. He said to me,

"I may well have to consider again coming to live with you in your lodgings." He did not look as if he relished the prospect, and Mr O'Loan would find him even more capable than himself of persuading someone else to finance his thirst.

Mind you, to look at him as he flourished his cuffs, you would take him for an idle blade, with a country house and twenty thousand pounds a year. A closer look, however, would uncover flaws in the nankeen, scratches on his boots and an overpowering desire to acquire a touch of the ready.

As I had already dined, he was trying to pin me down with another of his lucrative projects. As ever, the broad sweep was as grand as the strategy that won Waterloo; the narrow sweep was not so impressive and would have provided gun-powder for the horses and hay for the guns. Quentin was never a man for detail.

In brief, he wanted us to become Resurrection Men. In fact, there was not much more to the scheme, though he filled in the gaps with enthusiasm. Our opening night was to be in Inveresk churchyard digging by moonlight and the map of the battleground was what Quentin had managed to drag from Mr McBeen's uncertain recollections. Quentin's reconnoitring had been scant; the presence or absence of an enemy was unknown; we would discover our escape roads on the night. What the Iron Duke would have made of all this I hated to think. Quentin was babbling on.

"I do like the name Wesuwection men; it sounds so much more thwilling than Body Snatcher, don't you think? Just imagine—ten pounds a body evewy other week. We'd be up to our necks in blunt and," he added, thinking to dispel my fears with a professional touch "we could study some surface Anatomy before we sell them. What do you think of that? Haw, haw, haw!"

I took the glass he had refilled for me. To tell the truth, I did not think much of the idea at all. The tales of the Resurrection Men were as rife as the tales of the Peninsular veterans. There were even poems about them, and I remember my father once telling me one that began,

"Geordie Mill wi' his roond-moo'd spade,
Is aye wishin' for mair fowk deed . . ."

Twelve further stanzas hinted darkly that he did not always wait for them to die either. But the surgeons had to operate, and to operate they had to be conversant with Anatomy, and to be conversant with Anatomy they needed bodies, fresh, young, undeformed, and frequent.

One source, we all knew was the Law, and the Surgeons Hall and the University and the extra-mural schools were all conveniently placed near the Grassmarket, where the Law reached its perfection in a scaffold designed by Deacon Brodie. As if the rope were not enough to face the mob of Edinburgh would seethe around these gallows, stopped only by a circle of soldiers from devouring the hangman or the prisoner, according to their fancy. They had their own sense of justice.

The hangman's job did not require a great cranium. He had first to tie a knot and place it behind the ear, then wait for a pastor to save the soul before he despatched the breath. When he was done, the theoretical procedure was to hand the corpse to any relatives that might lay claim. If no relatives appeared, enterprising Body Snatchers might masquerade as heart-broken cousins and uncles, only to be attacked by other Body Snatchers who might or might not be convinced of their authenticity. One way or another, out of these frequent disgraceful scenes, Knox, Monroe or Liston would acquire another dissecting specimen—for a price!

During one such spectacle, the corpse, inexpertly hanged, got up and walked away into the folklore of Edinburgh as "Hawf Hangit Maggie". Such escapes were rare.

Quentin busied himself to persuade me by telling me legends of the Body Snatchers. I knew them to be apocryphal; he knew that I knew but it did not stop him from relating them as personal experiences. As far as they went, they differed little from the O'Loan epics, excepting perhaps in the size of the hero. I had to give it to Quentin that he had the knack of turning the most ludicrous episodes into heroic caperings that you might have found in the pages of Rifleman Harris. He told me of two of his associates (or so he called them) returning from a mission to Bonnyrigg Kirkyard, with a £10 sack for Dr Knox.

"Just thwee days dead, would you believe it."

To allay suspicion, they propped their corpse up between them on the seat of their cart. Feeling that the subtle reason for this had escaped me, Quentin explained,

"So that it would seem that there were thwee of them, and not just two. You see. Haw, haw, haw!" He slapped his thigh and horse-laughed loudly.

Half-way to Edinburgh, overcome with cold, they disappeared into a tap-house, leaving the corpse under a sack on the floor of the cart, whilst they roistered and warmed themselves within. A vagrant similarly affected with the Scottish November night, tried to warm himself under the sacking in the cart and fell asleep.

Out came the Resurrection Men, full of tippeny and whisky, and they fell on what they thought was their merchandise and, propping up the comatose vagabond on the front of their cart, resumed their journey.

A mile or so up the road they became aware of some movement between them, and were ascribing it to the drink or the road or a rat, when the tramp announced that he was,

"Cauld fit tae dee."

"Just imagine their fwight!" snickered Quentin. "I believe the twamp said, 'If ye'd been where I've been these last twa' days ye'd be cauld tae. Haw, haw, haw!'" He managed to get his tongue round the West Lothian gutterals marvellously. "Then they abandoned their cart, and didn't stop wunning until they weached the Camewon Toll."

He ran off to find Mrs Cudleigh, who was not answering his call for wine. When he returned after a curious delay, he was clasping a bottle and was already well into another fable. That I had missed the start affected the impact not a tittle. Quentin communicated his confident exuberance irresistably, and had his narrative not concerned Professor Monroe, I would still have found myself listening.

I gathered, between mouthfuls of brandy, that two of the fraternity had been wetting their throats in a sawdust den not far from the Nether Bow (strange how the professions have more than bodies in common). They were on the prowl for revellers who might not survive the evening's capers. At any rate they saw a likely cove sliding to the ground. They helped him out for a brief gasp of fresh air, before popping him into a sack. (They always have a sack at hand in these stories it seemed). They then staggered up to the University, and sold him to Professor Monroe for the usual fee. Just as they were disappearing, Monroe found to his horror that the sack was moving and ran after them, shouting,

"The corpse is alive! The corpse is alive! And alive in these circumstances means . . .ah—ah".

"Kill it then," they shouted back. He never saw them again.

In my later tranquil moments I realised that a year before, my decision would have been reached with a clear head. Now I took the plunge without giving Mr MacWrath's advice a second thought and for that matter the first thought had not been too clear either.

Whatever, Quentin and I drank to our new firm of Body Snatchers, By Appointment to the House of Hangover. The sharp if foul air of Robertson's Wynd blew away the effects of Quentin's brandy and his persuasive eloquence. I now grasped what a fearful business I had let myself in for. However, honour forbade my withdrawal. I slept that night in a state alternating between torpor and sheer terror.

By morning only the terror remained, and the remainder of the week passed, highlighted by the bungling performances of Professor Monroe and virtuoso versions of the same thing by his brilliant rival, Knox. Each time I saw either, I was haunted by visions of irate relatives dealing me mortal wounds in my rump with a blunderbuss, or of ignominous expulsion from the University in public disgrace. Either would destroy my mother, enrage my father and drive Mr MacWrath into ecstacies of foreseen reproof.

Lucy wondered at the cause of my malaise. When I told her, she burst into peals of laughter, then she became serious and told me to be careful and not let Quentin spoil my career. But she did not tell me, or beseech me, or order me or advise me not to go. She was obviously excited at the prospect, and I suspect would like to have joined the expedition. I was pleased after a fashion and equally pleased that she did not faint away from so unladylike a subject.

"What's so interesting?" said the Professor. "Mmmh. Hah. Mmmh."

"Leave them be, James. They're coming to an understanding," said his wife. And we were too, for I had to swear on my heart to tell Lucy exactly what happened on the evening, down to the very contents of the coffin itself.

Friday came, and with it a welcome mist. We dressed inconspicuously in coarse fustian, collier's boots to the knees and blue neckties. We sported short clay pipes, that enveloped our crumpled headgear in a thick grey smoke.

"Off to find the cart now," said Quentin airily. Easy for him, I thought, he's been a soldier. But then I thought again, the most active service he had seen had been fox hunting. He led the way down Paton's Wynd, where one of his murky friends was to lend him a cart and tell him where the most recent burials had been. We found the friend in a dilapidated stableyard beside a long cart and a senile horse. There was a muttered exchange between them, then a muffled villain of middle height came out from the shadows and took my hand in what briefly seemed to be a small clamp.

"Harry Plunderleith tae you," he said. "That's no' ma real name, ye ken," he added candidly. Now that my eyes had grown used to the gloom, I was prepared to believe that was one of the few times he had been caught telling the truth.

Half an hour later we were trundling out towards Duddingston Manor to Inveresk. The night closed in on us, and my teeth betrayed my cold, my fright and my despair. A fitful moon showed us infrequently that we were on some sort of a road, and all the time flung hideous shadows across our path. By the road margins, great trees and bushes creaked and swayed in the wind, like giant sentries taking sight along their muskets. Mrs O'Loan's establishment, when I began to think about it, had concealed attractions—well concealed to be true, but growing more obvious the further we drove away from it. I longed for the dirty sheets, and the cracked ewer of cold water to shave in.

We came into open country and crossed the Esk Bridge, where, on a similar night, Prince Charles Edward's Highlanders had passed on their way to destroy Johnny Cope's army and his reputation. I found myself singing,

"Hey, Johnny Cope, are you waukin' yet?"

and took that to mean I was feeling bolder.

My boldness vanished in an instant as we approached the wall of Inveresk Churchyard at the top of a stout brae. Quentin became serious. We tethered our horse under some bushes, a needless gesture, for he showed no signs of spontaneous movement. He lit a small oil lamp whilst I assembled our equipment: two heavy spades, a large thick sheet, and two steel hooks like grappling irons on long ropes. I shivered and tripped over an exposed tree root that crooked over the earth like a witch's finger.

Quentin had no real need of his lamp, for the random moon guided us with ease to the recent graves which lay beneath the far wall— fortunately for us, as it turned out.

To our left stood the Inveresk Church, a ghostly shadow, and its spire a half-silvered beacon for the bogles and phantoms that I could clearly see glowering and trailing across the moon.

"Wight," said Quentin, "now lay that sheet on the gwound here."

"You'll be mourners, I take it," said a menacing voice behind me. I did not need to turn far to see a square pit prop man behind me; but what caught my eye first was an enormous musket he was pointing at us. Quentin fixed him with a cool stare.

"And you'll be out for geese, I pwesume. Well, you'll find them down by the mud flats, I would think. As a matter of fact we're out to take a bweath of the pure night air."

"Nae doot ye've brocht yer ain sleeping materials as well," said the pit prop, gesturing at the sheet with a sizeable thumb. I laid a quaking hand on Quentin's arm.

"I think we ought to go," I said. I could barely speak because my teeth kept obstructing my tongue.

"Ye're bloody Body Snatchers." There was no denying it; his assessment of the situation was sharp. "Come on, lads," he was shouting now, and two knotted friends cut from the same trees as himself, suddenly loomed out from behind a large burial cairn. They also carried firearms as large as themselves.

Quentin reacted rapidly.

"Let's hoof it," he shouted superfluously, for I was already heading over the wall with musket balls whining about us like angry hornets. We ran about a furlong and flung ourselves into some tangled undergrowth and panted in sheer' fright.

"Jesus, that was a near wun thing," said the cucumber hussar. "All we need to do now is to wait for them to get dwunk.

"Quentin," I whispered, "you're not contemplating another attempt surely?" I began to tremble afresh.

"Indeed I am—you can't fail me now. Look, we need not suffer in the meantime." He produced a flask of whisky from some inner pocket and offered it to me. I never had much of a taste for raw spirit, but at that moment it seemed like fiery honey.

We lay and listened and kept warm from the flask as required. Waiting was tedious. It must have been two hours; it felt like six when the three wooden guards stumped by, laughing loudly and exchanging coarse ribaldries. Several flasks had been emptied in the graveside vigil. Never a doubt, for their muskets now hung loosely in the couch of their arms, and their feet hung loosely from their legs in all directions.

We gave them ten minutes to move clear, then returned to our objective in the cemetery. Quentin peeped over the wall and laughed softly.

"The clowns have left our equipment. Haw, haw, haw!"

This time we worked fast, without interruptions and the moon, swinging across towards the western sky, marked our time. We dug furiously, taking care to lay the earth on the sheet and not on the grass. Quentin's spade suddenly struck wood, and I thought for a moment that the noise might bring the armed bruisers back. Nobody appeared.

"Quickly now," he said leaping down into the grave to place the hooks around the edge of the coffin lid. He bounded up again in a flash and threw me a rope. "Pull on that," he barked, "when I tell you. Now—heave—heave—heave." With a crack the lid gave way, and Quentin was down again, wrestling with the contents, still wrapped in its shroud. "Help me up with this," he ordered. Corpses are heavy, and they don't help you one little bit.

"Damn me," he chided himself, "I've left the sack in the cart." Quentin swore again, but went off to fetch the necessary bag, leaving me on guard over our grisly booty. I felt ill, and vowed before God I would dissolve forthwith our new company and give up drinking beer, and devote myself to studies, and remember all Mr MacWrath's stern admonitions, and, oh Jesus, I wished Quentin would come back.

I heard his step—unnaturally loud on the crisp ground.

"My God, what if it's that bloody sentry again?" I half whispered, tensing to leap the wall if necessary. Quentin appeared almost immediately with a voluminous canvas sack. I could not but admire his nerve. He opened the sack and we worked it around our prize, tying up

116

the end with a long rope. The shroud and the earth we tipped back into the grave, taking care to restore it to its original neatness. As I worked with the spade I was troubled by a swift unpleasant flash of some wife or mother or son mourning over that empty coffin, while Knox or Liston or Monroe or some other detached scientist was shredding their lost one to ribbons somewhere else. At that moment I hated all doctors and wished that I had chosen the Law or the Army, or even assistant to our parish minister.

It took two journeys to the cart to transfer all our equipment and our gruesome capture. Not a moment passed but that I was expecting divine retribution in the form of a thunderbolt, or at least a musket ball.

Quentin whipped our lethargic cuddy into motion and for a brief moment I thought we were going to have two corpses on our hands, but eventually he began to clip-clop away down the hill towards the Esk and the bridge. A feverish chatter now took the place of our previous silence. The trees now looked like trees; the shadows of our outward journey had lost their terror; it mattered not now whether the road was clear or not.

Since it was almost one of the morning, we decided to spend the night in our cart in the park of Duddingston Manor, for no-one would be on hand to buy our merchandise much before six. I have spent happier nights.

Generally at dusk and dawn, or when the ambient light was sufficient to allow man to move incognito, furtive back doors would open in dark corners in case the Snatchers had been out on a successful foray. The first light was turning the clouds over Dunbar to a lurid churning gray as we slipped out of our harbour with about as much confidence as Villeneuve had when he left Cadiz for Cape Trafalgar. We decided to go to Professor Monroe as fast as our sleepy cob could take us.

A few loiterers were stirring; I could distinguish here and there a water caddie and a night watchman, but no-one wanted to ask us what we were carrying at that hour. My panic mounted again as I considered how we might explain away our illegal cargo. I shut my eyes and my brain began to spin with phantasy conversations.

"My cousin has consumed too much wine, sir"—no, that would not do for an explanation of strange behaviour in a town where such a condition was standard.

"We came upon this cart when out for a little walk." Damn me, if that wasn't weaker still. "Our postillion has been struck by lightning and we had to make him decent with this sacking. He does not feel uncomfortable—I assure you."

"By lightning you say, sir; I didna hear any thunder. Did you, McFetters?"

"Na na, Mr McNab."

"Unco' useful carrying a wee sack about with you like that. Have you ever seen a flunkey on a cart withoot ony livery, McFetters?"

"Na na, Mr McNab."

I opened my eyes to answer McFetters and McNab but they had been replaced by further alarming visions. I tried over another one to Lord Braxfield and a jury of Mr MacWrath's who were now taking shape behind our cart in wigs and bedsocks.

"We have been body snatching, Your Honour."

"A hanging offence," said his Lordship.

"Guilty," said the twelve MacWraths.

The University, taking shape out of the morning mist, put a welcome end to my whimsical dialogues.

Quentin managed to find the way to Monroe's back door, despite the hour. We trotted at snail's pace past Brown's Square, drawing up, if such a description were meet for our drowsy steed, in a small lane. He jumped off, looking in the back of the cart first to make sure that our ten pounds was still there.

"Now," he shouted, "here we go." He strode up to the door, but before he could knock, Monroe's lame attendant, Marble Willie, hirpled over.

"Whit hae ye there fer us, gentlemen," he whined. I have never seen a man more in need of a corpse than he. He ran an expert hand over our body.

"Aye, this yin's no' been lang in the grund. Whit were ye thinkin' then?" Quentin glanced at me like Shylock.

"£10," was his sharp reply.

"Ooooh, that's awfu' dear."

"Well, it's no' aff a rabbit," said Quentin in mimicry. "Well, we'll just have to take it up the woad to Dr Knox." Marble Willie gave us a crafty side look.

"Na, na, na. Dinna dae that. Here, gie me a haund in wi' it." We obliged, all three of us struggling with our cold unhelpful burden.

The Professor's rooms looked different to us in these servile clothes. I glanced about before Willie ushered us out.

"Now," he said, "thank ye kindly."

"What about our money?" said Quentin.

"Whit money?"

"For our body, Mr Bwiar."

"There'll be nae siller for yoose," said the cripple. "If Professor Monroe kent that his students had ta'en to the grave robbin', oh dearie me." He shook his head at the very thought of it. "Na, na. Off wi' ye, an' Ah'll say naethin' aboot it." Quentin began to advance on him, clenching his fists. "Dinna you threaten me," said Willie, retreating rapidly to the mortuary.

"Give me my money." Willie's answer was to fasten the chain, leaving the door open but unbroken by Quentin's furious charges. My rising panic substituted a gallows now for the City Guard. It also gave me voice.

"Come on, Quentin," I said. "We've lost this one."

Quentin whipped up the cart, and I could still hear the crippled Willie, cackling and laughing as he watched us from behind the door, for our horse now refused to walk another inch. "Give him the bloody horse too," hissed Quentin, now too enraged to think clearly. "I'll dwag the damned cart back myself."

I will not say how we made it home—or when or how we persuaded Mr Plunderleith that we had not deliberately damaged his senile horseflesh which he would, I felt sure, soon be selling at a profit as prime beef to any clown unwise enough to see an honest merchant behind the ready smile.

But I kept the two of the vows I made that week. I told Lucy exactly what happened—well, almost exactly; there was nothing to be served by telling her that I had been somewhat less cool than Quentin during our crisis moments, though I suspect she knew anyway.

I forgot about the beer drinking vow and my stricken promises to Mr MacWrath's shadow, but never again did I put my foot inside a graveyard with a spade and grappling hook.

11

The Royal Infirmary of Edinburgh was an imposing pile. The main part of the building faced North, set back from the High School Yards, whilst two buttresses formed the sides of a quadrangle, whose fourth side was made up of a railinged wall broken by a large gate, that for some quaint reason nobody ever used. Above the main doorway perched a full-length statue of King George II in the dress of a Roman emperor. When I first saw it, some wag had tied an old fiddle to his outstretched hand.

On entering the main building, there was no escaping the bust by Nollekins of George Drummond, the man without whom there would have been no Royal Infirmary at all. Turning from that you would next encounter an oil portrait of George Drummond, and for all I know there may well have been smaller parlour versions of the same in other rooms throughout the hospital. Along the walls hung blackboards which recorded in gilt letters the names of those who had bought space with a donation to the Infirmary funds.

Architecturally the building was plain, for it was felt that external decoration would waste important money that might be otherwise diverted to the healing of the sick. This embargo on spending did not, however, apply to the Administrative Department which was adorned with a pillared facade, surmounted by a specially designed attic and cupola. The architects still managed another gesture to economy; they placed the Operating Room in the attic, and the Theatre for two hundred watching students, angled above the attic, could then be used as a chapel; the cupola then allowed an unrestricted view of Heaven for divine worshippers, and indeed at other specified times, for astronomical telescopists.

The building was divided in half, according to sex, the West Wing being Male, and the East Female. There was a Fever Ward, where I had seen so many succumb during the spotted epidemic; a small Maternity Department, and beds for the mentally unbalanced. Each Wing contained public baths; indeed King George IV had doffed his kilt and manoeuvred his large bulk into one of them during the celebrated 1822 visit. Whether the bath attendants had 'carled then because the King had come,' was not on record. There certainly could not have been a great deal of room left in the bath for water after the royal buttocks had settled to the bottom. Neither was there a great deal of room for surgery or surgical students, for in keeping with the traditions the hospital requirements had been planned by men about to retire; men who had in their youth fought on the frontiers of medicine but thirty years previously. When their advice was sought, they not unnaturally viewed the problems in the light of their waning need for surgical beds. But help was on the way. A new hospital was planned in 1807, and its completion the following year had been confidently predicted ever since. We were all still confidently waiting. I believe they still are.

Our shuffling group of medical students that November morning, however, did not have to wait long for the Clerk of the House. A uniformed slavey directed us to where we might catch his attention. Mr Grovell was a small globular man, whose hair was disappearing rapidly under the combined stress of a junior post and the senior staff. He would have had a lot to discuss, I am sure, with Mr Collick. Above him was suspended a likeness of George Drummond. Hospital frugality doubled his duties on one salary to that of Hospital Registrar and Resident House Surgeon. As Registrar, he had to inform the prospective patients of their forthcoming admissions, and as House Surgeon, he had to write down a history of their symptoms and illness.

As Registrar, he told the visiting surgeon of their duty day, and as House Surgeon he accompanied them on their rounds, noting details of the patients' diets, treatment, recovery or decline. As Registrar, he kept all surgical instruments under lock and key, and as Registrar again, accepted from the surgeons who might choose to use these instruments, the price of their renewal as an earnest of their safe return.

As Registrar, on Saturday mornings he would read out his ledger of interesting cases, and in return for a sixpence, not returnable, he would give us transcriptions of their behaviour. As Registrar, he allocated Aeneas, Quentin and myself to be surgical dressers to Mr Damwell, for the month of December.

Mr Edward Damwell's fame filled and bellied like a sail from one of the men of war where it had been acquired. He was full and grey-haired, and his nose had taken its shape from a youthful addiction to pugilism and, it was suspected, a poor left hand guard. He regarded dry land as a poor substitute for water; he was frequently heard to bay,

"I am really a quarter-deck surgeon—nothing like the dip and roll of a broadside to sort out those who keep their hand steady from those who don't—eh, what?"

The naval pose was not an affectation. He had spent less time on the beach than he had on the deck. After his return from the West Indies station he wasted no time, as might have been expected, in finding a bride whom he bore off to his country seat, acquired with his prize money and which lay off the South Queensferry Road. From here he would sweep into town in a smart carriage with two tidy ones in hand, which he reined himself. He was generally regarded as a first rate whip, and could take a fly off his leader's ear as easily as he might dislodge a stone from the bladder. His students feared and respected him; his patients loved him, and the more he threatened to excise the more devoted was their love.

On the morning of the third of December, we carried out a shivering vigil on the steps by the locked front gate of the Royal Infirmary. I did not feel well, but ascribed it to Quentin's brandy which I had been taking over the last month for fever caught on the Inveresk road.

"Here's the Admiwal now," muttered Quentin, and sure enough up he rattled, in his gleaming conveyance, pulling aside in time to avoid a peg-legged soldier who had tottered before his chestnuts.

"What do you mean crossing my bows like that," he hallooed at the startled veteran. He did not wait for an answer, but tossed the man a groat for his pains. He looked us up and down in silence, as he might have three ill-dressed midshipmen. Quentin broke the silence,

"Good morning, sir. We're your new dwessers."

"Humph. Well, don't just stand there. Follow me in. I've an unconscionable amount to do today. Can't waste time. Busy man. Several procedures to be done. Must be off to Cramond by two o'clock." All this while bouncing up the steps; meanwhile the coachman got out of the carriage and drove off. We trailed after our new master into the main building.

Grovell greeted him with rather overdone humility, I thought, and led us all up to the Male Surgical Wing on the second floor.

"What have you got for me today, Grovell," snapped the Chief.

"There is a hernia incarcerata, a compound fracture of the tibia, and a woman was admitted this morning after having vomited several ounces of red blood, sir."

"You're sure it was not black blood?"

"No, sir, I'm sure it was red blood."

"Well, she will not survive the morning, unless you can persuade her to swallow some ice. See to that now."

Grovell truckled out the door backwards.

"Now you," Damwell turned on us, "where is the hernia incarcerata?"

"We do not know, sir." Quentin was our spokesman.

"What do you mean, you don't know? You must know. It's your duty to know. Ah, Grovell, you're just in time. These fellows need to sharpen up. They don't seem to know a damned thing. If they don't learn something fast—depend on it, I'll have the press on them. Eh, what?" I could see Grovel making a mental note to give us an unpleasant month.

122

He ushered the way with great ceremony to the bedside of a thin, wan little man. He read us a peroration from a long sheet.

"This is Mr Grough. He has had a hernia inguinalis on the right side. He has not worn a truss, and he tells me he used to slip the hernia in and out without discomfort. He strangulated seven days ago. He has been vomiting, retching, and has had severe colic and no stools. I do not consider it reducible, sir."

"Do you not indeed, sir? Have you tried taxis in a hot bath?"

"Yes, sir," said the House Surgeon defensively. Damwell surged forwards, his hands spread and his face alight with determination.

"Lie still there, my good man," he boomed confidently, as though addressing an adjacent ship through a loudhailer. He placed his thumbs on the swollen hernia, paused briefly, then suddenly pressed with enormous energy into the groin.

Grovell gazed silently. Aeneas turned pale. Brown passed out. But the hernia had passed in.

"There," he said. "Apply a truss to that; put him on milk and barley meal porridge and he will be emptying his bowel famously tomorrow. Splendid; first rate." He brought his stern round and glared at us.

"Put them in a hot bath first, then reduce just as I have shown you, but never cut if you can avoid it," said he, before we walked on to his next bed. "If you cut, the body will fill with pus, and if the patient doesn't pull the gut out himself, then it will burst out itself under pressure, and if you rub the gut with your finger, you will make a hole in it. Just imagine if that were to happen inside the belly. In these cases surgery means death.

"None of this applies to you, Grough" he shouted, "You'll be ship shape, Bristol fashion at the first light. What!"

Grough had now recovered enough to murmur his thanks. I could see that Damwell was touched by the man's gratitude, but he fidgeted with his cravat and pretended he wasn't.

Grovell by now had moved on to the bedside of our second patient, for no doubt he had heard all this before. We had not. Nor had we seen before a leg that resembled a leg only because it was where a leg ought to be. I listened to Grovell's recital with half an ear, while I watched the young man before us. His face was dry, his breathing hard, and his complexion jaundiced. Damwell frowned at the bone end, jagged and yellow red, that poked through the blackening skin. A fine crepitation of gas was audible as his fingers made contact. The foot was gone, removed by a new fangled reaping machine. Damwell's frown remained and deepened and he took the young man by the hand.

"We will have to remove the leg," he said and suddenly softening he added, "it will be over as quick as it happened—that's a promise."

"You mean below the knee, sir?" asked the house-surgeon.

"No. Below the hip. Here." He drew a figurative demarcation line across the mid thigh. "I shall do it this morning at the start of my list. See to it, Grovell." As house surgeon, he waited long enough to note down orders for leeches to the swollen skin, vesication to the chest to ease the breathing, and emetics and enemeta to clear the system.

Mr Damwell continued around his charge, rather like Lord St Vincent on a tour of the dockyard, stopping here for a diagnosis, or a decision, or a word of comfort, or a word of reproof. Despite my initial fears I found myself liking the man. He belonged to that breed of men who saw life as a series of decisions that had to be taken—preferably at once. Men who could dispose of a leg or a tumour or a colleague's opinion, in a morning, whilst the lordly physicians, who made a virtue of their erudite languor might take a whole day about some line of action that would probably be made needless by the patient's recovery or death in the evening.

Two other thoughts disturbed me. The first that, although I might admire and envy surgical directness, I did not have the temperament to let me survive what I did to my patients any more than they might survive what I did to them. The second disturbing thought was that I could not face the idea of being a stately phsician either. But that was for other reasons.

The rest of our procession passed off in a majestic flurry; fibrous breast lumps, cervical cancer treated successfully with caustic potash and silver nitrate and acid muriaticum. He always paused to tell us why he did what he did, and even more honestly why what he did sometimes went wrong.

We followed him on to the Operating Theatre, where he proposed to remove the gangrenous leg. We changed for the operation, taking off our neckcloths and outer coats. Damwell put on a large apron and rolled up his sleeves, gesturing to us to do the same. Looking up to the chapel and astronomy laboratory above us, I could see a hundred or so students of our year smiling down with sardonic interest. Quentin's eyes followed mine. He snorted.

"Look at those damned flash boys up there on Mount Olympus. They think they're pwime and bang up to the mark—damn their eyes. But they wouldn't come it so stwong if Damwell had them down here. Haw, haw, haw!"

I was not sure that I was coming it so strong either. Our patient with the gangrene, already screaming despite his incipient lockjaw and opium, arrived in the arms of two burly porters, who laid him on the central table.

"So that's what the holes are for," said Aeneas, watching with horrified fascination as the two giants roped the poor lad into total immobility. When they had tied their knots, for good measure they fell upon him as well, in much the same way as I had seen during Knox's operations; one on the chest and one across his belly, and they took a firm expert grip on all his moving parts.

Surgery was Anatomy at speed, with compassion; I had heard Dr Knox say this many times. Mr Damwell had all these attributes in abundance. He flung himself on the doomed limb in a frenzy. I could barely see his right hand as it hacked down to the bone with the saw. The left hand held the femoral artery closed. Within twenty seconds the man had one leg, and there was not a drop of blood on Damwell's shirt. The screaming haunts me to this day. Now I was familiar with the principles and with the principles in action. The arteries were ligated, the wounds washed in rose water, and the skin flaps apposed with silk stitches. These last manipulations were no less agonising than the first. I was now certain I did not want to be a surgeon.

When it was over, Aeneas was delegated to wash the instruments and Grovell stood back, his eyes closed as if in contemplation. I was sure he just did not fancy speaking to any of us, but his appearance was too ethereal even for Damwell to risk disturbing it. His eyes remained that way until the next case arrived.

For men younger than twenty, death is a fate that happens to other people. In spite of these daily reminders of my own mortality, I could not accept it as an inevitable part of my existence. I felt that if I could turn my back it would just go away. I found my mind deliberately planning a world where none of this would involve me or my loved ones. I was innocent enough and free enough of disease, to dream it possible. My world was somewhat wanting in detail but I half designed it—a little world, poised in time, where Lucy and I would walk hand in hand through October trees to the sound of our Mozart Larghetto.

I could hear Damwell again, teaching with the same refined exuberance that characterised his surgery. He charted Quentin and me through the anatomical shallows of the last procedure and where we might founder during the next.

The next case was to be the removal of a breast lump from a young girl in her twenties. There was the usual preliminary manoeuvring, but all very briskly to give the unfortunate girl no time to reflect on what was about to happen and to mask her embarrassment, he placed a cambric handkerchief across her face. Then Damwell suddenly translated his scholarly description into a controlled fury; scalpel through skin and fat, down to the mass, widening the incision, ligatures to the branches of the mammary artery, the tumour in his hand in its neat capsule, silk stitches to the wound. The girl did not scream, for she had fainted. I retreated into my russet forest. Though I did hear Damwell saying,

125

"That scirrhous is almost certainly not cancerous—it came out easily like a hard-boiled egg out of its shell."

When his patient was sufficiently awake and composed, he thanked her with ineffable charm for being so good and told her that she would be well.

The list proceeded relentlessly—the large porters, the opium, the ropes, the blood, the rose water, the stitches, the unearthly screams of pain, and in the middle of it all Surgeon Damwell, precise, deft, cool and fast.

It is about this time, this half way point in a medical course, that students tend to develop a surface hardness to disguise the terror they feel for the diseases they effect to laugh away. How often had I heard, "Why damn me, I saw an interesting case of diabetes the other day. At least his urine was sweet. Very thirsty he was, and he said that he was not seeing too well. Professor Home told him he was suffering from loss of vision, and wondered if there might be some morbid affection of the retina, but could not be sure." Or something similar.

The same student would be away to his lodgings that night, tasting his water in tremulous anticipation for a saccharine matter, for all the world like common sugar and all this behind the privacy of his locked bedroom door. The next day he would be emptying tankards of ale at Ross's without an apparent qualm.

It was after a month of this surgical horror that I suffered my first mortal illness. It happened one cold December afternoon. I felt breathless and suffered acute chest pain and diagnosed Syncope Anginosa, on the first step of No. 3 Robertson's Wynd. By the time I had reached the second floor, I was afraid I was going to die. I struggled to my tiny room and lay on the two-legged bed, waiting for the pain to go, which it did.

I then ventured gently off the bed to see the worst in Cullen's *Practice of Physic*. I searched for some information on my condition. I tongued my finger through all four volumes before running the disease to its lair in the first book that I had picked up. The exhaustion of the search made me fear again that I was about to die. The products of the search convinced me. I read,

"The paroxysms which, in the incipient stages of the disease were only brought on by walking up a steep hill, by mounting stairs or by walking or riding against the wind, or by gusts of passion, or by mental anxiety, or by hard drinking." It went on for several more discouraging pages.

I might have asked myself a history. If I had, I would have told myself that I had fought three rounds hard-fist with Dominic Corrigan the day before that could have well explained the pain underneath the sternum and the unaccustomed dyspnoea. I did not ask myself a history. I read that I might try Digitalis, squills, calomel or gin punch. I kept only the last in my room and it did me no good whatsoever.

I picked up Cullen again and saw that wine negus was often not tolerated and that the stomach was frequently morbidly affected, becoming unusually irritable and rejecting whatever was swallowed. I did not think it necessary to tell myself that I had consumed five mutchkins of heavy beer just eighteen hours previously. I continued to lie on my bed, and my malaise began to clear. I now feared that I might not die.

A knock at the door was followed by the gay figure of Quentin, all boisterous good humour.

"You can't lie here all day," he brayed. "There's a cock-fight in Plunderleith's stable yard at half past eight. Let's pad the hoof down to Paton's Wynd and see if we can waise the wind. Haw, haw, haw!" I padded the hoof, as he suggested, down the same lanes that had landed us in Inveresk Kirkyard. Plunderleith's premises were as dank and uninviting as an old well, but himself was there all a-welcome. He greeted Quentin as a prime spectator and told me he was calling himself "Harry Bull the nicht".

"For pwofessional weasons," explained Quentin jovially. "Cock and Bull, d'ye see—attwacts the lads. Haw, haw, haw!"

A ring of mufflered men had already formed around two scrawny bantams that were stabbing and screaming at each other in a flurry of thin feathers. Money and curses were exchanged; the vanquished died, the victors being dragged off by triumphant owners, and the whole performance repeated endlessly.

The sport cured me, and when I left Plunderleith's yard, my symptoms had vanished, as had my last ten shillings.

Now that I had got cured of my heart disease, I had to earn my title of dresser to Mr Damwell. This meant staying in hospital day and night. Had the room been any smaller, it would have been impossible to sleep stretched out. Not that we had much time to sleep, for the night porter kept disturbing our rest. We had to patrol the wards, handing out the medicines and making sure that Mr Damwell's suture lines did not burst apart like old boots.

We were well off for nurses in the Surgical Ward, for we had one full time ordinary nurse to clean the ward and to carry medicines from the apothecaries' shops. From time to time a supernumerary was engaged if they had a case that was considered beyond our care.

I saw my first surgical death on my very first night in the surgical wards. The woman who had come in vomiting blood, had continued to, despite the ice, and Damwell had shaken his head sadly at the sight of her.

"She'll not last the night. She must have some erosion or ulcer in the stomach wall, and the artery is just pumping her to death." He was right. She became pale and pulseless, and in death took on a beauty that had been denied her before. Serene now, in a tangle of auburn hair. I had to turn away, for my eyes were wet, and I knew well an auburn head just like that in another part of Edinburgh.

I saw my second surgical death on my second night in the surgical wards. Our amputee of yesterday began to rise into the agony of a traumatic fever. His body convulsed sporadically. We applied antispasmodics and tried to give him some barley broth. I drew three ounces of blood and placed leeches to ease the tense swelling over his stump. His breathing now came soft and rapid and, of a sudden, it came not at all.

"Mr Damwell will want a post mortem," said the egregious Grovell behind me, transferring the name of our recent patient from his portable register of the living to another book reserved for those we failed to cure. It was a thick book and well thumbed.

Still, in Damwell's charge, there could be no doubt that our methods were clean. And, after all, when it came to compound fractures, only forty or so out of every hundred patients failed to survive the injury or the curative surgery—incredibly few compared with what happened in other charges.

Attendance at post mortems was a formal part of the dresser's duties. We followed the signs directing us to the Mortuary, a gloomy low cottage hidden behind the main hospital building, where a large notice "SECTIO HODIE" told us Latin scholars that the surgical pathologists would be finding out where we had gone wrong again.

The surgeons did not like the pathologists, because they were always right when it was too late, and were wont to say,

"The ossified state of the kidney clearly contributed to your patient's demise, as you can see here, and here," when it had not been at all clear yesterday. The physicians did not like the pathologists either, for very much the same reasons, and they despised the surgeons as well for their faulty education. The pathologists disliked all clinicians for their lack of humility in the face of their proven mistakes and their larger incomes.

The Post Mortem room had the chilling coldness of a stone cellar that has never seen the sunshine and indeed it never had—deliberately so to keep it inhabitable for its main occupants. Its temperature was further reduced by its compass setting which placed it directly in the path of the north east wind that swept out of the Arctic seas, collecting a unique odour across the alleys of the Old Town before blowing itself out against the mortuary and the undertakers' carts that clustered discreetly around the back door.

There was a front door too, not unlike the back door but on the leeward wall of the building—possibly as a concession by the architects to the bodily temperature of those who preferred to walk in and out. It was opened to our knock by a ghoul decked out with a bloodstained apron and a grin like a mouthful of yellow tombstones. He beckoned us to enter a wide hall, ringed with lecture benches and lighted by a broad skylight that trembled in the gale. The floor was of stone, tilted and furrowed to drain into a large channel at its far end, into which a colleague was casually sluicing away odds and ends that had escaped being stitched back into the last case. Although these sights were arresting in their own special way, it was the smell that made me falter— a smell that fouled the palate for the entire day and which I found to my horror could be duplicated by mixing a grapefruit in milk.

We took our places around a grooved marble table, where lay our patient of yesterday, and one of John Thomson's minions began to expose the contents of her body with grisly expertise. He drew a flowing incision that slit the skin from the suprasternal notch down the mid line to the pubic bone. Then he dug a sharp bistourie through the fat to the costal cartilages, unearthing the heart and lungs, like a grocer lifting pickled eggs from a jar. This was followed by the stomach, the intestines, the kidneys and the bladder. I looked on in a state of impending lunacy. Was this really happening? A snow-covered hillside with heather and rock, and this could have easily been a deer shoot, Thomson's man, the ghillie, gralloching a stag; Grovell and Mr Damwell frowning about like Highland factors, making sure that the best cuts went to the laird and themselves. I could take no more. I shut my eyes and sent my thoughts spinning out of the window but, despite the effort, I could dimly overhear the ghillie muttering,

"Bleeding from varicose veins in the oesophagus; liver hardened. There could have been no hope, you know." And Damwell grunting in bad temper as each finding was revealed. This was someone's wife, someone's mother, someone's sweetheart, and here was this eager necroscopist tying off her last meal with a length of twine at either end of the gut. And to make the insult worse, all her sliced organs were then tipped back into her body cavity, after which the fiend with the graveyard teeth cobbled her up from pubis to neck with black saddler's thread. She was now sufficiently restored to take pride of place at her wake, and relatives, maudlin with grief and whisky, could babble about beauty after death, happily unaware of the unthinkable invasion that had taken place beneath her shroud. If this was the price of medical advance, I vowed I would recover no part in it.

An easy vow when you are well and twenty, and it was all gammon too, for at the first worrisome symptom I would be in a lather, shouting for Professor Home to tell me that I would recover and to cut me or leech me or prescribe any poison that took his fancy. I was twenty and had not yet learned how infirmity makes mock of youthful convictions, which are just ageful bigotries without the wrinkles when all is said and done. The range of careers open to me was now narrowing in an alarming fashion.

I made my responses to the usual litany of alternative occupations, but this time found no solace. I did not know how I would survive my next post mortem. As it turned out I did survive it, and in fact I also survived my second fatal illness. The site of affection had descended somewhat in the body, and I was now about to succumb to some sinister malignancy in the lower bowel. During this terminal complaint I was allowed no time to ponder my imminent doom, for Quentin whisked me off to watch a turn-up in Canongate or, as he persuaded me,

"Come and see if we can waise a guinea on the gentleman of the fist tonight." He was all optimism—indeed when was he not?

We went, and we lost two guineas, but as well as explaining away his misjudgement of the form he told me my malady was not unknown after debauching with red wine of an inferior quality and "some fellahs in the 11th Hussars, don't you know, wecently weturned from Cawnpore, inform me after excessive quantities of hot pilau, chillis and cuwwies of evewy descwiption."

But curries of any description could not have scorched my emotions in more ways than did an urgent message delivered to me at the O'Loan residence one Saturday afternoon while I was dragging some information from Thomson's *Military Basis of Surgical Pathology*.

I recognised the interruption behind my prodigious landlord as Mrs Peddleclap's go-between—a freckled, toothless urchin, short of breath and filthy.

"There's been a wee stramash," he gasped. "Mrs Peddleclap wants you to come at once, sir." This was fame—Physician by Appointment to Mrs Peddleclap's brothel, and I was not yet qualified. I put on my frock coat and, remembering the medical maxim that if you have to run it's too late anyway, I followed him up and down the wynds and closes at a dignified trot.

At Number Four there was a certain degree of agitation. I could see Madame herself gesticulating at three guardians of the law who, with brawny arms, were clutching three struggling women. Mrs Peddleclap was opening and shutting her Waterloo teeth as if uncertain whether to invite the constables in would produce arrest or freedom from the same. I began to feel uneasy for no-one seemed to be ill; then came my shock. The two nearer women I recognised as vinegary dragons from our parish charitable ladies' guild. The third, from the back, had a familiar shape. As she and the constable lurched round I could see it was my betrothed, wrestling like a maniac.

"She says they know you, sir," declared Mrs Peddleclap scornfully. "But I know their kind—just creating a disturbance, so that I would take them in to my house. The streets are the place for the likes of them." Grizel broke free from the constable's restraint and Mrs Peddleclap retreated in fear for her throat.

"I tell you, I'm here to start a benevolent fund for your fallen women," shrieked the minister's daughter.

"That slut," continued the brothel keeper, when she saw she was safe again, "is ruining my good name. It's the Liberton Wynd lock up for her."

I could sympathise with the old bawd for, as with so many of her clients, she was unable to advertise her virtues and depended on word of mouth and an unsmirched reputation for continuing custom.

"Do you understand?" shrieked Grizel. "I want to save your whores."

"That would never do surely," said the withered strumpet. "Where would I be then?" By this time I found my voice.

"I do know her, Mrs Peddleclap. She is not what you think. You can let her go, constables."

"Is it safe, sir—she's a tough yin that."

"Ooh, ooh, ooh," screeched my intended.

"Come with me, Miss MacWrath. I shall look after you," I said reluctantly. They let her go cautiously and stood about, half fearful, half hopeful.

"Come in, constables," cooed Mrs Peddleclap. "We'll make your evening worth while." And she ushered them into her house before slamming the door on the rest of us.

"This is too much this time, Miss MacWrath," I declared sternly. "I demand an explanation for these—these—disgusting cavortings." They were no theatricals. I was just saying what I honestly felt. She was defiant.

"I, that is we," she gestured at her leathery companions, "have just founded our new society, and we were tired of waiting for Father who said he would join us in our journey of mercy. I suppose he couldn't find his way here." And there followed a long rigmarole of justification, which I did not listen to.

By the time she had exhausted the flow, I had escorted them back across the North Bridge where I abandoned them in their hotel. My position was no less uncomfortable than it had been that morning. How long could I survive the insanity of loving one person and shaking on the brink of marriage to someone else. Still, she hadn't mentioned that marriage, and she must have seen that I was not in a mood to be trifled with. At least that was what I thought. I felt I really ought to be telling Mrs Home and her daughter about Grizel, but not just yet.

By Christmas we had become hardened to the daily sight of fever, suppuration, post mortems, and heart-broken relatives. But we did learn how to distinguish inguinal hernia from femoral hernia; how to lance for pus; how to fill abscess cavities with lint; how to set simple fractures and how to behave like surgical gentlemen—when working. What we did away from the wards and out patients was at our discretion, and often indiscretion.

There was unfortunately another side to our surgical training. Surgeon Damwell showed us the craft in practice including the late diagnoses in the post mortem room. The theory was provided by Professor James Russell, a rheumatic relic from the days of the minuet, who sported a red wig, tail coat, knee breeches and black silk stockings. He was the man who had prompted Hatchett to destroy Dr Ball at the meeting of the Royal Medical Society. When I saw him in action I could not believe that he could prompt anyone to do anything, and his cleverest manoeuvre was to yawn while continuing to speak.

He did not owe his appointment to any special talent, although he was well practised in the art of pleasing the mighty. In truth, he owed his appointment to the talent of others—namely, Syme and Liston, whom the Town Council were determined to exclude from the University at all costs. He had the questionable distinction of being the oldest man ever appointed Professor in any University in any part of the world.

He gave his course in the usual precipitous amphitheatre, demonstrating from colourful posters that he had had pinned to a board behind him.

There were huge red arteries pumping against frail silk ligatures, keen-edged knives tracing incisions that the Professor had surely never managed in the flesh, bladder stones as smooth as a pebble on a strand, and leeches clustered like hungry plums on a fevered abdomen. They were the liveliest part of his course.

When thankfully I clambered down from the cliffs of his last lecture, I was now finally convinced that nothing could induce me ever to be a surgeon. The trouble was that I was also now finally convinced that nothing could induce me ever to be a physician either. Quentin had a different kind of problem—the inability to live within his income. Although I had seceded from his moonlight company, I suspected that he had kept it going. I never asked him, but he disappeared sporadically, coming back in the early hours of the morning, jangling gold coins in ragged pockets.

Poor Aeneas in pursuit of opposing chimera did not always share that lunacy of the majority we call 'normal'. It could not be long before the strain of all this landed him in Andrew Duncan's Hospital on the Borough Muir, which had recently replaced the town "Bedlam" for the mentally embarrassed: he had the consolation that in the event of an enforced incarceration he would not be put on display in fetters for the delectation of the mob.

As usual, the answer was a tankard of the foaming, followed by another. I remember our conversation become rapidly philosophical, as it tends to amongst those with no immediate responsibilities and a taste for cakes and ale.

"I wonder," I said, "is there any way that I could use a Medical degree without actually practising medicine, without seeing patients whom I can't cure, in fact without seeing patients at all, for I don't think that I'm well enough to treat anyone else."

"You could become a specialist in Pathology," said Aeneas darkly.

"But you'd still be obliged to see patients. The only diffewence is that they would be dead before you were called in for an opinion. Haw, haw, haw!"

I was beginning to think that Quentin had the full laugh that betrayed the empty mind.

"Seriously though, there must be some way. What if several hospitals, in different towns say, were to be controlled from a central area—Edinburgh, for example. There might be a lucrative sinecure there. You might even get an official residence somewhere—yes, Charlotte Square even. Now that would be quite suitable. You would be able to see what the professors were up to."

"Egad! It would be just like the Army," said Quentin all excited. "Just imagine, official luncheons and dinners, with the best of clawet; spending other people's money, and a knighthood at the end, and," he added, "there would be no danger of being shot either. Why, damn me, I would be pwepared to pawn by vewwy togs for such a post. Haw, haw, haw!"

"It will never happen," I said amused. Quentin thought differently.

"Why, damn me, you're wrong. I can see the system now. You need a doctor administwator, who may find he cannot get up easily at night, who is no good at making his own decisions but finds that he is awfully clever at making other peoples! Yes that's it—haw, haw, haw; and of course an income wising with the amount of interfewence, Haw, haw, haw."

"Ach, you'd just be another time server on the Town Council," glowered Aeneas. "Promises you cannot keep, feathering your nest at the expense of the rate-payers, lies to stay in power. Doing nobody any good except yourself. Ach, it's disgusting. Aye, and you'd need to be glib too, and the only folk I know who are glib are lawyers and ministers."

"On the contwawy, I believe I would find the position charming to a degwee. I would suit me to perfection. I am not a pink of the hard work. I would put the tickle in my wibs, setting the west of you to clean out the Augean stables awound the Woyal Infirmawy. Haw, haw, haw! Sir Quentin Deelatwumpe, K.B. And not a dwop of honest sweat on my bwow. Haw, haw, haw!" Aeneas continued to stare bleakly at his empty tankard.

"Come, Anas. Bwighten up and let's wet the whistle again. You can always be a teacher of Latin if all else fails. Haw, haw haw!"

At this point in my career I had the faintest vision that I was rapidly acquiring information that could only lead me into a state of unemployment. I had seen enough of the professors and their work, and what they had to do to achieve their position, to sicken me of that ambition for life.

Doctoring in the country also carried its problems. It would mean driving about in all weathers at all times of the night in an open trap. Grizel could still change her mind about the necessity of being a University wife though I had noticed her letters had been less frequent than before. And even if Grizel did forego the pleasures of being my wife, Lucy would certainly be forced to do the same by her snobbish father.

As ever, in times of paralysing uncertainty, I sought a judgment of Solomon from Professor Thomson, whither my feet had brought me like a drunken farmer brought home from the fair by his horse.

The overworked scribe in his office told me that the Professor had gone to the Law Courts. I was not surprised, for I generally regarded his office as the start of a trail that might lead anywhere. At the doors of the Law Courts I was stopped by a clerk who said alas the Professor was not there.

"I understand, sir, that he is expected at the College library, hourly." I thanked him, marvelling at his optimism.

Professor Thomson was neither at the College library, nor at the Gladstoneland apothecaries, but I did find him sipping punch in the Oddfellows' Club off the Lawnmarket. He was surrounded by folio parchments and quills and in his hand a closed book; on the wall above his head I saw what I presume was the roll of members, names written upside down as was the custom.

"Ah, my boy," he smiled, shaking the punch out of his head, "I'm due at the Law Courts." He tilted his face to examine his watch through spectacles poised on the tip of his nose, and went on, "Yes, an hour ago—there's still plenty of time." He now altered the angle of his face to gaze at me across the top of his spectacles. "Have a drop of punch." He summoned the waiter to attend to my dry mouth.

I told him my problem, which he heard in his usual fashion, eyes closed, head nodding, with the occasional pursing of his lips, a technique no doubt acquired at his many committee meetings, which could certainly have passed for keen attention.

"Well, you must decide what you want to do," he said sagely.

"I know that, Uncle John. That's why I'm here." He sat up, now quite awake, seeing my dilemma with the clarity of thought that had taken him where he was with so little actual work. He looked at me again over his glasses.

"You don't want to be a country doctor because you think it's not grand enough to let you ask for the hand of Professor Home's daughter. How he ever produced so nice a daughter I shall never know. You therefore want to be a great success in Edinburgh, though it would seem you have your doubts about that too. But if you are, you would feel obliged to marry Miss MacWrath. Is that so?" His face disappeared into his glass for a second or two, then he was at me again.

"How is your campaign to avoid Miss MacWrath progressing, by the bye?"

"Disastrous."

"Aye," he said, I felt a trifle smugly. "Your affair in the brothel caused a good deal of merriment, I might tell you." Which affair was he referring to? But he was going on,

"It's a fearful thing when you find yourself damned by the folly of your own careless actions, and then stepping into traps of your own devising." He was beginning at this stage to sound horribly like someone I knew well, and he was not done yet.

"He that steppeth up to the alter may make an unhappy wife, but he that steppeth away may be happy for ever, and so may she. Have you ever considered that?" Of course I had not.

"There's a lot of things you haven't considered." He scratched his forehead wryly. "Have you ever thought, for example, what it entails to be a success in the big city? You give away your best years in penury, struggling, carrying out work you don't want to do, for which your professor will claim the credit. That's not all. To get a chair you have to keep in with the Town Council. You will yawn with boredom at committees composed entirely of monkeys, who don't know how to speak or how to stop speaking. You dare not be wrong in public and if you are, you must make sure that the blame goes elsewhere. Aye, aye,

aye. A sad business it is. And when you get the professorship you have been dreaming of you'll be too old to enjoy it. You will speak only to people who drive a close carriage like yourself. Phaetons and gigs are all very well for your son and his smart friends and you'll have to pay for it all and provide a dowry for your daughter commensurate with your style. Oh, dear dear," and down went his chin in that droll way he had.

"But Uncle John, you seem to have thriven on it."

"Ah well that's true, but I've always specialised in subjects that no-one else can catch me out on." The punch always freed his tongue in a way that he tended to regret later.

"You see, Surgical Pathology is now hotching with young brutes who know a hundred times more than I do. Though that's one fact they doubtless are not conversant with yet. It's time for a change for me. Rumour whispers that the Professor of Medical Jurisprudence—you know—Christison, is not too well. The Town Council want to be prepared for any sad eventuality and think I am their man. So I have just been reading a few books on the Law this last month because they will expect me to know something of the matter. Mind you, I had them all round to dinner last week." A rueful head shake dispelled the memory of the cost in coin and the boredom of that evening.

"You must find it hard entertaining without a wife, Uncle John," said I all innocent.

"Well, er," said he inscrutably, "I have attended to that. I'm told the Professor of Medical Jurisprudence is better with a wife." He quizzed me over his spectacles briefly and a faint smile played around his lip corners. "I have therefore succumbed to Cupid's little darts, and I am pleased to say my suit for the hand of Miss Grizel MacWrath has been favourably received by her father." His ghost of a smile became now a full one.

So perverse is humanity, I was angry with him for having succumbed to her dowry, which I am sure he had nosed out long before Mr Dunsome had read the will. And here was this scholarly wag, not at all put out at the prospect of tying himself to a gorgon, who had driven me to the doors of the madhouse. And my reluctance to marry her seemed to cause him some amusement; it also touched his sympathy.

I tried to recall his last words exactly. What was it he had said? "Go and tell that old clown Home." Yes, that was what he said, "Go and tell that old clown Home that you want to marry his daughter and see what he says." And so I would have, had the Professor of Botany not got in the way.

136

12

While striding along the main thoroughfares of Medicine and Surgery, we had to take a serious stroll into less trodden pathways, like Chemistry, where exciting new elements like iodine were being discovered daily; or like Botany, which was still struggling against the rigid classification forced on it by the obsessive Swede, Linnaeus; or Materia Medica, which hopefully translated all these brilliant discoveries into healing balms. We were taught how to roll pills, to smash solid drugs with mortar and pestle, to dispense unguents in oyster-shells and to write expensive prescriptions in Latin, at great length too; this was important for fees could rise with the classical fluency of our recommendations.

The great impedimenta of the dark eighteenth century were yielding to our modern advances. Chemists had already convinced all but the most bigoted that the vital life force that held animal and plant life together did not enjoy a rarified haven exempt from the laws of Physics and Chemistry; that blood was pumped round the body for a reason and not just to give the heart something to do.

In the chemistry laboratories, learned and eager men shared with us the elements of their art, and we re-lived those exciting moments of first discovery—watching the contents of separate bottles giving birth to, say, Oil of Vitriol, behind a sinister smoke screen. The physiologists taught us of an instrument devised by James Currie to measure if a patient was too hot. We heard how consumptive ulcers of the lung might be healed with inhalations of hydrogen or decoctions of hemlock and myrrh or might disappear spontaneously, following pregnancy or an attack of mania.

Sadly in Botany, we re-lived and learned nothing. The field was rich and new to be sure, and the heathland around our town overgrew with potential therapeutic agents, from which the chemists had taught us to make aqueous and alcoholic extracts—foxgloves for the dropsy and male fern for the tapeworm. The real problem was the Professor of Botany himself—Adrian Mucklequhair, whose staggering altitude pushed his elegant head almost into another world and it belonged there.

But it was not always so. Mucklequhair had been the youngest and brightest man ever to hold a chair in Edinburgh. Indeed, so appropriate were his qualities, that some cynics wondered why the Town Council had ever appointed him in the first place. In Germany, he collaborated with Runge to extract caffeine from the coffee bean and had been quick to recognize it as the "foul enemy of sleep and other nocturnal activities." He reorganized the town's Botanic Garden and for some years, his course of lectures in Botany used to seduce truants even from the classes of Dr Knox. But when it was our turn to study plants, things changed.

The trouble was not lack of brains but rather too many, his curiosity bubbled beyond the confines of herbs and flowers and before long we knew that there was more than simple curiosity at work.

He was a strange man of many talents. In his hands the fiddle could pour out honeyed music that had brought him weekend invitations from all the important houses in the Lothians. He gave his lectures in English or Latin or Greek, whatever mood took him.

These moods were the clue to his behaviour. He now seemed to spend his life on a large wheel. At the bottom of the cycle, he would retire to his house and bow endless dirges on his violin, or just look out of the window. At the top, his whole being was consumed in a furnace of furious activity. If he went to bed at all, he was up again at four of the morning, writing concerti for three violins and two orchestras before luncheon. In the afternoons he would be up slaughtering more pheasants than anyone else on a shoot. The evenings he would devote to dining, singing, carousing and visiting, and when his family and friends had finally collapsed, he would while away the time designing tartans.

Any attempt at teaching took place late in the morning—about five of the clock. When the notion was on him he could usually cover the entire course in a morning. Nature rambles turned into frenzied cavalry charges, with Mucklequhair filling his specimen satchel at a fast gallop. Indeed, when Quentin had brought the equestrian comparison to his notice, he arrived at our next ramble with a cavalry bugle, from which he produced a wild and insistent braying.

"Over the bank lads," he shouted while the entire class thundered into a hidden ditch of uncommon depth and width.

"As well we're not clad like Scotsmen," observed Quentin dragging himself in some discomfort and disarray from a thick tangle of nettles and thistles.

"Ah, the nettle—a curious plant," declared the professor gazing down upon us like Beowulf into a pit of foul trolls." A curious plant," he repeated, "armed with fine and feathery needles of a rare acid to protect her person against coarse and unlettered marauders; to motect her cerson from moarse unmettered parauders; to cotect her merson from . . ."

With half my mind on the dock leaf that folklore falsely proclaims as a sovereign cure for nettle stings and the other half on the stings themselves, I lost the thread of his ode but I did think at the time that there might be something wrong with our lofty poet. So did the light dragoon whose life in the mess had given him an unparalleled experience in the recognition of madmen.

And so did others in our well exercised year for about midway through term, after two dawn lecturers, another country scamper and a string trio, the class geniuses, Charles Darwin and Dominic Corrigan, decided that they had had enough. On their own initiative they wrote to the Town Council and complained about the professor.

The Town Council were not pleased at all and there was a prolonged exchange of sharp letters. They refused to believe that Professor Mucklequhair was failing to measure up to their expectations which was reasonable given his earlier reputation. The student rumble grew louder, and the *Caledonian Mercury* carried menacing though vague reports of student unrest in the capital.

Meanwhile Mucklequhair's wheel suddenly swung over its summit, and down the other side. He was heard in the front room of his home playing a funeral hymn for solo violin, but no-one saw him for three weeks. Some agitator arranged an inflammatory meeting of students to discuss what action we might take over the professor. I arrived full of optimistic enthusiasm, but witnessed what the passing years have sadly shown to me to be the standard performance of doctors in conference.

Something that has always baffled me about medical men is their genius for disagreement. When it comes to the haemorrhoidal flux, a physician might agree that his own recommendation for a cold bath is right. He may also agree that the infusion of oak bark recommended by a colleague is wrong, though he would not say that in public. But ask fifty doctors to realise that today is not yesterday and you will get fifty different opinions. I have no doubt that an agitated meeting was called when the Town Council threatened the Barber Surgeons with an end to their ancient privilege to make and market one annual gallon of whisky. There would be suggestions:

"We must take care not to press this too vigorously lest they think us not gentlemen."

"Were that not in doubt, there would have been no threats to start with."

And so on, with an occasional bleating,

"nobody spoke like this when I was a lad."

Then they would emerge from their full and frank exchange of views to find their still already confiscated.

Our students had nothing to learn when we debated our course of action. Some wanted Mucklequhair run out of town; some wanted the

Town Council; some wanted both; some wanted neither. Whatever, they all discoursed at length with a remarkable blend of irrelevance and self deception.

Our assembly poured out into the street, muttering and rumbling fire and brimstone. The debate continued in the sunshine. Little clusters of agreement formed into special cliques—confronting each other with shared convictions.

I almost felt confident, listening to all the bluster of rebellion and insurrection, until we heard one day that the Town Council was prepared to meet us. At once we called another revolutionary council to decide who should meet them. The bluster gave way to a whimper. From all sides I heard,

"Perhaps we've been too hasty," or

"I rather enjoy music while I study," or

"I don't really mind getting out of bed at five o'clock of the morning."

Without ever knowing a summer our budding insurgents vanished, like wrinkled leaves before an autumn gale, leaving as spokesmen Darwin, Corrigan and me. Quentin had romantic business to attend to, and Aeneas, reasonably enough, felt he had too much in common with Professor Mucklequhair to complain.

When I had time to think about what we proposed to do, I knew I had blundered again, nailing myself to a cross of my own making, for the benefit of others who were lukewarm enough or wise enough not to kick against the authorities before they were in a strong enough position to do it safely; and then they wouldn't know whom they could kick safely. As John Thomson always enjoyed telling me in the presence of our parish minister,

"If it's martyrdom you're after, laddie, you will always find someone with a cause he wants you to die for. Then when you've rotted away on the gibbet, there he'll be, headside down and backside up before the king for the wee tap on the shoulder. Is not that right, Mr MacWrath?"

If I believed John Thomson was right I also believed Mucklequhair was deranged, but as the day of our meeting approached I was not so sure that I believed so much that I wanted to destroy myself to prove it. After all, Mucklequhair was nothing to me. His botanical parades would last only a term, when all was said and done, and moorland scampers at five o'clock of the morning with a lunatic professor would always make for an amusing after-dinner tale to drink over—like Father with his leg.

Lucy knew that something was going on. I had not the courage to tell her and she had the grace not to ask. However my little idylls could not delay the circling clock. The day of our appointment arrived.

We met where students always meet, and took what courage we could

140

from the familiar containers. Then we walked up to the Parliament buildings to meet a committee of City Fathers. We were breathless by the time we climbed from the Cowgate. A flunkey showed us into a large hall, where we were kept waiting for thirty minutes or so. It was the usual Scots baronial, with high mullioned windows criss-crossed with lead chevrons. There was no fire in the grate, God knows we could have done with it. From time to time officials rushed about on important business.

Suddenly we were called into another hall. This was decorated along the lines of the first one, though the roof was more vaulted and the walls set farther apart. It was equally cold. In the centre stood a large table, at which sat four of the City Fathers. I have no doubt that Deacon Brodie himself had frightened plaintiffs from behind that selfsame table, before the gallows had done for him.

The City Fathers seemed to have assembled their most daunting quarter for the occasion. The spokesman, Bailie Flaytess, larger than the other three, addressed our representatives from a curious orifice that at first glance appeared to be his nose. His head was egg-shaped, and I suddenly saw that the expanse where his mouth ought to have been, was in fact all chin. Two rheumy eyes glowered at us from his forehead, which itself was saved from further embarrassment by a total absence of hair.

Beside, fidgeted a smaller version of himself, a man of little features; little ears, little eyes, little mouth and little sprouts of hair that had escaped his razor; a man beaten by life and already acknowledging it. His role was to repeat everything that Flaytess said. The central pair were flanked by what Darwin took to be two Gibralter apes in official garb.

"Well, after all," he said later, "the prognathous jaw and the angle between the face and the brow clearly indicated that they belonged to the anthropomorpha."

Flaytess opened fire first. He tried first to out-stare us, and we just stared back silently.

"Well, er, gentlemen," he began, with a faint sneer at the title. "We hear ye're no' happy wi' the way we run oor University."

"There is one particular problem," Corrigan was quick to counter.

"Dinna quibble, sir—ye're here tae complain", said Bailie Flaytess.

"Dinna you dare quibble," said the unshaven assistant.

"We feel we have just reason, sir." Darwin took up the theme now.

"Spell it oot, then," said Flaytess testily.

"He says 'Spell it oot'", said the echo. The two apes said nothing.

Darwin told them the story—rather confidently, I thought. Flaytess heard him out impatiently, then began his attack again.

"Ye're ungrateful laddies. Ye should be thankfu' that he shifts himself enough tae gie ye sae comprehensive a course in sae short a time."

Corrigan replied before the echo had time to translate these remarks into even more unintelligible language.

"But, sir, the Botany course lasts for a term. He gave it all in a morning, and at five o'clock too."

Five o'clock ye say—a verra healthful hour. Many's the time I've got oot o' my bed at five of the clock. I never gied it a second thought."

"Ahah," I said to myself, "when did you give anything a first thought, except perhaps your own advancement?" Luckily I was not called upon to say it to anyone else for Corrigan was following up fast. He said,

"I realise that Medicine is a liberal profession sure enough, but we do not feel Botany is learned best to music."

"I disagree," grunted the egg shaped bailie.

"Bailie Flaytess disagrees," said the minion.

"Ye should consider yerselves fortunate to have sae talented a man as a teacher. Just imagine, instruction in leaves and stems and at the same time lovely music on strings and flute. I never had music played tae me when I was a laddie," he finished tearfully. "But listen tae me," said he, suddenly all friendly, "What can we dae tae accomodate yer complaints. There must be some wee manipulation tae make ye all happy—uhuh, aye, uhuh—there's aye the possibility of another faculty."

"He says ye can git oot o' here."

"I said naething o' the sort, Bailie McCrawle. I was merely beginning a speculation when ye interrupted me. As I was saying, before this wee brute here opened his gab, it would be criminally prodigal not tae make use of Mr Mucklequhair's undenied talents, noo that we have paid for them, if ye follow me. Supposing noo we were tae persuade the mercers and haberdashers and tailors of the city to found a chair in Highland Studies. Yer man's aye warping and woofing wi' coloured threads and the tartans right popular since his Majesty, God bless him, so graciously covered his hurdies wi' sae much of it."

He stopped and preened himself, piqued with his little whimsy before giving his imagination the bridle.

"And if they wouldna bite we might use oor influence at St James tae have him made Royal musician in Scotland, at the disposal o' the Town Council when the King is no' in residence of course, tae compose holy cantatas and sacred oratories; or he could pen Latin couplets and wee sonnets for the Faculty of Arts. The possibilities are boundless and as varied as the man himself. What a prodigious brain he must have."

He leaned over on the table towards us, arms stretched, fists clenched, face awrinkle with smiles. I could see that Bailie Flaytess was not the man to neglect any opportunity for changes that might make change needless.

"But ye see," he declared with his faint air of conspiracy," ye might as well hold on tae yer botanical troobadoor; his replacement could be worse. Ye know—professors are an unco' strange breed o' men!"

So ended our tilt with the authorities. And perhaps it did not end there, for I had the slightest suspicion that the whimsical bailie would make sure our subsequent careers would be as hard as it was in his power to make them.

As we struggled back to the Cowgate my dominant thought, I am ashamed to say it, was what Professor Home might think of me. Would he regard my involvement as evidence of dangerous revolutionary trends and part of a general contempt for all professors. I was becoming grisled enough in my dealings to realise that such a view was reasonable, especially if your name was Professor Home. I worried, and I continued to worry, and I worried none the less when an invitation to dine at Charlotte Square arrived the next day. At any other time I would have been pleased to join the Homes for an evening; this time was different. The dust from our brush with the Town Council must have tickled the Home nose into a disapproving wrinkle by now.

I rang the bell with some trepidation and even their jocose butler failed to raise a flicker of joy in me. It is funny, when you have your peepers open for trouble, you tend to see trouble everywhere. In the drawing-room Lucy smiled at me as she always did, but I wondered if she was unhappy about something. Mrs Home beamed graciously, as was her wont, but was she rather less gracious than she had been last time? It was impossible to tell with the Professor. He never looked at ease, even with himself.

The evening passed. We chatted about this, and we prattled about that; the grand aunt prowled about with her ivory counters. Lucy sang *Flow gently, sweet Afton,* and her father asked testily why she never sang a Scots song. It was on the surface a normal evening at Charlotte Square. Yet I felt a nameless apprehension. The meal passed too, and when the port arrived the ladies retired. Surely now the Professor would express his displeasure and ban me for ever from his house and the society of his daughter.

He made a great ritual of passing the decanter clockwise. Only he could have managed that with just two people at the table. But at least he did not knock it over. I took this as a bad omen. He sipped his port and smiled and sipped it again. Why could the old ram not come to the point? He did, in his usual circumlocutory fashion.

"I hear there has been—um—ah—certain difference of opinion over the Professor of Botany—acrimonious disagreement, if you prefer it so." He wiped some stray port off his waistcoat front with a stained napkin.

What could I do but say,

"Yes, there has been, sir. It has all been very embarrassing. I hope you do not deem it a personal attack on the status and title of Professor."

He emptied his glass, this time into his mouth, and said surprisingly,

"No, not at all. In fact, I would have liked to have led the attack myself, but you realise it is difficult—a source of some unease, you might put it—for one Professor to attack another, although I know Gregory did so once, and with a walking stick too." He sighed, almost wistfully, and filled his glass again. I followed his lead, and agreed that this was true.

"I had trouble with Mr Mucklequhair when I was in the chair of Materia Medica. Do you know, I asked him to lay out a private botanic garden, for myself, behind our house, you understand. Well, he did so. He arrived with several cartloads of plants and shrubs, and he told me that he had arranged them chromatically—that is, I take it, according to colour."

"It might have been a musical allusion, sir," I ventured.

"Of course. That would explain it," said the Professor. "I could never bear to look at that garden, and could not have managed even a potful of broom tea from it. It even sounded unpleasant," he added doubtfully, still abraded by the memory, "when ruffled by the wind you understand."

I was beginning to enjoy my port now. The Professor resumed his sad tale.

"We, in fact—that is, the professors in the University—advised the Town Council—counselled them, some might have said—not to appoint Mr Mucklequhair. We considered his was too lively a mind to be properly academic. But what can you expect when you fill a Chair? It is never different. You know, I think professors are an uncommon strange breed of men, do you not so think too?"

Well, I did and so did his daughter but I wasn't going to raise his ire by agreeing with him. The day after, events, as the books say, moved rapidly to a climax. We were called to a five o'clock lecture, which, for some bizarre reason, the whole class attended. Mucklequhair was already prancing about in a lilac cape. He held a ream of foolscap in his right hand, and a music stand in his left. If anything, he looked even more fevered than normal.

"I have something new for you today, gentlemen. I wrote this last night after dinner." He began to read to us his latest masterpiece—a comprehensive course of Botany in rhyming couplets, and as a sop to us, because we were medical students, he had added a section on Materia Medica as well. It ran:

"Thrice the learned sage hath mewed,
Thrice the student body spewed,
Round the Borough Muir we go
In search of Senna, Aloes, Sloe,
To make decoctions sweet and rare,
That charm the bowel from blocked despair.
And Syrupi Extracta Tincturae
Will all our ghastly ills allay.
But our noble Botany
Will only bring us obloquay,
Unless we find the genus 'neath the cloak
Of Jerusalem artichoke.
Root, bulb, rhizome, corm,
Providing food in time of storm,
That feeds the stem and leaves in all,
Despite the snowflake's heavy fall.
Greater burdock, buttercup,
Otto Brumfeld Vinder Nupp.
Stamens, petals, forms sublime,
Scents to make us fell divine . . ."

So it went on for twenty sheets of foolscap, and if a rhyme or a rhythm
failed, he would put in a Latin word or a Greek word, or one of his own
devising. It was a formidable document. And that was not all. He had set
it to music—scoring the piece for three tenors, two baritones, flutes and
violas.

"Now I would like you all to come to the Lecture Room after we break
our fast for our first rehearsal, when we will select the best voices
amongst you. I cannot believe that we cannot produce from such a
talented group of men tenors worthy of *Die Zauberflöte,* or baritones
who might appear with distinction in *The Messiah,* not to mention all
these exciting fragments by Glück, Hummel, Grétry or Paisiello".

He sprakled and gabbled and prattled, inventing words as he went
along. He was still in full voice when Quentin said to me,

"I can't tolewate any more of this. Let's toddle now. Come on."

Others had come to the same conclusion, and were already beginning
to shuffle out of the hall. Sheep-like, the rest followed. We peeped back
through the door and marvelled that Mucklequhair was still outlining
his new plans for our class for the next term, and not a soul of them was
remaining.

Into the pale April sunshine we rushed. Small mutinous groups had
formed around our two ringleaders. Now that I was not going to be
expelled from Charlotte Square I played my role of third ringleader with
great exuberance and verve. The Professor's lunacy was now so clearly

established that I was sure no-one would dispute it with us and in any case there was no-one important about at that time of the morning who might have noted down my unseemly militance.

As it was, these warlike threats all proved unnecessary, for shortly after the appearance of his metrical variations on a theme by Linnaeus, Mucklequhair's mind took flight on wings of poesy, to lute accompaniment and never came back to earth. He was invited to stay for an indefinite period in Andrew Duncan's hospital, where he created forty-five further oratorios on subjects diverse and miraculous. As a final irony on the Mucklequhair legend, I would now lay a groat or two that his teachings still remain with us all long after Professor Monroe's fabled remarks have been buried with his subjects.

13

Students exposed to the caustic of Surgery and Medicine develop a hard face to our exit from this world. They see the young and the old sinking quietly or violently into the grave, and accept the sad inevitability of it all. And at least in the short term, they know where their former patients have gone. Where they came from in the first place is something else. It is a mystery that excites the fancy of everyone from the moment they begin to think.

I had shown as much curiosity as the rest over my origins, and was assured that I had been laid under a berry bush at the foot of our garden by a passing stork. When my brother was on the way I accepted these confident, if coy, explanations at their face value. I ascribed my mother's increasing girth to gluttony. As for the screams at her confinement, when I was banned from the room I assumed that she was giving exact instructions to the stork, which would no doubt be circling round the garden just at that time.

The years passed, and if our own family did not increase, that of Farmer Grumbell's cows did. As I became older still, I watched, and finally helped, to drag kicking, slippery little calves into the world from suffering dilated cows. It would be about this point in my life that the stork and berry bush theory became untenable, but I suppressed the logical comparison between calves and me. Then I saw Farmer Grumbell's bull, Jock, in action, and a fierce sight it was. The bull's determined exuberance was baffling, and when Grumbell, a coarse rustic in nicky tams and a fustian coat, laughingly encouraged his bull,

"Aye, Jock, ye're a braw lad. Ye're aye payin' fer yer keep," the bafflement only increased.

Sandy Leer provided the next link in the chain of my sexual instruction. Sandy Leer, a precocious Adonis, whose father was the town butcher, was the class bad boy at Beattie's School. He was the first boy of my age to shave, and he told us things about himself and his mother's kitchen-maid that struck a chord in my memory over the bull Jock. He even carried his knowledge with great daring into Beattie's history lesson. Beattie was a scholarly giant with a taste for rhetoric and a long cane for discipline. The exact details escape me now, but I recall he was giving us the benefit of his scholarship on the great issues that brought Charles I into conflict with Cromwell and Parliament.

"Now where," he said expectantly, "do you think sovereignty lies?" In a flash came Sandy in an unnatural stage whisper.

"Between the thighs of the Queen." And he was only fourteen years old too.

Beattie went white, then he went red, then he picked up his cudgel with savage intent. It was a day I shall never forget.

From that moment Sandy Leer went the way of all class bad boys— banned by every parent as a foul influence, and sought out by every child as a source of otherwise unobtainable information. He also lent me a copy of *Moll Flanders,* which was on the Reverend MacWrath's proscribed book list.

The Reverend Gideon was not one to miss the chance of a meal and a sermon over Sandy Leer's exposure. He came over to our house one Thursday evening—I think it was some two or three days after the scene in the classroom—certainly it was the same week. I watched him stride up our path, a present day reincarnation of saintly fortitude. I was not very clever that day, else I would have reckoned on the Achilles heel of his stomach, and controlled my trembling; as it was, I could have done anyway without his lengthy homilies on pitfalls, lust and his own holiness.

He settled comfortably in the parlour in Father's favourite chair. He thanked my mother for the whisky, but no—he would have it later. No doubt the old fraud would need it after he had finished with me. He spoke affably enough, edging gently towards my association with Sandy Leer.

"Did you enjoy reading that—that book?" he asked.

"Yes, sir."

He made a sudden start forwards, and I thought he would choke.

"What! You mean you did not sense its innate filth?"

It seemed an unreasonable view to me, but he was not to be gainsaid. Indeed he was not to be stopped. He fixed me with his emaciated sincere look.

"You must realise, laddie," he said, "the Devil is at work in all these acts of fornication."

"What is fornication, sir?"

"Illicit carnal connection," he said quickly. I was none the wiser. Sandy Leer had given it another far more expressive name. Instead I asked another question. "Is the Devil working in Farmer Grumbell's bull, sir?"

"Now for why would you be comparing us to the lower animals? But yes, the Devil is at work in Farmer Grumbell's bull too."

"But God made the bull, sir, did he not?"

"Indeed he did—no-one can dispute that!"

"I had a good look at the bull, sir, and I found great similarities between it and me. I mean in the . . . I mean, well, I mean, well, surely it's like you too, sir."

"Aaargh." The Reverend Gideon clutched his throat and eased his neckcloth. The comparison with a lecherous bull for once paralysed his speech, but he soon recovered.

"Aaargh. You're even more polluted than I had thought. You will be telling me next that you've been—ah—ah—experimenting with the—um—ah—apparatus." He paused as if searching my face for some sign or other, which he seemed to have found, for all of a sudden he began to tremble and clasp and unclasp his hands. Finally he found words.

"No. Don't tell me. Do not tell me. You have. It cannot be. But it is. It is true—you evil boy. Aaargh. You are defiled beyond recall. It behoves me to remind you that the retribution for the sin of Onan is swift and sure and well deserved. The eyes glaze over, the tongue swells, the lips go slack, the mind coarsens to the level of God-given insanity. Oh, may the Lord protect you from these dire consequences, and from his just rage."

He said a good deal more in the same vein, and had I not known him for a squalid glutton, I would have begun searching in earnest for all the signs of the Onanous blight that he had threatened me with.

He skipped quickly back into 1819 after his eloquent Old Testament travels, took my mother's offer of whisky, and left a book for my father's edification—"De Signis Manustuprantioris Certioribus"—it was a treatise of infallible signs for recognising self-abusers. He made the obvious gesture of leaving it where I should see it, and no doubt read it to my benefit. He then gobbled and drank his way through the remainder of his visit and strode home with a step less sure than that with which he had arrived. I heard him mutter to himself, "a rift in the hump is worth two in the thrapple", and he demonstrated loudly to himself (he thought) the pleasures of both.

My father, returning from the real world without, actually laughed as he glanced through the Reverend MacWrath's gift.

"What a canting imposter he is," chuckled my father, leafing through the volume. The sound of his laughter reassured me, not only for its lack of gravity, but for the fact that I could still hear it. My eyes seemed to be intact as well.

"The Reverend MacWrath," went on Father, "you will recognise, selects carefully where he directs the anger of God. You will notice the good Lord is never called upon to interfere with his healthy appetite. I would hazard a guess, what was the word he used—apparatus? Yes, I would wager his apparatus has never bothered him much, so he can resist it the more easily. You likened him to a bull, did you? Ha ha! He should have been flattered—perhaps he was." I survived the Reverend Gideon's warnings, and my own experiments.

These dramatic episodes now came flooding back to me as I was starting out on our course of Midwifery. Only recently had this study become obligatory. This had been a curious freedom of choice, considering how regularly babies came into the world.

The explanation perhaps lay in history, for there was, and still is, a vast army of female midwives who bring their practical wisdom into the delivery room. Men were considered unsavoury there, or at least unnecessary—that was until Hugh Chamberlen invented a forceps for pulling the baby from its cosy womb into the cold world. These large curved head-forks at once gave men an instrument not only for levering the baby out, but for levering themselves up into the medical hierarchy. Their titles changed from men midwives to gentlemen accoucheurs, and when one of their society was chosen to deliver Louise de la Vallière, their status was permanently assured.

Edinburgh was justly proud of its senior gentleman accoucheur, Professor James Hamilton. In his field he was supreme. His views were quoted over the whole of Britain. His patients, private or charity, received his undivided attention; his opinion was sought everywhere, and if it was not sought, he had a tendency to give it anyway; and if it was not listened to, he had a tendency to anger. This anger was not limited to a spurned opinion. It could boil and bubble even when his opinion was accepted. It frothed into his relations with his staff at the University, and it was only their lethargy that spared his back from their walking sticks as well. Despite it all, he was still a great teacher.

Although his inclination lay towards bickering and wrangling, the wrangling was used to collect money to build up a service that made sure that no married woman in any part of Edinburgh need deliver her baby alone. If the promise of a gilt memorial failed to separate a skinflint from his donation, a few irate threats usually made certain of the gift. He could sense benefactors like a ferret senses a rabbit, and he unearthed them with the same ferocity. The result was a separate Lying-in Hospital off Brown Square—named after a merchant banker; a midwives' teaching school named after the Guild of Builders; and a collection of midwives' bags named after the Inveresk Hunt.

The course followed the usual pattern—lectures, demonstrations, visits to the lying-in wards, visits to the private houses with one of his midwives.

This devoted band of women swarmed all over the city delivering any baby they could find, offering spiritual help if things went wrong, and a suitable catalogue of names if things went well. The French called them "wise women", as though the remainder were anything but, and a nation's heritage of folklore rested on their keeping. They could advise infusions of mugwort, briony and penny royal for the infertile, more secret remedies for the over-fertile, and when these latter failed, there was slippery elm or a fall off the mantlepiece to make everybody happy again.

There were even wiser women who offered physically to ease the sorrows of an illicit love, but these added manoeuvres usually ended in painful fever, and sometimes death.

The Professor drilled his midwives like an army. In fact the first time we saw him, he was inspecting a detachment in the foyer of his lying-in wards. Quentin was most impressed.

"Give them muskets, and they could pawade down the Esplanade quite the thing. Haw, haw, haw!"

They didn't of course carry muskets, but they did carry midwives bags stuffed with lint, scissors, twine and needles and linen thread to tie off the cord and to sew up any tears in the birth canal. From this formidable band I remember two especially, Annie Paynes and Aggie Dulliver. Annie was a tall grey angular woman, whose view of life was just about the same. She regarded all men as barbarous beasts, who violated her mothers in search of their own gratification. To conceive, she felt, was a fall from a state of grace and it took me several weeks to realise that when she talked of her mothers' falling, she meant pregnant and not down the stairs. Her eyes rarely opened fully; she either looked to heaven or at her feet, and was never known at any time to smile.

By contrast Aggie Dulliver was fat and jovial, and her whole being and diet seemed to consist entirely of dumplings. She tolerated everyone, even Annie, and found a reason to excuse everyone's failings, regarding us medical students as possibly human and not merely drunken brutes whose brains were consumed with lust when not confused with strong drink.

None the less it was a relatively happy study. For the first time we seemed concerned with assisting the relentless role of nature instead of deflecting it.

Like Russell, Professor Hamilton illustrated his disquisitions with colourful illustrations. I looked in wonder at coy little babies, curled up in snug, protective wombs, and marvelled where all the arms and legs went. He showed us other pictures of the baby leaving the womb on its perilous journey into the delivery room.

"If the wee bebby comes doon with the head first, we ca' that a vertex birth, and generally the back surface of the head is the surface that looks

151

up at ye when ye're huddin' it back." While we were absorbing this information, he went on.

"If the backside of the bebby comes doon, we ca' that a breech birth."

It became clear after some weeks of this that babies did not always want to be born. They sometimes lay athwart the uterus like the diagonal of a St Andrew's cross, or occasionally the head would stick sideways. In these situations it required more than even the Professor had to offer to persuade them to unstick. As the birth postures became more unreal and fearful, so did he become more and more excited, and he kept this exuberance going for the entire lecture course.

If the head threatened to obstruct the birth canal, you could pull down the feet, "podalic version" he called it. If it was an arm presenting, you put it back where it came from, then pulled down the feet. He told us how to foretell the baby's position by tracing its back through the abdominal wall, and how to tell whether a head or a breech was presenting by groping for the baby directly. Whether this manoeuvre told you anything about the baby or not (my fingers never became sufficiently educated) it certainly gave you skill with your hands in a confined space, and it also gave you time to think what to do next.

We learned to take rhythmic contractions seriously, especially with the waters broken, but to take our time over those colicky twinges, which sent everyone into hysterics but left the baby where it was. At this point he expatiated on how long a woman should be allowed to labour. There was a non-intervention school—all men—who thought nothing of letting deliveries go on indefinitely, for they believed in the godly virtues of a natural unassisted delivery. This school lost the Royal patronage and all of its reputation, when Sir Richard Croft allowed George IV's daughter to labour to death. After two fruitless days, a dead child was born, but the afterbirth was not. Port wine was prescribed and Princess Charlotte died, but not before telling her confidants that Sir Richard had made her tipsy. Not belonging to this school, Professor Hamilton felt that labour should be hurried along, as one with his peppery personality reasonably would.

Towards the end of the course, he then turned to happier topics, and for comparison he began to show us illustrations from the History of Midwifery from an ancient Mediaeval text—*The Woman's Boke* by Thomas Raynold. This showed delightful curly-headed manikins prancing about in a large uterus like dwarfs playing in a balloon. Had they been in any way accurate, the profession of midwives would never have happened at all. These ready-made adults could have stepped out into the world without a forceps intervention and certainly without a podalic version, since they were pointing that way anyway.

As June followed May, so did manipulated deliveries follow natural deliveries. Like a magician he produced his forceps from a dark bag. He glowered at us for a second, and then said,

"These blades, in the wrong hands, are a diabolical instrument." He left no doubt that he did not include his hands in this group. "Ye would dae well tae remember the remarks of William Hunter, not that all his remarks were worth such conseederation. He said that it was a thousand pities that they had ever been invented, and if ye're imaginin' by noo that our new century has brought us to the pinnacle of knowledge, then I would counsel ye to read this document, an extract from Raynold's book on the sewing up of a torn birth canal. We read,

"After replacing the uterus, and washing the wound with wine and butter, the midwife is instructed to 'sowe togeder yat pece that is broken with a silken threde with a quarell needle in thre places or in foure and sithen do pitche on a softe lynnen cloth and leye it to ye prevy membres. After this operation the woman is to be kept in bed seven to nine days, to eat and drink little and to avoid cold or anything which might make her cough."

"And that was written three hundred years ago," he yelped. "There are some who would like tae forget the past tae impose new fangled notions upon us. That new hearing tube they call a stethoscope; I believe they are now employing it in France tae listen tae the bebby's heart. This means placing your ear near the belly of a naked woman. Now this may be all very well for people like the French but no' for us. I therefore will not countenance its practice—I conseeder it indecent and therefore unnecessary."

Unlike Professor Russell, he was quite happy to put his theories to the test, and he took us frequently to witness live demonstrations of his illustrations. We went to the Delivery Room in the Brown Square Hospital. This was an open, airy chamber. In the centre lay a high bed with two pillars at either side, curved at the top like rams' horns—the Professor's own innovation.

Babies had hitherto been welcomed out with mother lying on her side. Hamilton's sense of propriety had been outraged by his discovery that babies arrived more easily with mother on her back. However, with a characteristic flash of casuistry, he resolved the dilemma by tying their feet up off the bed.

Scattered around the room were various trollies containing basins and instruments, and in the corner was a little crib to take the new-born baby.

"He forgot to add the smell to his dwawings," said a voice in my ear. This was true enough, but the lack was in the drawings. In a brief space of time I came to like the warm sticky smell of mothers and babies, and could have told that I was in a Delivery Room with my eyes blindfold.

The Professor brought us to see our first delivery. Our mother was already abed, with her legs attached to the ram's horns, and her belly like a mountain. Hamilton seated himself comfortably at the lower end and began to talk her into activity. Quentin, Aeneas and I stood respectfully behind him, whilst behind us stood the angular Annie, muttering and grumbling. She was doubly mortified, firstly because she had been ousted from her central role, and secondly, because Hamilton was a man.

"Push, mother," he shouted.

"Pair lassie," snarled Annie. "The beast's been botherin' her again."

"Perhaps she enjoys having babies," said Quentin. "She's had thwee alweady."

"Not a word of it. Sure he's been demandin' his conjoogals again, the pig." Hamilton broke into the argument.

"Stop that affray over there at once, Annie. And bring me that water. Push, mother, push." The mother groaned and screamed and it was obvious even to our inexpert eyes that something was happening. Annie glowered. Aeneas said,

"My God, how does anyone ever get born?"

"Push, mother." Hamilton was now half standing and guiding the head out with his left hand, while protecting the perineum with his right. More screams, and one of a different pitch.

"It's there, mother! Grand! It's a boy. Annie, the twine." Hamilton laid down the baby on a towel.

"Anither man in the wurrld," growled Annie.

"Annie, the twine," repeated the Professor. She brought it this time, and he tied two ligatures round the cord and with one snip severed the baby for ever from his mother. Annie took the baby, and showed him to his mother, who began to cry.

"Now gentlemen," said Hamilton. "We pull on the cord and gently press on the fundus of the uterus and bring away the afterbirth. Like that, d'ye see." He was very deft and the cord quickly began to lengthen, bringing with it the solid umbrella and its trailing membranes.

"Lord save ye, lassie. Anither boy," said Annie, before disappearing to perform some mystery with the screeching baby.

We watched Hamilton sowing up the tears in the birth canal. It was a shattering experience. And there was worse to follow, but that was later.

Annie and Aggie and their colleagues filled in the practical gaps in our education. They added some theory as well. I joined Aggie one lovely June evening to a confinement in the West Bow. Quentin was not with us, having temporarily abandoned midwifery earlier that day. I had last seen him heading off in the direction of Greyfriar's Churchyard.

We trudged down the steep but curling West Bow, while Aggie chattered happily on her preferred topic, in a stream of rural superstition.

"If a child be conceived by the full moon, 'twill be a boy," said she. "If the moon be on the wane, 'twill be a girl." I think that's what she said, or was it the other way round? She gave me no time to think, because she was off on a new subject.

"Ah, the barren ones! Now they're the sad ones," said the globular Aggie happily. "There's a fine way to tell if they'll ever manage to conceive. The lady in question must wrap herself up tight in a blanket, then the attendant must fumigate from below and if the scent passes through the body to the nose, then she will be fruitful."

While I was trying to recall the precise tracts by which this happened, she told me that the late French Emperor hated naval warfare because his mother had almost foundered in a rowing boat on the River Tiber. She was certainly a fund of vital information. She was also well-known and popular, people had a cheery word for her every few yards. She took me up a tenement close and put me through the hoop of my first home confinement.

Aggie exuded confidence. She bustled into the room, issuing a string of orders to the husband and the children, and the aunts and the cousins, and the neighbours who just happened to be looking in to see if there was anything they might do. There were so many people in the room, I felt sure the arrival of yet another would lead to instant suffocation. Aggie's instructions were practised though and so timed to keep everyone out of the way until the baby was safely born. She shouted at the young mother,

"Mrs McLardy, this is a young doctor from the Infirmary, come tae help me."

"Ah'm no' in trouble, Mistress Dulliver?" gasped the woman through her pains.

"Nae trouble, wifie. Now you," she added to me, "tell me which way the baby's comin'," There is nothing so unnerving as a delivery to expose your ineptitude. As a physician you can take a week over a decision. As a surgeon you can at least decide when you want to make the decision. But when a baby's coming, the decision is made for you.

I shut my eyes and groped for the baby and felt what could be anything. I began to sweat, and pushed more firmly. I even felt that I was suffering more than Mrs McLardy, who called me back to reality with a memorable observation.

"Doctor," she gasped, "ye're a wild wee man." This was clearly the time to retire to a more secondary role. Aggie completed the delivery for me and handed me the baby.

"Dinna drap it, laddie," said Mrs McLardy. That might in fact, have been less damaging than its passage through the pelvis. You see, the pelvis is just a funnel of bone—wide into the belly and narrowing to the outlet. The hip joints hang from the side walls that curve round in front to the pubis and in the back to the scalloped shell of the sacrum. With all its internal bends and twists it presents at the best of times, a hazardous road. At the worst of times, disease, hunger, injury or ill-luck can all conspire to block the road entirely, to trap the baby behind a girdle of mis-shapen bones. Faced with such an obstruction, the womb only doubles its efforts; it may then rupture or weary itself into inertia and kill the child and mother.

Man's ingenuity does not permit these crises to proceed without interference and as well as the forceps, has devised all manner of ways to interfere. The accoucheur can try to drag the baby past the blockade by a chin or a leg with a leather fillet, whalebone stiffened. Sometimes he succeeds, sometimes he may leave the head behind, sometimes he elects to perforate and crush the head with suitably designed weapons of steel. The mother does not always lose consciousness.

When all else fails, there remains the Caesarean operation, "which takes its name frae the Latin verb 'tae cut' and no frae the Roman general," as Hamilton phrased it. After anguished indecision, the accoucheur turned surgeon cuts down for the baby through long incisions in the abdominal wall and the uterus. It is not a widely favoured procedure but I did see the professor perform it once in circumstances I have no wish to see again.

He was in attendance on Lady Kilbuddo of Kilbuddo House and I was in attendance on him, lest he require an informed messenger in a hurry. His sedan chair he deemed too cumbersome, for Kilbuddo House lay some miles up the Queensferry Road. No-one could have been persuaded to carry it that far for him anyway.

It was one of those frolicsome June days where your good humour just swells at the sight of it—what we could see of it through the carriage window. Our third member was Aggie Dulliver. Aloft, the coachman enjoyed the weather even more, whilst in tow trotted two spare horses for the summoner and the summoned.

Within, the Professor was at his happiest, his colleagues being too far away to disturb his ruminations on his best-loved subject. He sketched in for us the coming case. She was a pretty little thing, very pert and vivacious and in a fret to give her husband an heir. Only eighteen, she was always on the gad, falling off horses and getting into every kind of scrape. He had been engaged to see her through her delivery as soon as her pregnancy was established and he would now be seeing her for the second time. He stretched back into his seat and smiled peacefully at Aggie.

We now left the road, for the gates of Kilbuddo stood back at the end of a line of old elms which we now passed. Our way inclined through flowering bushes and deep green laurels to a pilastred Jacobean manor of honeyed sandstone, just visible behind clumps of larch and oak at the end of the driveway.

We continued our journey along a series of butlers and flunkies to the blue pastelled birth chamber prepared and designed on the Professor's instructions. It was now four o'clock.

Greetings over, the Professor looked at his patient. He listened to her cheerful description of her now regular contractions. He felt the line of the child. He smiled. He prescribed a little port, said he would check the head presentation later and pronounced himself satisfied. Lord Kilbuddo met us in the vaulted ante room where he offered us the run of his library and grounds to while away the time which proved to be long. First deliveries always are. And should the time prove to be even longer rooms had been prepared for us off the long gallery. We left Aggie behind to bustle and fuss and took a turn over the park.

The Professor maintained his continuous monologue, oblivious of the frou-frou of leaves and the capering skylarks, whilst I maintained a respectful silence. We might have passed an hour or so like this when the Professor said, "Right, Mr Bryson, let us proceed to assess Lady Kilbuddo's labour pains. And we did. They were coming now every five minutes and gaining in strength. Professor Hamilton prescribed more port and pronounced himself satisfied. It was now seven o'clock.

The Professor told his Lordship he would now go to his room and of course, I was expected to escort him there. On the way back I found time a-plenty to compare the Kilbuddo family portraiture with that of the Fairley-Dunn's. The evening light allowed little to choose between them. There was the second Lord Kilbuddo routing an entire French brigade at Fontenoy and the fifth following Nelson out of Portsmouth with a giant optical device. Thereafter, the group dwindled into the usual collection of younger sons, poor relations, rich benefactors and timeless dowagers.

Tiring of this, I strolled on to the library which would have filled in the waiting hours happily had I had the patience to read. It was well stocked and up to date too, so I took down his most recent Scott—*The Antiquary*. Just at that moment arrived the butler, who might have walked out of the opened pages, bearing a decanter of fine claret that Monkbarns himself would not have sneered at. After a glass or two looking down on the elm park I gave way to Sir Walter's talent for making Scotland seem as Scotland is not and emptied the decanter.

The same butler wakened me between pages twenty-three and twenty-four with an air of urgency. Professor Hamilton was already arguing at the door of the delivery chambers. He was saying,

"It is of no moment that the waters are broken these two hours, Mistress Dulliver. I will not listen to the bebby's heart. You know my views on that!"

Aggie muttered and grumbled under her breath.

The contractions had eased off and Lady Kilbuddo managed to smile a boisterous smile at her husband who rather more anxiously awaited his heir. Professor Hamilton walked about confidently, soothed away all the worries, ordered a little more port and pronounced himself satisfied. It was now one o'clock.

The next I knew was the hubbub that brought me to Lady Kilbuddo's room before the butler could reach my door to waken me. I remember racing along the corridor towards a rising drama. Lady Kilbuddo now lay pale and shocked and spasmodically in the grip of fearful torment. Hamilton was even now measuring the dilatation of her uterine cervix. His face was grave. When he withdrew his bare hand it was smeared with a blood from a stream that began to trickle with increasing speed into a flood.

"My God," he muttered half to himself, "the after birth is coming before." He looked up at Aggie. "I shall have the bebby stethoscope now, Mistress Dulliver," he capitulated. He placed it on Lady Kilbuddo's belly and placed his ear to the tube for a full minute.

"The baby is still living, my lord", said he, "but the after birth is where it shouldna' be, unless I'm much mistaken." In went the hand again. Lord Kilbuddo stood back discreetly. Aggie and I closed in. Of a sudden he began to mutter again.

"The Lord save us. The pelvis is narrower than I ever thought possible." He closed his eyes briefly as if in prayer. He glanced at us again. "That fall she had frae that horse must have narrowed her transverse diameter as well. How in the Lord's name could it have happened? It shouldna' be." He gestured Aggie to the bed head with the laudanum bottle, then turned to Lord Kilbuddo who paced, wringing his hands, by the fireplace. Hamilton nodded to him to follow us to the ante-room.

"My Lord," he whispered," your lady is in dire trouble. She will burst her womb if we leave her. She is bleeding tae death even now, as you can see. Your child will die if we do not bring him further, and there isna' room even tae drag him out—dead!"

Kilbaddo paled before this merciless list of choices. Hamilton spoke again. "There isna' any choice left tae me, sir. I must do the Caesarian operation."

Kilbuddo crumpled into his butler's arms, agreeing feebly. Hamilton, in the teeth of this catastrophe, did not lose his composure.

"Bryson," said he, "take the horses to Damwell's estate" He told me where it was and added, "Tell me I need him at once—and tell him why."

I rode away into the Summer night. It was again four o'clock and the morning mists were creeping through Kilbuddo Park when we returned, as blown as our steeds. Surgeon Damwell listened in silence to the recital and agreed that the available lines of action were limited to one. Our patient was fortunately by now comatose from pain, shock, opium and port wine. Aggie assembled the instruments and resumed her place at the bedhead.

They slit down over her swollen, tense, still contracting belly, through the skin, through the fat, through the muscle sheath, through the uterus itself and, amidst a torrent of blood, drew forth the seventh Lord Kilbuddo—limp and pulseless. Throughout, his mother had whimpered not a word and when they felt for her pulse, it was gone as well. It was now six o'clock.

14

I trundled home for the Summer, straight into Mr MacWrath's "Return of the Prodigal Son", now in its second edition and no less irritating now that I was a reprieved son-in-law. The Kilbuddo tragedy gave me the power to snub his fawning pietism without caring a damn what he thought.

In other directions, my welcome was quite the reverse. I settled into the old easy ways, delighted to have someone remove my chamberpot and bring my water in an imperforate ewer before I rose to meet the day just when it suited me. And no more obligation to pay court to Miss Grizel at the manse. It seemed life could hardly be improved upon.

Imagine my surprise and delight then when another Miss made an appearance early in July. I was emerging from Camerons, the grocers in Dalkeith High Street, one of these little cellars piled high with bottles, sweetmeats and acres of cheeses for the flies to rest on, and there she was, Lucy Home, side-saddling down the road, escorted by a woman altogether larger and older, and a groom. So astonished was I, my bag of tea almost ended in the street.

"Hello", she hailed me over and I needed no further invitation. I skipped up to the flank of her courser like Sir Lancelot to Guenevere's palfry, bowing the more easily for not being encased in metal.

"Aunt Clara," said she pertly, "meet Mr Bryson—he is one of Father's favourite students. Is not that so?" she appealed to me. Aunt Clara—another relative—must have been the Professor's sister. The nose for a start and the air of disconnection, but it all added up to something less grave than her brother. I met Aunt Clara as requested and discovered that Lucy had persuaded her father that it was not right to neglect old friends like the Fairley-Dunns. The entire menage of Charlotte Square, including Aunt Gertrude and her backgammon board, had shifted from Edinburgh for the month, although the Professor would have to return to the city frequently to attend to the demands of his practice.

With such an inventive girl staying at Garbeige House it was no time at all before Sir Donald said we must all come to dinner, "by Jove, you must, ha ha ha." In a little more time Lucy convinced them all that a riding expedition would suit everyone to a marvel. Mother joined her good sense to Miss Home's and agreed it was an excellent idea even before I told her, and when I came to think of it she had been most insistent that

I buy that tea at 10 o'clock sharp—not a quarter of an hour before not a quarter of an hour after, and it had to be Camerons shop. So a riding expedition it was to be, and Mother said that there was no hurry to tell them that she would not be present herself.

On Thursday morning the horsemen of the party assembled on the gravel in front of the columned portico. Sir Donald and the Professor did not join us: instead they went off to visit the mine workings, at least that is what they said. As for the rest of us—we were an optimistic group trying to maintain a connected chatter against our conspiring mounts who dropped their necks, raised their necks, checked their bits for later possibilities and generally tittupped and snickered and whickered and shifted about when inertia would have been most convenient.

We set off at last at a walking trot across the Fairley-Dunn park, towards the river—a gentle dappled ride through gnarled oaks—thinned only by Sir Donald's patriotic contributions to Nelson's naval victories. Ahead cantered the hunting Gavin, followed by a chestnut gelding with Lady Fairley-Dunn aboard; Aunt Clara, Father, Lucy and I trailed after them. Lucy and I trailed further still, partly by choice, partly by the natural taste of the sleepy hunters that she had chosen for us and as we trailed we laughed. We laughed over the adroit manipulations that had brought the Homes to Dalkeith, we speculated where her father and the knight might really have gone, we wondered how our cuddies managed to anticipate our intentions. So we tethered them to a slim birch tree and wandered off into the woods.

Meanwhile, Aunt Clara must have tumbled to our absence—or, more correctly, she tumbled as late as she reasonably might without risking her name as a duenna. Her hoofbeats grew louder and more urgent. "Quickly, that's Aunt Clara," cried Lucy. She pulled my hand and darted behind a thicket. Aunt Clara now galloped up in a lather of agitation. Lucy did a mime of Aunt Clara and ran on. Then came a hideous snap that seemed to drag her down; she screamed. In dread I reached for her where she lay twisted across a mossy stump—sobbing and shaking. Her right foot was trapped beneath an exposed root. Her left foot had disappeared, clamped in the jaws of an atrocious gin trap, the trap itself disappearing behind a wash of oozing blood.

"Lucy, my darling!" I gasped as I came down beside her and worked out my fury on the spring which finally gave way after a fierce struggle. I turned again to Lucy but she had now fainted beyond the recall of her Aunt's smelling salts. We placed her on the grass. There, with my neckcloth, I fashioned around her calf a tourniquet that allowed me to see and grow pale over the broken ends of her tibia that were mocking me through the torn skin.

We carried her back to the house in a hammock of riding capes and I fell prey to the most fearful depression, for I had seen too many similar injuries find their way to the infirmary mortuary to let me anticipate anything but the worst. Hoof marks in the gravel, as well as telling my downcast eyes that we had arrived, now fretted cruelly at my memories of our carefree start. Without yielding up my burden I managed a coherent account of our disaster to Sir Donald's old liegeman who must have seen us struggling across the lawns. He nodded then dispersed his gaggle of maids on a hundred vital errands. He said gently,

"It's upstairs the noo for Miss Lucy, sir. Would ye no let me help you? Ah well then follow me if ye will." Aunt Clara followed us all, weeping silently.

By the time my father hurried into our sick room, the sight of my wounded sweetheart had reduced me also to worldless tears. Father now came over to her bedside. Wakened by the door she held up her hand to him and crinkled her face in pain as well as recognition.l He clasped her hand in both of his.

"Well my lass," said he, "No—do not explain. I know what you have been up to—you are asses—the pair of you."

"The fault was mine, sir." she murmured. "The idea was mine too but it was a good one, was it not?"

"Well now—hark at her—that's what I like to hear—a girl with spirit. You'll make my son a fine wife yet!" He chuckled at our surprise then asked Aunt Clara to let him see the wound. His brief examination set his lips in a way he took care to hide from Lucy. He called me up with his bag.

"Some of my favourite remedy for you, my girl," he declared, taking a large measure from the laudanum bottle.

When she was sleeping, he was brisk again—and to me, "Off you go to Sir Donald's man; have him send fast to Turner's Mill for some potter's clay—fast, mind you."

And fast I was. I galloped off myself, glad to drum away my nightmares. What Father wanted the potter's clay for I could not think. Nor did I bother, for a brain haunted by death visions cannot think clearly enough to practice medicine.

When I returned with the clay I found the entire house party in the bed room and indeed in alarm, watching Father replace and realign the smashed bones, while Lucy howled through a veil of opium. I thought I would go mad. The three mothers silently passed courage to each other through clasped hands. The Professor betrayed no emotion. Sir Donald broke the silence.

"Your daughter is in safe keeping, Professor." he barked cheerily.

"Indeed she is." echoed his lady.

"Is she indeed?" said Home sourly. "That is a matter of opinion. I want her treated in Edinburgh; to put it another way, by one of my colleagues."

"Nonsense," shouted the knight, "we are all well here by grace of Dr Bryson. Look, sir," he separated his right eyelids to show off his corneal scar.

"Upon my word, sir, she will not benefit from the eight miles to the city—even if we had one of Larrey's sprung ambulances." said Father tartly. "In any case, Edinburgh means nursing home gangrene."

Persuaded of the sense of this, the Professor moved off on a new tack, "It we cannot take my daughter to Edinburgh then I insist on calling Professor Russell to see her here. Father shook his head,

"We are wasting valuable time."

"Yes indeed—valuable time." repeated the Laird.

The Ladies said nothing. Gavin gazed into the fireplace against the mantlepiece, idly smacking his thigh with a riding crop. Lucy slumbered. The silence was chilling.

"I want Russell." said the Professor again. "You can send a groom, Sir Donald, to Queen Street. He can be here within the hour—that is to say, reasonably soon."

"But Professor Russell is near eighty," cried Father in disbelief. "He will not stand the journey out!" The Professor now came about again.

"What is that?" he queried, pointing at the board of potter's clay at my feet. Father explained—

"I aim to encase and splint her fractures in this, it will let them heal in place."

"You will not touch my daughter's leg with that filth," shouted Home.

"Mayhap Dr Bryson is right," it was Lady Fairley-Dunn now joining the argument. "He treated many such wounds in the Peninsula."

"It is possible," added Mrs Home.

"Russell must be sent for. My daughter's not a soldier!"

"As you will sir," said Father evenly. "Sir Donald, have your man bring the Professor of Surgery."

Sir Donald's man arrived three hours later with the surgeon. Russell tottered into the sick room, his red wig in his hand, and declared himself to be ill. He had the air of one plucked from a stick in a nearby field.

"I have not long for this world." he quavered.

"Russell," Home raged, "my daughter has fractured her leg. I want your opinion, sir, your views, sir, your proposed line of treatment!"

Russell answered by swooning into his servant's arms. They dragged him off to another sick room and Sir Donald asked my father if he would undertake his care as well. The silence began to chill again.

I watched the minutes tick away on a gilded ormolu by Gavin's head. Lucy slept still, her bones set but the wound open. It was obvious Father could barely curb his impatience. The ladies sensing a further battle slipped out of the room.

"We will have to call Mr Damwell then," said Professor Home, at length. "He lives in these parts, I understand."

"He does not; he lives near South Queensferry, sir." I cried. "It will take three hours to fetch him and he may not be at home."

"What pray, do you think ought to be done, Professor?" asked Father heavily.

"I would expect a surgeon to open the wound—to let the pus out, that is!"

"Pus, sir! There is no pus!" exploded Father.

"And," continued the Professor woodenly, "if the wound goes bad the leg would have to come off."

"Professor Home," Father's voice was urgent now, "your daughter's leg can be saved as indeed can her life if you will but permit me to cover it in this potters clay—before the wound becomes any dirtier."

"Why would you put that on my Lucy's leg?", wailed the Professor.

"It will stop needless interference, sir."

"It is contrary to established practice," pleaded Home.

"Whom else would you have me call then?" said Father. I was not prepared for the Professor's reaction. He collapsed like Lunardi's first balloon. He sat down, head in hands and said,

"No-one, Dr Bryson. I have no other friends on whom I could call." Father gestured to the Professor.

"See to him, Sir Donald. Now," he turned to me, "there is much to be done and we have already too long delayed."

"Do what you will, Dr Bryson", said Lucy's father weakly. Sir Donald led him, trembling, away. Before Father could start with the clay, Mrs Home returned to the bedroom.

"Has my husband relented then, Dr Bryson?" she asked.

"He has done more than that, ma'am." said Father most gently. "I venture to say he would benefit from your presence." After one last look at Lucy, she went below to succour her spouse. Father returned to the bedside. "Now, at last—to work." he sighed "Mix that clay with a little more water. That will do nicely."

He took it and moulded it around Lucy's leg from the toes to the knee. She looked so peaceful, my medical reason began to return. I looked on, mystified. I was sure Damwell would have taken the leg off but I did not say so. Father answered my unvoiced question.

"This is the cleanest way I know to treat a compound fracture," he declared, "Larrey told me he used a straw-lined cover when he could not find clay. It keeps prying hands out of mischief and holds the bones straight. You could not ask for more!" My medical reason fled again. I

164

wept on his shoulder. "What will become of Lucy, Father?" I looked up at him.

"I cannot promise, laddie, but if anything will save her, this will. The next forty-eight hours will tell. Now we shall leave her asleep with her mother. You can tell her we are finished. Sir Donald has already arranged for us to stay here. Now I must go to see what has happened to Professor Russell. Away you go! Take a bumber of whisky and follow it with two more."

I took his advice and passed the first twelve hours of my next period of waiting untroubled. When I awoke next day, the sun streaming through my window only reminded me, by its very brightness, of the shadow that threatened to destroy my love. I lingered briefly to splash myself clean in an ornate basin then ran to her room where I found Aunt Clara and Father already in attendance. Her pulse was regular and unhurried, her forehead cool.

At first all went well. Even her tetchy father agreed, with only a little quibble, about the open curtains, the open windows and the general air of cheerfulness insisted upon by my father, that she was flourishing. Lucy, for her part, agreed with no quibble at all and it was not the opium alone that made her so reasonable. We talked as long as she wanted, whilst about us bustled maids with broth, cooling cordials, warming pans, wet towels. Mr MacWrath came by to read us a book or two of scripture. When he had closed his bible he said, "You will no doubt be lunching soon, Sir Donald?"

"I fancy not," said the knight, "Our victualling is knocked awry at the moment!"

"Ah well, I shall return later to read more of the holy word!" sighed the ravenous prelate.

By the evening it was clear our patient was well enough for us to go home. By the next morning she was ill enough to have us all recalled. She was flushed. Her pulse was hurrying; she was discinclined to speak. Her father stood by the window in colloquy with mine; some might have called it disagreement. Evidently, the natural aggresion that had brought him his chair had survived its temporary collapse of the day before. A flood tide of powerful remedies, now raged themselves into a spray of doubt against father's rocklike scepticism.

"She is fevered," he roared, "She must be bled, cupped if you prefer the term." Father took it all like an old breakwater.

"With respect, Professor Home, she has already lost a great deal of blood. She needs more, not less. Would that it were possible," he finished sombrely.

"If you do not do something, I will send for Abercrombie!" I watched Home's fury rising as my father's patience was falling.

"Professor Home, what would you have me do?" He asked the question with even greater irony than he had yesterday.

"Do? Do? What you mean 'do', sir? Do? You have a choice of bleeding blistering or purges. You have already rejected bleeding. Then blister, man, and purge: it is the only way. Your son knows my views." He glanced at me bleakly and his anxiety for his daughter did not allow his customary double phrasing.

"I will neither blister nor purge." said Father. "Because she is hot, I will cool her—with cold compresses. If she wants to eat she may do so. If she does not, she need not. My only injunction is that she drink water or milk and I will give her laudanum should the pain return, which it has not done yet." I could see Aunt Clara silently praying to heaven.

"But her leg; you are ignoring the cause of the fever." bleated the Professor. Father shook his head.

"Her fracture may have been the exciting cause but it is not so now. Look, sir, the skin is neither swollen nor angry above my clay. There is no spreading red weal on the thigh." He stopped his harangue and took the professor's arm. He said, "Professor Home, you are not yourself. It is always so with one's own children; it quite takes away the judgement. Look, she is sleeping now."

"Maybe so, maybe so", said the Professor weakly. As he stumbled past his daughter's bed he murmured, "Lucy, Lucy, what will become of you?" I saw the tears cascade down his withered cheeks.

With the Professor gone and Aunt Clara bending over our patient, Father now put his hands on my shoulders.

"You must be strong," he said, "If that leg begins to swell now—she is lost."

"And if it does not, Father?" I choked.

"Then she will recover. I can only treat her symptoms as I find them; you know that". Indeed I knew that. He went on: "We will know in about forty-eight hours. Now," he said more lightly, "I must see our other patient next door. He is suffering from acute indecision, coupled with deep convictions. I must have him home before an encounter with his distinguished colleague causes him to relapse."

Another forty-eight hours were to pass as I settled now to my longest period of waiting between Lucy's sick room and the library. In the latter, Sir Donald, remorseful as only the owner of the offending gin trap could be, came frequently to ease his anguish by easing mine. Although his faith in my father's painless remedies was unshaken, he clearly did not expect his fair visitor to recover. He heard she had begun to rave. He even speculated that the leg might be better off. I was too numb to refuse his speculation. Whenever I turned my eyes a black pall settled. The Laird's wine touched everything except my devilish imagination. His consolation made it only more vivid. I could now clearly make out a long ebony box being lowered out of sight near a cypress tree in the Dean cemetery. I did not even care if Mr MacWrath were called upon to officiate and, when he arrived in person at dinner-time, I could not raise even a frisson of anger. That day and that night I waited for Lucy to die in her delirium. That day and that night Father arranged the rest of his practice around her needs.

The following evening he came to tell me in the library that her fever had now broken, that her leg was not swollen, that she had now ceased to rave. My hours of restraint poured on to his shoulders in a gush of defenceless weeping.

From then on, her recovery was swift. The delighted Professor abased himself before my father and agreed to our unofficial engagement, that was to say, to our being promised to each other in marriage, or indeed wedlock. He then dashed away to Edinburgh. Mrs Home's relief was, I think, not for Lucy's good fortune alone and she and my mother now wept tears of joy over their joint daughter. Garbeige House rang with the noise of cavorting, shouting, dining and drinking. Sir Donald took me to view his ancestor and the wild pig. MacWrath's mealtime theology provoked my usual febrile response. Everything was normal; Lucy was going to live and even Gavin said my entire family must really come down to visit the Thredbairs in Selkirkshire—sometime.

15

The year continued to wear away. I had planned to teach my father the subtleties of midwifery, but Lucy's joust with death in his care had made all my academic antics seem a passing sadness. Older now than I knew, I became a senior medical student. We plunged into a study of Mental Disease, Dietetics, Medical Jurisprudence, in short, into what every educated student should know before daring to face the Final Examination.

New students asked me where the best taverns in town were to be found, and was it true that Professor Monroe was a clown? I could enjoy having suffered him, now that I had to suffer him no longer. I decorated my advice a fraction, possibly, but told them the truth as I saw it.

We were now free of the anatomy rooms, and Quentin was the only one of our year who continued to frequent them. He usually came to the back door, where he exchanged his graveyard trophies for ten guineas each. I didn't know what his motives were; perhaps the thrill of the chase, with himself as the quarry, raised the blood of a fox-hunting man; perhaps Edinburgh life bored him; perhaps he just needed a fat wallet to give him courage.

His real trouble was a talent for getting caught, and this is where the big scandal started. We had known for some time that there was more than the kitchen between him and Mrs Cudleigh, but for a plunger, Quentin was reticent. When the scandal finally broke I was in fact listening to Dr Archie Plainfayre telling us all he knew about the art of planning a diet. He was a kenspeckle Physician eccentric, who was on the staff of the Royal Infirmary. He always wore a dark black coat, and a shaggy white beard, cut short enough to retain his patients' respect and their fees. His deep distrust of modern farming led him to grow his own oats and barley and turnips, in fields manured by his own horses. The cycle of purity continued, as half his produce went back into the same horses, who then roamed his farm, fertilising the ground as they chose. He carried this belief to the extreme of eating only his own food. In fact he carried anything necessary around with him in a large case. Arriving at a friend's house, and finding him out, he would sit on the doorstep to eat his supper, which he would arrange with great delicacy in the case lid. He told us,

"The Lord commanded the people of Israel to enter a land flowing with milk and honey. An excellent counsel, and I would add only eggs to complete the divine advice, provided of course the hens have foraged for themselves amongst barley grown in pure dung."

As you can guess, there was a limit to your tolerance of such quaintness, and I had reached mine, so I slipped out into Brown's Square. My head was spinning with information ranging from butter to line the blood vessels and so guard against apoplexy; and iron filings in hot wine to cure the lassitude. Any further dietetic ruminations were dispersed by the sight of Quentin across the road. He looked as though he had just charged with the Greys—as a mount. His hair blew wild, and his eyes rolled like those of a frightened steed trying to see round a blinker. He came across the road and took my arm in a fierce grip.

"My God," he said, "I am beat to a dead standstill. I must have a canister cap of Max. I feel like getting as dwunk as a Fwench sow."

"Well, what's up? What's happened to you, Quentin?"

"Come here and I'll tell you," said he, dragging me into a filthy taphouse.

"Surely not here." My tastes were now selective.

"Yes," said he urgently, "come on." He called for and devoured a large measure of gin, and started immediately on a brimful of dark ale. His story came out in the dry periods between long mouthfuls. Whatever had happened had left indelible scratches across his dragoon glitter.

In fact, what had happened was Mrs Cudleigh, or, to be precise, her husband. Quentin's fluctuating financial status allowed him to engage Jenny Cudleigh officially as cook but with other duties as took their fancy. His recurrent trips to the graveyard financed a cosy menage. His tastes made certain it remained cosy. It was a menage of heaving bosoms, sly innuendos, direct invitations, where only one of the four bedrooms was in permanent use.

Imagine then his horror when a wolf in the form of Mr Cudleigh, and his entire baggage, came to the front door one bleak November evening—all a-hunger, his face blotched either from the weather, the drink, or both. The liveliest aspect of his features was a black patch poorly disguising a deformed socket. Just a bed for the night and he would be on his way—emigrating, he said, "tae Canada". Four months later he was still there; that is when he was not lurching back and forth across the North Bridge to attend to his consuming interest in the White Horse Inn.

Quentin and Mrs Cudleigh resumed their delicious little trysts that had been so impolitely interrupted by her husband's unannounced arrival. All this continued smoothly for a few months. The one-eyed Mr Cudleigh would spend his nights on the floor in the hall; he could never find his bedroom in the dark, and in the end a bolster was routinely thrown into the hall in readiness for his evening collapse.

But one night his habits changed. He did not fall down on entering the house. Instead he continued up to his bedroom, where Quentin had taken over the role of husband, and flung open the door. He swayed there for a while, uncertain of what he was actually seeing. He stared at Jenny staring at him around Quentin, who had doffed more than his breeches.

"In the name of the wee man, it's himself," screamed Jenny, paralysed as much by fear as by Quentin.

"Aargh, aargh," roared Mr Cudleigh like a Highland bull, his red-rimmed eye glaring balefully in all directions. He blundered out laboriously, but deadly earnest.

"Quentin, Quentin, he's awa' for his gun." Jenny clutched first at her throat, then at Quentin, then at her clothes. Quentin was not in a situation new to him.

"Help me on with these damned bweeches," he commanded. But Mrs Cudleigh was too busy tugging at her own, and with a woman's ineffable eye for useless detail, was smoothing away little morsels of evidence in the hope that Quentin, the ruffled sheets, and her total absence of clothes, might escape the notice of her furious husband. She was brushing her hair, can you imagine it, when they heard a furious roaring outside the door. In burst her outraged spouse, staggering under the weight of a monstrous blunderbuss.

"Jesus, he's got the artillery," barked the untrousered hussar.

"Quentin, he's going to kill us. He's going to kill us."

Quentin leapt forth as heroically as a pair of ankled breeches permitted, to do battle. Jenny hid behind him—a remarkable achievement considering her shape.

"Put away that damned firearm, Cudleigh!" Quentin tried his best quell-the-rioting-mob manner.

"Ah'll blast ye baith," he barked. "Oh, ye deceitful whore ye. And as for you, and me trustin' ye the while. Aargh, this bloody gun." He began to lever the gun horizontal, sadly for him, by the trigger, and a discharge of grapeshot raked the bed, a porcelain ewer, Quentin's calf boots and his own foot. He subsided at once, groaning, then silent; felled by his own marksmanship.

"I didn't know what to think," Quentin went on. He continued the tale with furrowed brow. He took Mr Cudleigh's wrist, patted his cheek, then tried kicking him as a greater stimulus. Jenny, consumed with remorse, began to shriek.

"John, John, ye're deed," and fell across his neck sobbing. In a trice she turned on Quentin.

"Look what you've done to ma husband," she hissed. "Ye've killed him."

"I never touched him. The dwunken lout shot himself. In fact, he didn't shoot himself. He died of shock at not killing you, you silly bitch." He stretched for his glass, then pressed his eyes closed, as though trying to squeeze away the memory, then spoke on.

"The old fool was dead. He must have had a bwain storm or something."

"No."

"Yes, damn me. Dead, and obviously not going to wecover. Just imagine. What could I do? And half the bloody neighbours in these unspeakable houses must have been able to give a verbatim weport on our pwoceedings. Pwobably even before Cudleigh came in at all. God help me!" he went on. "what could I have done? What would you have done?"

"Quentin, there was no choice. You went to report the accident." There was no change of expression on his face. "Quentin, you did report the accident, did you not?"

"No, damn me. I didn't. I sold him to Pwofessor Monwoe. The old skinflint gave me only eight guineas. He said the feet were a little mis-shapen, and that one-eyed specimens were not in gweat demand. The tight-fisted old stoat!"

"Quentin, that was insane. The neighbours must have seen it all. They must have seen most of Jenny as well, come to think of it. They'll have blown the gaff by now."

"Yes," he said grimly. "That's the pwoblem. I had to bowwow Plunderleith's cart. I took him down the stairs at midnight, and I dwove like the fires of Hell to Monwoe's back door. I thought I could leave the cart there, and come back by the mawwowbone stage." He sat there shaking, quite unlike him, and I had his glasses filled for him again. He did not notice, but reached out to drink without thinking. And there was more to the story.

"I was finishing off the business side of the twansaction with the Pwofessor," went on Quentin with dignity, "when two guardians of the city peace arrived and began to ask questions. Cudleigh was alweady on the marble next door by this time. My God!" he shook his head at the thought of it. It seemed that the two stony-faced men in fustian grey and cocked hats had steered the shabby Professor in his own dissecting room.

"We are lookin' for a missin' person," said the larger of the two to Monroe.

"And why have you come here? What I mean to say, you are surely not expecting to find him on my premises?"

"We're leavin' nae stane unturned, Professor,"

171

"Now, my man, you must know that only hanged felons find their way here, and we have not had a hanging in the town these last three weeks. And the last went to Knox too," he added under his breath. Quentin managed a weak smile at this deflection of Monroe's specimen onto Knox's dissecting slab.

"We were just comin' tae warn ye, sir—in case ye happened tae see the person we had in mind."

"And how would I recognise him?"

"He hasna got twa eyes and his feet's full o' lead balls."

"An admirable description. Upon my word, I could not fail to recognise him if I saw him; indeed I will tell him, if I see him, that you are searching for him."

"Ah'm thinkin', sir, he'll no' be hearin' ye." They gave him one final disbelieving look, and bowed their way out.

Monroe had now turned his unweildy stained bulk on Quentin, who was pretending to examine the skeleton on its stand.

"Well, Mr Deelatrumps, what have you to say for yourself?"

"That I think eight guineas a fair pwice, sir. If you will excuse me, I . . ."

"Hold a moment sir," cried the Professor treating Quentin to a closer view of his face. "How did you come by the specimen? One eye, and lead balls in the feet; there cannot be many specimens like that in Edinburgh. One could say, such qualities must be rare indeed. Do you not so think?"

"Oh, I would agwee, sir. Indeed, sir, I would," said Quentin humbly.

"Let us go and examine the new body, Willie." Monroe turned to his crippled slave who hirpled ahead, flinging open the mortuary door, which Monroe now flung shut so hard on Quentin's heels, that he all but joined John Cudleigh who lay on the marble, his face set in dismay at what he had done to himself the day before.

"Rare qualities, I would say," muttered Monroe, running his fingers over the monocular face and the leadened feet. "Aye, rare. So rare as to be uncommon, would you not agree, Mr Deelatrumpe?" Willie smiled malevolently.

I could have given him a facer. In fact I could have given the pair of them a facer apiece," said Quentin clenching his fist in regretful despair.

"Then the buffoon began to ask me about my family. At first I could not see what he was about." Poor Quentin, I could share his misery as the shameful recital spun along, for I could see that what the Professor was about did not come under the heading of Christian charity or Sunday morning hypocrisy.

"Ah heh heh—now Mr Deelatrumpe, you don't happen to have any

172

church connections of any kind—that is to say, any relations who might be in the—eh—clergy?"

"An uncle of mine was once a Bishop," replied Quentin. The Professor clutched his throat as though it had been transfixed.

"Aaargh. Papish," he choked.

"No, sir. Anglican," said Quentin.

"The same thing. But tell me, you say 'was a Bishop'. Is he dead?"

"No, sir," said Quentin. "He was unfwocked."

"I see," said Monroe unseemly once more. "A tragic end to a noble calling. What are the rest of your family? Have you any relatives in the—er—Army or Navy—er—or in high Government office? What I mean is . . ."

"Well, I knew damned well now what he meant, the sanctimonious old stallion," said Quentin bitterly. "I was so confused I hadn't time to invent an Admiwal Deelatwumpe, or at least an aide-de-camp to the Duke or to Castleweagh or even Canning. Well, it was fwightening, you know," he added. "I was sure he was to have me sent down. So I told him that my father was almost bankwupt, and that the estate was mortgaged beyond wecall. I thought he would be kind to a poor student. And all he said to me was, 'I think this makes your case simple, Mr Deelatwumpe.' I thought Monwoe was going to succumb to apoplexy." He continued to look miserable.

"He began to swell like a fwog. His eyes bulged, his face was awfully wed."

"What did he say to you?"

Monroe apparently had subjected him to a grand homily, shifting from foot to foot and looking as if he had just come across something odd in his mouth.

"This University is a noble institution for the education of young gentlemen, and young gentlemen do not steal bodies, Mr Deelatrumpe."

"I did not steal it, sir." Quentin denied the charge hotly. "I found it."

"And," the Professor sententiously ignored Quentin's interruption, "young gentlemen, if they find bodies do not sell them. They give them to us gratis to further the cause of humanity."

"But young gentlemen need money to continue as young gentlemen, sir."

"Gentlemen should have money, Mr Deelatrumpe. That is to say, they should not need it. But this is beside the point. Whether you need money or not is irrelevant. I have grave doubts about the origins of this body. Did you murder him, Mr Deelatrumpe?"

"What! Do you think I look like a murderer, sir?"

"No, you haven't the courage. That is to say, you are not brave enough, but I am not sure you are not soiling God's temple in some evil dalliance or another. That is to say—em—er—you were—er—dabbling in things you should not have been dabbling in."

"At this point," said Quentin, "I knew the only escape was to gwovel, so I gwovelled bwavely. Squared my chest all gentleman-like and bowed to the gweat man. 'Pwofessor Monwoe, I am guilty of this lechewous charge you level against me. I am a sad disgwace to my father. I would bweak his heart to hear that his son's a blackguard.'"

"As well he might, Mr Deelatrumpe. For his son is a blackguard that is to say, a blackguard indeed."

"Then, sir, I am totally lost. My name is wuined. I will go and pwepare to wemove myself from Edinburgh at once."

"No," said the Professor, "we need not take things to that extreme. We need—er—only go to—er—a lesser extreme. First of all, give me back the eight guineas, and we will forget about the body this time."

"Thank you, sir. Thank you." Quentin was delighted to skip off the hook so lightly.

"And," the Professor droned on relentlessly, "you will be a gentleman."

"Of course, sir. Anything, sir. I'm a gentleman, as you know, sir." Monroe and Willie both smiled evilly, even Cudleigh the musketeer seemed to share their amusement.

"I mean the gentleman we were describing," said the Professor. "I mean, those who hand over gratis any bodies they might discover from time to time. I want one fresh specimen every month, Mr Deelatrumpe, until the summer term is over. That is to say, when the summer vacation has commenced. The cost of these specimens to me will be nothing, do you understand, Mr Deelatrumpe. You will provide them gratis, as a gentleman should."

"The swine," said I. "He parades to Church on Sundays, smiles away as robbers swing, and steals from you bodies you've stolen from somebody else. There's no justice in this life." Quentin accepted my sympathetic bolstering for what it was worth.

"I have to do something else for the Pwofessor. He said to me before I left (Quentin now dropped into a perfect imitation of Monroe) 'It would be of benefit to medical knowledge if you were to dissect some specimens for me during the summer. You would need to pay me a small fee for the privilege—that is to say, for the—um—er—tuition. I think two pounds a month would be quite satisfactory.' You see, I not only have to supply bodies for the old scuffler. I have to pay him to do the work he's paid to do himself."

And pay he did all through the winter when he was not shivering into an empty brandy flask beside an empty grave. When I told the Rev. Gideon who had just arrived one sharp December supper time, to bless and sample the effects of his blessing on our festive bird, he detected at once all the signs of divine retribution in Quentin's sentence. His eye was full of bale.

"The Lord will set his face against the man that commits whoredom with Molech. The lecherous must pay the price of their lechery," he bawled, having no doubt done just that at Mrs Peddleclap's; he went on through mouthfuls of gooseflesh and turnip, "And the meek shall inherit the earth."

"Aye, and if your name happens to be MacWrath," I could hear Father muttering, "you inherit a good proportion of what's on the earth too!"

There was no response, for our parson was already debating the good or evil of an apple tart on the sideboard.

16

Hogmanay went and Spring came and with it the dangerous daylight to make Quentin delay those eerie poaching forays beyond even his usual bedtime. And that was but half of his problem, for come to think of it the whole medical course is rather like a prolonged poaching expedition. You sidle into alien territory, often by the back door; after some guddling, up comes a trout, or a salmon, or a piece of wood, and you occasionally fall in. At times you have to break off to celebrate your acquisition, whether it's venison, pheasant, partridge, or a buttockful of buckshot.

Awfully fine, you'll agree, till you have to persuade the gamekeeper at the gate that it all really belongs to you. It is at this point that the resemblance to a Medical Final Examination comes in. Instead of one gamekeeper, there are six, all of them Professors of the University, and in the place of stolen game comes Materia Medica, Surgery, and all the wisdom garnered and accumulated from centuries of suffering— experimental therapeutics. In succession, each of the Professors played host to the other Professors, and about a dozen candidates sat the examination at any one time. We then had to write our thoughts on any of the Hippocratic Aphorisms. In addition we had to commit ourselves to paper on the diagnosis and treatment of a case drawn up by a Professor, and finally had to demonstrate our powers of reason and logic in the defence of a thesis. As all this could be written without supervision, the more unscrupulous paid the more needy to write their theses for them. Quentin never said, but I suspect that after the judgment of Monroe, he was treading warily. In return for this act of penance, the successful candidates were granted the degree M.D.

Now about the same time of the year other lesser institutions also held their examinations. The Surgical College could confer a Licentiate of the Royal College of Surgeons; in Dublin and London the Apothecaries' Halls thronged with hopefuls (whose hopes had often been dashed elsewhere) in search of a Licentiate in Medicine and Surgery from the Society of Apothecaries.

The M.D. was recognised by the discerning at the highest, and showed its confidence by using the fewest letters in its abbreviation. The more gullible, however, if they could not read too well, chose their doctors by the procession of letters across his brass plate. Thus a failed M.D. could, on the production of a suitable fee, march up the career ladder, flourishing both an L.R.C.S. and an L.M.S.S.A., and if he felt more letters might help him to augment his income, he could add Dublin or London in capital letters after the Diploma.

About April time early, I realised with alarm that my Final Examination lay but two months away. We were all acquainted with the frightening details, for in every medical school you will find, without searching too hard, some veteran examinee who knows exactly how to pass, and why you will certainly fail. To ask him why he is still appearing, would be an act of lèse-majesté, even if you have the coolness to think of asking him in the first place.

I met such a man in the White Horse Inn.

He said loftily, "What you need is a grinder. The one I always use is MacKenzie. You'll find him in the Advocates' Close, Number Two. Now I must toddle," he finished grandly. "Take your reckoning, landlord," he called, tossing him a coin before clearing a way out for himself with his silver-tipped cane.

"He must be terribly senior," said Aeneas.

"Don't you believe it," said Quentin. "That's Allwood. He's thwashed his bwain half a dozen times at least, to my knowledge. And he still has not got his M.D. Why, damn me, I am told on impeccable authowity— the vewy last time he appeared in the examination, Pwofessor Monwoe, no less, asked him to comment on the femur. Allwood said, 'It's a bone, sir'. Monwoe asked him if he had nothing else to add to that statement and would you cwedit it, Allwood said, 'Pwofessor Monwoe, I just want to pass, I do not seek a commendation.' So you can tell him how to sit the examination next year. Haw, haw, haw!" I could see that Quentin had bounced up again following his humbling exchanges with Monroe.

I joined Quentin's laughter but I took Allwood's advice, and sought out the grinder, MacKenzie—a lank-haired poet of a man, who hoped that a few successes amongst his pupils might bring him a reputation, a little practice, and perhaps a little money for food. He offered to polish up my Latin as well for an extra sovereign.

I went to his modest hovel, four floors up in the Advocates' Close, three evenings a week. He took me up the arm and down the trunk, not forgetting the brain, to the legs. I recited in English and Latin the symptoms and signs of bladder stones, jaundice, putrid angina, farmer's lung, miner's lung, consumption, the dropsy and smallpox.

By the beginning of May we had moved on to surgical methods. He reminded me how to recognise at a glance an artery forceps, a tenotomy knife, the apparatus altus, bladder cannulae, and hernia trusses. What saws you would use on a leg, and what on the arm. We practised Larrey's bandaging for fractures of the tibia. By the end of May I was fluently writing for him lengthy complicated prescriptions like infusions of senna:

"R. Infus. sennae, 3 iii
Sal. Glauber. 3 ss
Tinct. Jalap. 3 i
Tinct. Aromat. 3 ss
M. f. haust."

and telling him how to concoct the infusions when the drugs arrived: for example,

"The more suddenly purges operate in acute rheumatisms, the more efficacious are they generally found: and as large diluting warm thin liquors considerably accelerate the operation of all purges, such practice is never to be neglected in these cases. Cream of tartar whey, mixed with twice its quantity of warm water, is a very proper drink to assist the operation of purges." And like a set of instructions from the Annals of the Cleikum Club . . . "Cream of tartar whey is made by adding to an English pint of milk (when it begins to boil), Cream of Tartar; the pan must then be removed from the fire, the whole suffered to cool, and afterwards the whey is to be separated from the curd by straining."

And if you were thinking that this might wear me out before I could carry it to my invalids, I had to do the same without thinking for Gregory's mixture, Hamilton's pill; and for a succession of enemas, emetics, purgatives, blisters and syrups.

The time came when the most recently acquired facts pushed the older ones out of my head and far away. Avoiding all the stern potions described in my books, I took the only honourable escape, unfortunately temporary, into oblivion, from which I awoke the next day with an untreatable headache. I set off glumly for my examination which, irony or ironies, was to be held in Professor Home's house in Charlotte Square, where I had visited Lucy on so many happier occasions. She had forbidden me to enjoy myself until the examination was over. At least she had cared that I was miserable with a purpose.

I went on foot to clear my head and to let me reflect on the penalties of failure. It also cost me less, and I thought to myself which part of the examination I would like the least. I decided they would all be equally bad, and nothing shifted this thought from my now thudding head as I trod up the same steps where Quentin had fenced the railings with his ebony stick on the night of the great Assembly Ball. In response to my bell came the laughing Jamie. He greeted me with amiable irreverence, and showed me into the dining room. Four or five examinees were already sitting, or pacing about, or muttering in soft whispers. They welcomed me with bitter-sweet smiles, as Christians waiting to enter the arena might have welcomed another jawful of lion fodder. They said little otherwise.

By and by we were joined by a hearty student, who had just now been through the mill. It was David Toomhead. I knew him well for an uncomfortable know-all, who was always offering unsolicited tips on investments, sporting guns and horses. At that moment he could not have been less welcome than a town crier in a Trappist retreat. He now began to give a blow by blow account of his late triumph. He was very confident. I listened with consternation to his smug narrative.

"Then Home asked me about the small intestine of a horse. Imagine that. Why bless me! I told him of course, that the first twenty-five feet contained only secernating glands, and that absorption of food begins after that. Then I told him . . ." And so on he went, while we wished he would have a seizure. I knew nothing about the horse's small bowel, or about its large bowel for the matter. I could not fathom how twenty-five feet of small gut could fit into a horse at all if there were to be any room for its large gut, and I did not know what a secernating gland was.

I wanted to rush out. Had I been alone I would have done so. Instead I looked at the sparrows frolicking on the cobbles in Charlotte Square.

"My Bryson," droned Jamie. This was it now.

"Good luck," croaked the lads, barely audible. I could hear Toomhead as the door shut,

"And when we got on the action of bile, I was able to tell him that . . ."

I followed Jamie out of the door which, thankfully, cut off Toomhead's caperings in the gall bladder. He led me at snail's pace across the hall, muttering to himself the while. He slowed down, if that was possible, as we approached the double doors of what I knew was Home's study, then he stopped suddenly to adjust the buckle of his shoe. I saw in a second the reason for this clumsy little scene, for Lucy limped down the stairs to give me her locket as a talisman for the coming ordeal. Jamie rose and coughed, pretending not to see her. She fled aloft without another word. I watched her till she disappeared. At least one of the Homes was on my side. No, two, for her mother would be in the drawing-room wondering what was happening. Jamie became all fatherly.

"Dinna fash yerself, sir." said he. "They're a' in a braw spirits in there. Even Professor Hamilton. Smilin' a' over his face. Och, ye'll be a' richt." He pulled at the door handles, found a resistance that he must have found a thousand times before, but he still managed to feign surprise.

"The wood in this hoose is a disgrace. Wha'-ever built the hoose must ha' made a fortune oot o' the wood. It's bent, and it isna seasoned." With

179

a tug he finally managed to separate them. "Mr Bryson!" he announced, and I was face to face with the big guns. The biggest gun was sitting behind the desk, flanked by equally frightening muzzles. What caught my eye, however, were books. Behind them, to right and left, and indeed to front of them, were books, books, and more books. Handsome leather volumes standing in neat racks on thickset oaken shelves. Whatever the architect had skimped on the doors and window sashes had been more than compensated for here. I almost forgot what I was here for, till Home rose before me, overturning a decorative mortar and pestle.

He came round, with what I took to be a smile, from behind his roomy desk, and took my trembling hand. I could see Russell shaking his red wig with as much vigour as he could muster at Hamilton, who may have been smiling when Jamie saw him, but certainly was not now. Hamilton's knuckles were white. He, too, was trembling over some slight or other. My entry interrupted whatever developments might have followed. Monroe was dropping snuff on the floor by the window.

Professor Home, as the host, opened fire first, and on the causes of swollen ankles. It was not my favourite subject. However, I struggled through and told him about digitalis, and how it had been discovered by William Withering in a spey wife's foxglove brew, and how cases of dropsy divided into those that responded to foxglove and those that did not.

"Yes," said he, "what do you call the second variety?"

"Essential dropsy, sir."

"Yes, that's right," said Home. "Correct, if you prefer it."

"Indeed it is not," barked Hamilton, bobbing about like Tom Cribb. "Richard Bright has just published a book, whose name escapes me for the moment. He says that essential dropsy is due to diseased kidneys."

"Well, it may be so," said Home mildly. "But that does not stop us from calling it essential, does it?"

Hamilton wanted to say more, but threatening grunts from Home's colleagues stopped the words on his lips. He began to sulk.

Home wisely led the questioning away from swollen ankles to consumption. We discussed the value of fresh air and proper exercise. He thought cold baths were a bad idea.

"But what other sort of bath would you find in Edinburgh, eh, heh, heh, heh?" Before he could go on, Monroe began to speak.

"There were other kinds of baths, you know, That some might say are of a different nature. These flourished for a long time in the south of England in a town called Bath, that drew its name from them. And do you know, they, the suffering men and women, used to bathe together there, without a stitch of raiment upon them. And it was only when they discovered a body lying in the silt at the foot, who had failed to appreciate the therapeutic qualities of the water, that they closed the place down."

"Thank you, Professor Monroe," said Home. "Now, what would you recommend in the way of drugs?"

"I heard that a solution of iodine has been used in Paris by Lugol."

"Well, that may be what they use in France, but I've had good results with extract of opium. Mind you," he added, with a weary shake of his head, "I've had some bad results too. That is results that do not bear contemplating, if you would phrase it so."

He then asked me the constituents of Dover's Powders. My spirits rose, for I had recited an account of this to MacKenzie just the week before. I had reeled off the details like a Holyrood man, fluent with profitable falsehoods about Mary Queen of Scots and David Riccio, to gentlemen beginning the Grand Tour in Scotland.

"It is a sedative, and a diaphoretic. It contains 1% of Ipecacuanha and 90% of sugar."

"Aye, uhuh. Uhuh, aye. Very good," he said. "Tell me, did you know that Dover was a pirate? He rescued Alexander Selkirk. The man we know as Robinson Crusoe. Defoe, you know. Aye, a great author was Defoe!"

I was about to tell him that I had read "Moll Flanders", but I thought the better of it. Still, I wasn't going to stop him rhapsodising. The more he spoke, the less I would have to.

He thanked me graciously, and handed me over to Monroe, who carelessly asked me to follow him through the entire bowel. When I emerged, Russell took over, with some of the horrible morbidities that could afflict the bowel, like escaping from the body where it should not—as a hernia, or worse still—becoming strangulated.

"You will have heard of the ligament of Astley Cooper, of course, Mr Ahah . . . ?" he scowled.

I had heard more than that about Astley Cooper. He had made his knighthood by finding and removing a fatty growth from the King's head. Just finding it, they said, might have been worth a baronetcy. I said, "Yes, sir, and it . . ."

"Indeed, who has not heard of it?" His envy aborted my answer and he grumbled on, "A successful publicist; indeed, I hear his servant makes £600 from showing his patients in, out of their turn; a dreadful practice, you will agree, £600 a year!"

We then turned to sadder matters, like that untreatable condition causing pain and tenderness in the lower abdomen and ending usually in fever and death.

"I am led tae believe, Professor Russell," it was Hamilton now

181

breaking into his ageing thoughts, again with proof of reading wider than one might expect from a gentleman accoucheur. "I believe, Professor Russell, that Thomas Addison has suggested that site of this malady may be related to inflammation in a small wormlike appendage of the great bowel. He calls it the vermiform appendix."

Russell erupted so violently, his wig slipped to the side, giving him the appearance of a discarded puppet. He screeched, "When will you learn to confine your interest to—confinements?" Pleased with his wit, he thought to deliver his coup de grace. "There is no way in which the vermiform appendix could possibly contribute to this fatality."

Hamilton, who had barely contained his impatience through this performance, laughed coarsely. Russell snuffed, all high nosed. In his black breeches he always managed to look like an emigre count, fallen on hard times. All this lordly pique meant nothing to Hamilton.

"Whit is the first sign you look for in pregnancy, Mr Bryson?" he rasped. This was hard, for there were dozens, and any one could be first.

"Increasing girth?" I cried.

"Na, na. Before that what do you look for?" I frowned in silence. What could you actually look for?

"The wedding ring—hah, heh, heh, heh. Very important, is it no'. Heh, heh, heh." You could not see his face for smiles now. He asked me to deliver a floppy doll through a silk-lined pelvic girdle. Then he asked me to deliver the same unruffled baby with the forceps, through a rather narrower opening. I think he was quite pleased with my efforts, for he was a poet when it came to mothers and babies. Start the labour contractions, and his truculence was transformed into a crusade to save them both.

"Ah, that's lovely," he said. "Now be sure to tie off the umbilical cord; none of this nonsense about draining off smallpox and other contagions with the umbilical blood. Leave it untied and you'll kill the baby. Is that not right?"

"Oh yes, sir," I said devoutly.

"Of course it is. Of course it is laddie." And that was it. It was over. I bowed goodbye. They bowed goodbye to me. Professor Home tinkled a bell, and I heard Jamie trying to open the doors.

I thought I would avoid Toomhead in the dining room, so I made straight for the front door, glancing briefly aloft, waved to Lucy who I knew would be there, hiding behind the balustrade. Jamie showed me out the front door, with a friendly, almost conspiratorial, nod. On the pavement stood Toomhead, telling more students how to pass the examination.

"You must have a thorough knowledge of prescription writing," he was saying. "If you cannot do that, you might as well just go away. Now, they asked me . . ."

There was no need for me to stay for this wayside lecture. I had passed my examination—or at least, I felt I might have. Whatever else I might have, I passed the rest of the day in the White Horse Inn with Quentin and Aeneas and listened to their tales of woe.

Aeneas had floundered badly in Dr Willan's classification of Porrigo and had recommended decoctions of poppy heads and tobacco for the wrong type of scabs. Quentin on the other hand had consumed enough ale to be amused by a joust with Professor Monroe that at the time must have been unnerving. The subject had been acute chest pain.

"Well I told the old goat it was more common in men—especially fellows with bull necks and a tendency to corpulency and I wecommended carminatives—you know cawaway and peppermint water, he bwoke in wather suddenly and said, 'We're not discussing treatment Mr Deelatrumpe—we're still on causes." So I told him it could be caused by ossification of the cowonawy artewies or walking at a quick pace after a hearty meal. He wasn't intewested in any of this; you know he's so tewwified of not seeing the wood for the twees that he misses the whole damned fowest.

"What about shock?' says he. 'a discharge of buckshot in the feet for example.'

'I cannot wecall this in particular', I said.

'Then your memory lets you down sir.'

I told him I had a good memowy, and he said.

'Aye—a good memory but a short one!' damn him." and he called for further refreshment.

The rest of my examination I wrote in 19 Hanover Street, which seemed to have lost its fairest flower now that Mrs Cudleigh had fled. For the first written part, Professor Home had selected a case of asthma and rheumatism. I found it straightforward. Inhalations of Friars Balsam, flannel vests next the skin, and exhibition of spirits in the form of whisky. The remedy was rather a pleasant one. No dictionary could give me the Latin word for whisky. I settled for Aqua Scotorum. The Professor did not quibble. For my commentary on an Aphorism of Hippocrates, I hovered uncertainly between:

"Life is short, science is long; opportunity is elusive, experiment is dangerous, judgement is difficult. It is not enough for the physician to do what is necessary, but the patient and the attendants must do their part as well, and circumstances must be favourable." I felt this left too much room for gratuitous insult.

The next left no room for anything.

"Drugs may be administered to pregnant women from the fourth to the seventh month of gestation. After that period, the dose should be less. Care must also be exercised in giving drugs to infants and children." This seemed so self evident that comment was needless. I continued my search for a smooth aphorism that was just contentious enough to let me expatiate without serious fear of disagreement.

"As for the daily changes in the weather: a north wind stimulates the body and makes it of good tone and agile, and makes for a good complexion and acuity of hearing; the bowels are constipated and the eyes sting. But a pain in the chest is made worse by such a wind. On the other hand, south winds relax the body, make the tissues moist, reduce acuity of hearing and produce headaches and vertigo. Movement both of the eyes and of the body generally is sluggish and the bowels relaxed." The winds around Edinburgh blew from so many directions that all these states might occur at once—with disastrous results. If Hippocrates were right then this could explain much.

In the end I settled for "Sleep that stops delirium is good." This was so sensible that the Aphorism hardly required defence—just a few words of praise from me for the Father of Medicine. I wrote a brief but beautiful rumination on the subject. Well pleased, I handed it to the Medical School, and a week later, well pleased, they told me I was now a doctor. I was just twenty-one years old.

The final steps taken at the University, after passing the M.D. examination, are down the large College hall, to be granted publicly the classical scroll entitling you to practise at the highest level of Medicine in the land. It was almost impressive, but before you could grasp the precious document, you had to pay the Bursar ten pounds the previous day, and, even worse, sit through a tedious homily from some aged savant the next day.

It was quite the family occasion. Aeneas shuffled about as he introduced me to his father, a harrowed cleric to be remembered by his parish as one assiduous in all his parochial duties, not immersed in speculation, but earnest in action to promote the merit he esteemed. His mother was plump and pleasant, and would no doubt merit the description of "making no pretence to speculative pursuits, but kind withall."

Across the hall I could see a faded gallant, who could only be Quentin's father. He was smiling graciously through a lorgnette at all and sundry, like a landowner looking with good natured bemusement at his cavorting tenantry.

After much giggling, the crowd finally settled expectantly. Father and

Mother at the back of the crowd could see my vantage point amongst the graduands at the front. Suddenly there was a knock on the large doors, and in came the procession, led by a College servitor, staggering under the weight of the University Mace.

"The College flunkey's got a popliteal aneurysm," said Aeneas. "Look how he keeps his left knee straight." I was too busy looking at the stately collection of learned heads nodding towards their seats.

The Reverend Maxwell Glebe spiritual advisor to the Town Council said a prayer for all young doctors and their patients. Behind him stood the Dean of the Faculty—a mountain of a man formed of self indulgence and piety. He gave another short address, explaining the nature of the ceremony. A Clerk read from a long scroll the names of the successful examinees of our year. We marched up in order for the handshake, and the Diploma which we had already bought the day before.

Up again stood the Dean, and he made us all take an Oath, to practise our profession without malice, grudge or partiality. He then gave a longer address. He called upon us to toil in the vineyards of learning. Why did he choose such a dreary metaphor, and why did he have to flight his remarks in such discouraging sentences?

"This Diploma is but a start," he thundered, "in fact it is but a start upon the real path of study and learning that must be followed now." I found his remarks offensive. After three years of hard grinding, I would have welcomed a few words of encouragement. But there was worse to come: an ethereal exortation to put ambition behind us, and to put service before self.

I looked behind him to the razor edge professional mountaineers, arrayed in a circle in their academic robes, and wondered whom he was actually addressing. But he was not done yet. He began to look like the Reverend Gideon.

"I would like to turn to more spiritual matters, and to remind all of you here how frail is the thread that holds you to life. You would do well to remember this, and to prepare for death now." This was just the impetus I needed to launch me on my new career. He resumed his throne amidst a round of weary applause.

"Well, that was a significant piece of humbug," said my father when it was all over. "Now, off to Dowie's for oysters and porter to see if we can be cleansed of that rhetoric." He had quite a way with words, did my surgeon-apothecary father.

"We must not overdo things at lunchtime, Father," said I, "for we have been invited to Charlotte Square to take dinner this evening."

"All the more reason to take some porter now," said he.

We paused to invite Major Deelatrumpe and Quentin to join us. The Major had travelled north with a large stallion, and the pair of them were staying at Thredbair Hall near Philiphaugh. From what I could gather, the stallion was the more important visitor, and both Lord Thredbair and the Major hoped to restore their respective fortunes with its hereditary talents. Tonight, however, only the Major and his son would be joining us for dinner with the Homes at Charlotte Square. I wondered what Lucy would make of the Major. The Revrend and Mrs McBeen graciously declined our invitations to oysters and porter in Leith, though, as we struggled into our hackney cab, the look of wistful sadness on Aeneas' face spoiled my appetite.

That evening we visited 12 Charlotte Square, where Professor and Mrs Home threw a large dinner party in my honour. Now that I was a doctor, with an established practice to go into, they thought it suitable that Lucy and I should be formally betrothed, or, as Professor Home had put it,

"Officially bespoken, if you prefer it so."

Well, I was happy, whichever way he preferred it, and to judge from Lucy's eyes, so was she.

Jamie bowed to us with exaggerated humility when we arrived, and winked at me and raised his brows at the "maister's mither", as he led our party aloft. After a brief struggle, he separated the drawing room doors, and announced in sepulchral tones,

"Dr and Mrs Bryson and Dr Bryson! Major and Dr Deelatrumpe!" He then drew the doors after him, quivering with hidden mirth the while. He reappeared almost at once to announce,

"Professor and Mrs Thomson" and gave me a huge wink as he did so. Grizel had obviously started elocution lessons from which she had not yet begun to derive any benefit. Her husband appeared to have lost some of his self possession. When the introductions were done she said,

"How chairming to meet you," as though she had never heard of Dalkeith and the banks of the Esk.

The gathering was a great success, made the better by good humour, good company and good champagne. The Professor made a speech, or rather two speeches side by side. He said Quentin was a splendid fellow; he said I was a splendid fellow, and that our mothers and fathers were all splendid fellows, that is to say excellent—er—ah—folk. He ventured to hope, nay to predict confidently, that the Major's stallion would help increase the Thredbair dowry.

Gavin glowered at this, and the Honourable Eliza blushed. But the Professor was not to be stopped. He further hoped that Lucy and I would be as content as he and his wife had been. Mrs Home and my mother dabbed their eyes. Lucy and I gazed at each other. Everyone smacked the table and shouted,

"Well said, sir." and, "more," a plea the Professor was in danger of responding to, but he thought the better of it.

The Major replied on behalf of himself, his son and his horse, and Father smiled blandly as the Professor gave him a lecture on blood letting. When Lucy sang, *Will ye no' come back again?* It dawned on me that there were two versions of this song, the one quite unlike the other. An unforgettable evening it was, but like all the rest of them it had to end some time. There was a great procession down to the hall, and I dawdled with Lucy as slowly as was reasonable. I had a bad moment going down the stairs, which did not escape Jamie.

"Aye, sir," he said, easing on my cape, "the maister's mither has that effect on maist fowk, even when she canna get oot o' that frame up there. But noo that ye're ane of the family, ye'll just hae to pretend she's yer favourite grannie."

As my parents were staying at Dumbreck's Hotel, I went the next day to collect my baggage from the O'Loan palace. I flattered myself that Mrs O'Loan now had a different opinion of the medical profession since my sojourn in her establishment. She gave me as gracious a smile as she could manage, and kept her fiery hound off my ankles for once. Taking her farewell by the hand cost me dear, but I went through with it as a gentleman ought. Her monstrous spouse was on sentry duty at the Close head as usual.

"Ah, it's yerself Professor," he promoted me one step as usual as I struggled down with my valise. "If it wasn't that you were doing so well with that bag on your own, I would suggest carrying it for you meself."

"Come and join me for a drop, Mr O'Loan," said I. His eyes bulged more than their wont. It was always he who did the inviting. But it was not an invitation he could refuse. He made a perfunctory gesture at helping me with my bag on the trail to Ross's, but he had enough to contend with carrying his own belly.

We sat in the old familiar alcove, with the old familiar tankards, and I paid in the old familiar way. Even the sawdust looked the original. We drank and sighed and talked of the old days that would never come again.

"Well, Professor," said he sadly, "it's sorry I'll be to see ye go. I've enjoyed taking a drop with you."

"Well, I am sad to be leaving too, Mr O'Loan," I lied, "but there's a good friend of mine looking for lodgings. David Toomhead is his name, and he has to stay in Edinburgh for another year. He knows all about horses. You'll like him."

There was no need to tell him that Toomhead had never been known to take a penny out of his pocket, and that he drank only water.

And so I became a Doctor of Medicine of the great University of

187

Edinburgh. Just as important, I became a friend of four distinguished dissenters—perhaps three, for Aeneas' remote postures led him each week to call for fierce retribution on all those who had shared his beliefs of the week before. His dreams differed on a similar basis, but I was sure that he would settle around Inveresk, where his reverend father's life of service had at least prepared him well for the lean early years of practice.

Like Aeneas, I was destined for country practice too, helped along by my father's reputation. No doubt we would fail to recognise each other at the next Coronation revels, and we would grow merry and shout,

"My God, you haven't changed one little jot, ha, ha, ha!"

I would also no doubt indulge my talent for private grumbling whilst I graciously grew fat on all the bounties brought my way by the system I grumbled about. Henceforth I could be safely contemptuous about my qualification. I could discuss it easily with a sneer and a shrug, perhaps adding patronisingly,

"Any clown can acquire an M.D. It doesn't prove you're educated, you know."

Darwin of the fuzzy head disappeared to Cambridge, where he had abandoned the study of medicine. Quentin tells me he went off in a boat somewhere. Well he's welcome to that. I should have thought he would be more suited to the life of a country clergyman. I might ask Professor Thomson's father in law to write to him about that one day.

Corrigan too, I hear about him from time to time. He drives about Dublin in a large carriage, and they say he has had a disease or a pulse named after him. I always knew he would do something remarkable.

As for Quentin, I shall not look on his like again. He had a sheer genius for turning disaster into victory, and indeed only last year got two pages in the *Caledonian Mercury* describing how, after a brilliant career at Edinburgh University, he has gone on to become Medical Advisor to the Navy, and that a Knighthood was only days away. Nothing like a glorious summit to make people forget the squalid rungs and the missteps on the ladder.

However, he was just clinging to that ladder when I went in search of him to say my farewells. Dawdling along in the warm June sunshine I had plenty of time to spare, which was just as well. As I entered the High Street I stopped to watch two women stumbling out of Maguire's inn, connected by their fists. Further up the High Street a detachment of the Royal Scots had fallen out to have an on the spot foot inspection beside John Knox's manse. I amused myself with them for a while before moving on to find Quentin hard at work in Monroe's laboratory, dissecting the brachial nerve and artery free of the armpit. He seemed in good humour.

"Well, well," said he, "what a surpwise. Come and look at my specimen. See—there is the Latissimus Dorsi; and that one there is the Pectowalis Major. I have wather a flair for this sort of thing, don't you know? Haw, haw, haw." He isolated the withered muscles with the confidence of a bold man selecting his supper from a scatter of mushrooms and toadstools.

"How long have you left to do here, Quentin?" I asked, all solicitous. His reply began with a humour-the-canaille smile, and he dropped his scalpel and forceps.

"The Pwofessor of Anatomy, God west him, if he is yet awake, will welease me when I have the distwibution of the ulnar nerve weady for pickling: that would be about August, I would judge.

"But what about the quota of free bodies?"

"Oh that!" said he with an airy wave of his hand. "That's alweady under way. Why, damn me, it's been just too simple. I say, could I persuade you to join me in just one little expedition before you become sewious old man?" He regarded me slyly.

"No more snatching, Quentin. I couldn't."

"Oh, no," he reassured me. "There is no gwave wobbing. I can pwomise that." Against my wiser instincts I agreed to whatever plan he had in mind. Quentin bubbled.

"Splendid, splendid. We will do it tonight. I have come acwoss a bwace of capital fellows. They've got their glimmers open for a swift guinea, I can tell you. What are they called now?" He leaned back from his decomposing masterwork and tried, hand on brow, to prise their names from his current fantasies. He said,

"Yes—one of them wuns some sort of lodging house down near the Tanners Close—calls himself Fewwet or Wabbit or some such, or no— Hare: yes, that's it—Hare; and his colleague—ah, his colleague—if I am not much mistaken he goes by the name of Burke."